A WITCH in WINTER

RUTH WARBURTON

Hodder
Children's
Books

A division of Hachette Children's Books

First published in Great Britain in 2012
by Hodder Children's Books

The right of Ruth Warburton to be identified as the Author of
the Work has been asserted by her in accordance with the
Copyright, Designs and Patents Act 1988

2

A Catalogue record for this book is available from the British Library

ISBN 978 1 444 90469 7

Typeset in Berkeley Book by Avon DataSet Ltd,
Bidford on Avon, Warwickshire

Printed and bound by CPI Group (UK) Ltd,
Croydon, CR0 4YY

The paper and board used in this paperback by Hodder Children's Books
are natural recyclable products made from wood grown in
sustainable forests. The manufacturing processes conform to the
environmental regulations of the country of origin.

Hodder Children's Books
a division of Hachette Children's Books
338 Euston Road, London NW1 3BH
An Hachette UK company
www.hachette.co.uk

For my mum, Alison.
With love.

CHAPTER ONE

The first thing that hit me was the smell – damp and bitter. It was the smell of a place long shut up, of mice, bird-droppings, and rot.

'Welcome to Wicker House,' Dad said, and flicked a switch. Nothing happened, and he groaned.

'Probably been disconnected. I'll go and investigate. Here, have this.' He pushed the torch at me. 'I'll get another one from the car.'

I wrapped my arms around myself, shivering as I swung the torch's thin beam around the shadowy, cobwebbed rafters. The air in the house was even colder than the night outside.

'Go on,' Dad called from the car. 'Don't wait for me; go and explore. Why don't you check out your bedroom – I thought you'd like the one at the top of the stairs. It's got a lovely view.'

I didn't want to explore. I wanted to go home – except where was home? Not London. Not any more.

Dust motes swirled, silver in the torchlight, as I pushed open a door to my right and peered into the darkness beyond. The narrow circle of the torch's beam glittered back at me from a broken window, then traced slowly across the damp-splotched plaster. I guessed this had once been a living room, though it seemed strange to use the word 'living' about a place so dead and unloved.

Something moved in the dark hole of the fireplace. Images of mice, rats, huge spiders ran through my head – but when I got up the courage to shine the torch I saw only a rustle of ashes as whatever it was fled into the shadows. I thought of my best friend, Lauren, who went bleach-pale at even the idea of a mouse. She'd have been standing on a chair by now, probably screaming. The idea of Lauren's reaction to this place made me feel better, and I reached into my pocket for my phone and started a text.

Hi Lauren, we've arrived in Winter. The welcome party consists of half a dozen rats and—

I broke off. There was no signal. Well, I'd known this place would be isolated, Dad had called that 'part of its charm'. But even so . . . Maybe I could get a signal upstairs.

The stairs creaked and protested every step, until I reached a landing, with a corridor stretching into darkness, lined with doors. The closest was ajar – and I put my hand on it and pushed.

For a minute I was dazzled by the moonlight flooding in. Then, as my eyes adjusted, I took in the high, vaulted ceiling, the stone window seat, and smelled the faint scent of the sea drifting through the open window.

Through the casement I could see the forest stretching out, mile after mile, and beyond a thumbnail moon cast a wavering silver path across the night-black sea. It was heart-breakingly lovely and, in that fleeting instant, I caught a glimmer of what had brought Dad to this place.

I stood, completely still, listening to the far off sound of the waves. Then a harsh, inhuman cry ripped through the room, and a dark shape detached from the shadows. I ducked, a flurry of black wings beat the air above my head, and I caught a glimpse of an obsidian beak and a cold, black eye as the creature hunched for a second on the sill. Then it spread its wings and was gone, into the night.

My heart was thudding ridiculously, and suddenly I didn't want to be exploring this house alone in the dark. I wanted Dad, and warmth, and light. Almost as if on cue, there was a popping sound, a blinding flash, and the light-bulb in the corridor blazed. I screwed up my eyes, dazzled by the harsh brightness

3

after straining into the darkness.

'Hey-hey!' Dad's shout echoed up the stairs. 'Turns out the leccy wasn't off – it was just a fuse. Come on down and I'll give you the grand tour.'

He was waiting in the hall, his face shining with excitement. I tried to rearrange my expression into something approximating his, but it clearly didn't work, because he put an arm around me.

'Sorry it's a bit of a nightmare, sweetie. The place hasn't been occupied for years and I should have realized they'd have turned everything off. Not the best homecoming, I must admit.'

Homecoming. The word had a horribly hollow sound. Yup, this place was home now. I'd better get used to it.

'Come on.' Dad gave me a squeeze. 'Let me show you around.'

As Dad took me round, I tried to find positive things to say. It was pretty hard. Everything was falling apart – even the plugs and light switches were all ancient Bakelite and looked like they'd explode if you touched them.

'Just look at those beams,' he exclaimed in the living room. 'Knocks our old Georgian house into a cocked hat, eh? See those marks?' He pointed above our heads to scratches cut deeply into the corded black wood. They looked like slashes: deep, almost savage cuts that

4

formed a series of Vs and Ws. 'Witch marks, according to my book. Set there to protect the house from evil spirits and stuff.' But I didn't have time to look properly at the scarred wood, because Dad was hurrying me on to his next exhibit.

'And how's that for a fireplace? You could roast an ox in there! That's an old bread oven, I think.' He tapped a little wooden door in the inglenook beside the fire, blackened and warped with heat. 'I'll have to see about getting it open one of these days. But anyway, enough of me rattling on. What do you think? Isn't it great?'

When I didn't respond he put his hand on my shoulder and turned me to look at him, begging me with his eyes to like it, be happy, share his enthusiasm.

'I like all the fireplaces,' I said evasively.

'Well you'll like them even more when winter comes, unless I can get the central heating in pretty pronto. But is that all you've got to say?'

'It's a lot of work, Dad. How are we going to afford it?' Even as I said it, I suddenly realized that I'd never really said those words before. I'd never had to. We hadn't been rich, but Dad had always earned enough for what we needed.

Dad shrugged. 'We got the place pretty cheap, considering. And I'll do most of the work myself, which'll cut down costs.'

'Oh God!' I said involuntarily in a horrified voice. Then I caught Dad's eye and began to laugh. Dad can barely change a light-bulb, let alone conduct major house renovations. He looked offended for a minute but then began to laugh too.

'I'll get someone in to do the gas and electrics, at least, I promise you that.' He put his arm around me. 'I have a really good feeling about this place, Anna. I know it's been a jolt for you, I do, but I honestly think we can make something of our lives here. I can do a bit of writing, grow veg – maybe I could even do B&B if money gets tight. This place just needs a little TLC to make it fantastic.'

A *little* TLC? I thought about the filth and the rats, and all the work we were going to have to do to make this place even liveable, let alone nice. And then I looked at Dad, and I thought of him back in London, sitting up night after night, his face grey with worry as he tried to make the sums add up, tried to find a way out for both of us.

'I think,' I said. Then I stopped.

'Yes?'

'I think . . . if anyone can do it, you can, Dad.' I put my torch down on the mantelpiece and hugged him fiercely. Then I noticed something.

'Hey.' I coughed to clear my throat. 'Look.'

I brushed away the dust that covered the fire surround, and shone my torch closer. Beneath the grime were twining vines and leaves, but that wasn't what I'd noticed. In the centre was a carved stone shield, bearing an ornate W.

'W for Winterson.'

'Look at that!' Dad said delightedly. 'Though it's W for Winter more likely, or maybe Wicker House. But it's a nice omen. Now come on.' He dropped a kiss on the top of my head. 'Let's go and do battle with that Aga, see if we can't get you some tea.'

Monday was the first day of the summer term, but you wouldn't have known it from the greyish light that trickled under the curtains. I lay in bed with the cover to my chin and listened to the wind in the trees. My body felt strange; every muscle was taut with nerves and my veins seemed full of some strange tingling liquid, as if my blood had been drained and replaced with carbonated water. It was terrifying starting a new school after ten years in the same comfortable surroundings. There had been only forty girls in the Lower Sixth of my old school – in comparison Winter High was massive. And scary. And co-ed.

Just to add to the stress, there was no uniform in the

sixth form. Which meant I had to think about what to wear to school for the first time in my life.

Dragging myself out of bed, I opened the door to my Ikea wardrobe, which looked strange and out of place in this huge, vaulted room. At the sight of myself in the mirror inside, I groaned. I've never forgiven Dad for bequeathing his hair to me: wild, dark and unruly, and ready to run riot at the slightest opportunity. I suppose the rest, the pale skin and blue-grey eyes, must have come from my mother. I wouldn't know, but that certainly wasn't Dad's DNA looking back at me from the mirror.

I grabbed a comb and began trying to tame my curls into something that wouldn't get people pointing and laughing on my first day. My best hope for Winter High was not being noticed. I wasn't planning on making any life-long friends; if I could just get through the next two years, get my A-levels, and get out, that would be good enough for me. But fitting in would be nice, and crazy-girl hair wasn't going to help with that.

I was only halfway done when Dad yelled, 'Breakfast!' up the stairs.

'Coming,' I shouted.

A leaden lump formed in my stomach.

* * *

8

It was two miles to town and Dad insisted on driving me. The car was parked in the middle of the clearing in front of the house, under a vast, spreading beech, and as we picked our way across the long grass, the dew wet the hem of my jeans. Far across the forest you could see the silhouette of some tumbledown ruin, high on the cliffs above the sea.

'That's Winter Castle,' Dad said, following my gaze. 'It's a ruin now, of course, but you can just make out the towers.' They were stark and black against the blue of the sea. 'And that lane'll be your walk to school.' He pointed to a cleft in the dense forest and a black tarmac road that snaked off into the distance over the cliffs.

'I still can't believe we can see the sea,' I said.

'As the crow flies we're not far,' Dad said. 'It just feels further going through the wood. Anyway, better get going. You don't want to be late on your first day. If we've got time I'll drive you past the fishing port – you'll like Winter village. I've always thought it was a pretty little place.'

He turned the key in the ignition and a clump of rooks detached themselves from the beech, startled by the noise. They wheeled around in alarm as Dad manoeuvred his way into the lane, and then followed us into the green shadows of the wood, swooping in our wake along the

9

leafy, curving tunnel, until we burst out into the stark sunlight of the cliff road.

Dad drove steadily down past the castle and through the outskirts of Winter, and we followed the tide of kids sweeping up the narrow high street until we came to a sprawling building that looked more like a Victorian prison than a school.

Winter High. It was huge. Winter was a small town but the school took in all the kids from outlying villages; there were five tutor groups in the Lower Sixth alone. I gulped – then realized that Dad was waiting for a reply to some remark he'd made.

'Sorry, Dad, what did you say?'

'I said, anything special you'd like for supper, to celebrate your survival?'

I shook my head. Food was the last thing on my mind.

'Anything's fine. Well, OK. I'd better . . .'

He nodded and kissed me on the cheek, and I slid out of the car with my heart beating in my throat. As I stood, fingering the strap of my bag, my mobile beeped. It was a text from Lauren.

Hi sweets. don't worry they'll love you. if they don't tell em there's a crew of Notting Hill beyatches gonna make their lives hell. Good luck miss you L xxx

The reminder of home and all my friends brought a

sudden prickle to the back of my eyes but I blinked furiously. Starting at my new school with tears in my eyes would *not* be a good way to go.

I scrubbed at my cheeks, straightened my back, and walked through the carved front door.

CHAPTER TWO

My footsteps echoed as I entered the hallway. I was gazing up at a mahogany board headed *In honour of those former pupils of Winter Grammar School, who gave their lives in the Great War 1914–18*, when a grumpy voice rang out.

'Hey you!'

I stiffened and looked round. A red-faced man in overalls was waving a mop at me. I pointed to myself and he nodded.

'Yes, you, Missy. No students in the main door!'

'Sorry,' I said, annoyed to find my voice was shaking a bit. 'I didn't know – I'm new.'

'Well you'll know for next time, young lady,' he said with obscure triumph.

'I'll take over from here, Mr Wilkes,' said a voice.

I jumped and turned.

Behind me was a small, elderly man wearing a tweed

jacket with leather elbow patches and a neat pair of gold-rimmed spectacles. He held out a hand. 'Anna Winterson, I presume? What a very appropriate name.'

'Yes, pleased to meet you, Mr . . .' I stopped in confusion.

'Brereton,' he completed. 'I shall be taking you for History. Usually it's the headmaster who welcomes new students to the school, but unfortunately he's unwell today. He has asked me to act as his deputy and welcome you to Winter, my dear Anna. I'm sure you'll be a great addition to our ranks. Mid A-Levels is not the easiest time to move schools, I realize, but I think you'll feel at home in Winter very soon.'

'Thank you,' I muttered.

'We are a friendly place, by and large, although a little old-fashioned I do admit. But we pride ourselves on keeping to some of the *old traditions*. And you may find our interests coincide with yours more than you realize.' He gave me a slightly sideways look, that seemed to indicate there was more to his words than face value. I had a sudden, horrible premonition that he was going to try to persuade me into some dire extra-curricular activity – dressing up as Tudors perhaps, with dodgy nylon costumes, and re-enacting battles with tin-foil swords.

'Um, I'm quite busy,' I said warily. 'I'm not sure I'll have much time for extra-curricular stuff at first, at least until I've caught up.'

He smiled, as if I'd missed the point of a joke, but only said, 'Of course. Now, we have ten minutes before first period, so I'll give you a whistle-stop tour of the school to orientate you. Mr Henderson is very keen on punctuality, but I think there's just enough time.'

'You're late,' said Mr Henderson without looking up as I sidled into a classful of staring eyes.

'I'm so sorry,' I said, slightly out of breath. Mr Brereton's brisk pace had left me wondering if I'd remembered to put deodorant on that morning. Altogether a *brilliant* start to my new school career. 'I'm new. Mr Brereton was just showing me around.'

'Oh.' He looked up and assessed me. 'Anna Winterson?'

'Yes.'

'Well, sit down. We sit alphabetically in my classes.'

I tried not to show my surprise. It looked like Mr Brereton hadn't been exaggerating when he said Winter High was old-fashioned. My old school was pretty traditional, but alphabetical order? What were we, ten?

'Madeleine, move up, please. Anna, take Madeleine's place.'

A tall, slim girl at the back of the class looked suddenly furious.

'Oh but Mr Henderson I'd just got all my—'

'Does Winterson come before Woburn or not, Madeleine? Unless you care to change your name I suggest you move up a place.'

'Yes, Mr Henderson.' She stood up, banging her books together with unnecessary force, and stamped along to the next desk, leaving a place free. I sat down, feeling my cheeks flame scarlet, and wished the floor could swallow me up. The force of her glare on my left side was like a blast furnace.

'Turn to page one eighty in the blue book please everyone.'

There was a universal rustling and I sighed inwardly and raised my hand again. Mr Henderson was writing on the board and didn't turn around.

'I will get you a book for the next lesson, Anna. In the meantime please share with Seth.'

The boy sitting next to me pushed his book across and smiled. 'Hi, Seth Waters,' he whispered under cover of the sound of Mr Henderson's chalk.

'I'm Anna,' I whispered back.

He put out his hand, and I shook it quietly. It was dry and strong and very warm, and I was horribly conscious of my own sticky palm, sweaty from trotting after Mr Brereton. There were callouses on his palm and fingers, and oil deeply grained around the short square nails. I wondered what he did that left his hands so rough.

'I hope you're good at differentiation, Anna. Because I'm beginning to think I should have taken Applied and Statistics after all.'

Actually I *was* good at differentiation, and I'd also already studied the kind of equation Mr Henderson was outlining on the board. Which was a good thing because I was completely unable to concentrate.

Seth Waters was possibly the most beautiful boy I'd ever seen. To say he had curly dark hair, dark eyes and tanned skin was all true, but still completely missed the point – he had an indefinable something that made me completely unable to tear my eyes away. I couldn't stop looking at him sideways as I sat there, pretending to read page one eighty, but in fact watching the muscles of his forearms moving under his tanned skin as he wrote, the string of beads round his throat, the movement of his Adam's apple as he swallowed.

As I looked down at the book I saw there were actual goosebumps on the skin of my arm and I bit my lip, hard, to bring myself back to reality. This was pathetic! Lesson one, and already I was having hot flushes and palpitations.

What next, was I going to swoon in English or something? It wasn't like I'd never met a boy before, for heaven's sake. OK, I hadn't had classes with them on a daily basis, but I knew *plenty* of boys. London wasn't exactly short of the male sex. But I had to admit, I'd never, never met someone like Seth Waters. Surely, though, there couldn't be many more like him in the school? If there were I was going to be in serious trouble with my exams, that was for sure.

It looked like I wouldn't be the only one. Maybe Seth was right, and he should have taken Applied and Statistics, because he certainly didn't act too enthralled by Pure. He day-dreamed through most of the lesson, staring out of the window at the sea sparkling in the distance. At the end of the lesson he scooped up his books and gave me a devastating smile that crinkled the tanned skin of his cheeks.

'Nice to meet you, Hannah.'

Hannah. Great. I'd clearly made quite an impression.

The next period was Classics and we were free to choose our places. I was early this time, but still hovered nervously by the door, not wanting a repeat of the hostility with Madeleine if I somehow chose the wrong place. In the end a pink-cheeked girl in a clashing red jumper took pity on me.

'Hi there, you're Anna aren't you? I saw you in Maths. Come and sit with me and Liz.'

'I'd love to, thanks.' I sat down gratefully at her table and said, 'Sorry, I saw you too but I didn't get your name?'

'I'm June. And this is my friend, Liz.' I nodded at Liz and she smiled shyly, hiding her face behind a curtain of blonde hair.

'Thanks for letting me share your table; I was worried about picking the wrong place.'

'Oh, what – after the business with Madeleine?' June laughed as she got out her books. She was sharper than she looked. 'Don't worry about it, Anna. Madeleine's just one of the thousand and one members of the Seth Waters fan club. Yawn.'

'Oh, I know,' Liz said. 'It's so boring. It's like he and Caroline are king and queen of the school.'

'Caroline's his girlfriend,' June put in. 'Thank God we don't have a prom here or we'd have to put up with them being crowned and all that crap. Although whether Mr Harkaway would allow that, I don't know. Seth's not exactly flavour of the month with the authorities . . .'

'What do you mean?' I asked. June rolled her eyes.

'Oh, you know, the usual. Drinks, smokes, got a tattoo against the rules. He was suspended a year or two back for getting into a fight and smacking some guy's head into a wall, but it didn't seem to do any good. Comes from a broken home, dontcha know. Anyway his reputation doesn't seem to put any of the airheads off. I expect every school has their official babe-magnet. Was it like that at your last school, Anna?'

'Not exactly. My last school was single sex.'

'Oh how awful!' Liz looked comically horrified. 'Poor you!' Then she blushed, as if fearing she'd been too critical. 'Though it must be nice too, probably makes life a lot simpler.'

'Yeah, there'd be a lot less bitching around if it weren't for people like Seth,' June added.

'He seemed OK when I sat next to him,' I said. Annoyingly unable to remember a person's name, granted, but not bitchy, I had to give him that.

'It's not him,' June said. 'It's the effect he has on the female half of the population. Plus Caroline's a total bitch. Sorry, I really hate that word but she is. She's always been a prize PITA and since last year, when she started going out with Seth, she's been unbearable. You'd think he'd conferred divine powers on her. If it's not snide comments about virgins, it's bitching about who's trying to steal him off her, and if it's not that, it's how amaaaaaaaaazing he is in bed.'

She rattled on to her Classics homework without

19

expecting an answer, and I was glad. There didn't seem a whole lot I could say to that.

By the end of the morning I was totally exhausted, but also slightly relieved. I was well up with lessons, or so it seemed, so I guessed the hefty school fees Dad had been shelling out for hadn't been a total waste. I'd made it through so far without disgracing myself academically or, if you discounted my run-in with Madeleine, socially.

I was dithering by the door of the canteen, trying to decide whether to buy a sandwich in town and save myself the mortification of sitting alone for an hour, when I heard Liz's voice from behind me.

'Hey, Anna, would you like to sit with us?'

I nodded gratefully. She and June swept me along to their table in the cafeteria and introduced me to their friends, who all seemed sweet. I answered lots of questions about London, like, 'Isn't it majorly, like, dangerous?' and 'Isn't there a massive drugs problem?' They all seemed quite disappointed to find out that I'd never been mugged, that I didn't go to a hellish inner-city comprehensive, and that anorexia had been a bigger problem at my school than drugs.

Only one faux pas spoiled the break, towards the end of lunch. Liz asked if I liked horses. I said an emphatic no, and then noticed the copy of *Horse and Hound* sticking out of one of her friends' bags. Oops. Closer questioning revealed that they were all ex-members of the Pony Club and at least three of them owned horses. One of them, a big-boned, solid girl called Prue, had hers stabled up near our house.

'Oooh, you live at the Witch's House?' Prue said when I mentioned it. 'We used to be, like, *so* scared of that place when we were little! I'd never let Mum drop me off at the main road by the stables after dark; she always had to go right up the track so I didn't have to walk past the gate.'

'The Witch's House, is that what you call it?' I asked.

'I know it's really called the Wicker House, but no one ever calls it that. It's always known as the Witch's House, like the wood is always known as Witch's Wood.'

'My mum says it should rightly be the Witch's House anyway,' Liz said. 'She said wicker is just a corruption of wicce, which is the Anglo-Saxon word for witch.'

'I told my dad that when he asked me why I wouldn't walk home alone through the wood.' June spoke with her mouth full of sandwich. 'And he says it's rubbish. He says it's called Wicker Wood because of the reed beds down by the river.'

'Whatever.' Prue waved a dismissive hand. 'It's bloody

spooky after dark, is all I'm saying. I don't envy you your walk home, Anna.'

'Oh don't worry,' I said. 'I'm not superstitious.'

History, after lunch, was fine, but fourth period English I was late again. The room was tucked away above the Chemistry lab and hard to find. I turned up just as the lesson was about to start and looked desperately around for a free seat. There was only one, next to a serious-looking girl with long dark hair and angular glasses, bent over a copy of *Macbeth*.

'Excuse me,' I said, 'do you mind if I sit here?'

'If you must,' she said, in a voice that plainly meant, 'Please don't'.

I looked around but the class was full so I was forced to sit down anyway. I laid my books out, looking at her out of the corner of my eye. She was wearing a skinny grey cardigan with fraying sleeves, and as she read her fingers picked restlessly at the loose threads.

What could I say? Something about *Macbeth*? Or would that be too swotty?

'Um,' I tried, but she ignored my gaze, and I was still trying to think of an opening for conversation when the class started.

* * *

22

At last the bell rang for the end of the day, and I gathered up my books with a feeling of profound relief that I'd survived the first day. The girl began packing up her bag, her long black hair shielding her face.

'It was nice to meet you,' I said lamely. 'What's your name? Mine's Anna by the way.'

'I know,' she said, and shoving her copy of *Macbeth* roughly in her bag, she walked off without a backward glance.

CHAPTER THREE

I lay in the cast-iron bath in the hateful lean-to, trying to ignore the wind whistling through the gaps in the corrugated roof. The water had been steaming when I got in but was already getting cold. Very cold. I pushed at the hot tap with my toe and a thin trickle came out, orange with rust, and dispersed into the murky bathwater. I shuddered.

I hadn't felt right since we got to Winter; I was constantly keyed up, ready for something – I wasn't sure what. I seemed to spend my whole time holding myself in; tiptoeing around Dad, trying not to offend anyone at school, trying to work out the rules in this strange new community. My neck and shoulders hurt with the effort of keeping it all inside – whatever *it* was.

Still, at least it was Friday. Only one more day of school to get through. The thought of school made me look at my watch, lying on the toilet seat: time I was getting out. I'd be late at this rate.

I was just gearing myself up to brave the freezing draught when there was an almighty crash from the living room, followed by an ominous silence.

'Dad?' I yelled. Then, when he didn't answer, more panicked, 'Dad!'

Then I leapt out of the bath and ran.

'Dad?' I wrenched open the door of the living room with a wet hand.

He was standing in his paint-stained overalls with a crowbar in one hand and a clump of paper and a blackened piece of oak about six inches thick in the other.

'What the hell!' Relief made me annoyed. 'Why didn't you answer when I shouted? And why on earth are you doing DIY at eight a.m.?'

'Sorry, sweetie,' he said mildly. 'I didn't hear you.' He held out the charred papers with a nod. 'I got that bread oven open – although, bloody hell, it was a struggle. Look how thick the door was! I was right, it was an oven, and I found this hidden in there – it looks like some kind of book. Could you stick it in the kitchen until I'm cleaned up?'

'Sure.' I took it gingerly by one edge. It was three-quarters burnt, covered in cobwebs, and slightly paint-spattered where Dad had touched it. Part of the cover was visible and I made out the words:

> . . . *e Hroc*
> *Grimoire*

What the hell was a Grimoire? Or a Hroc for that matter? It looked like an old recipe book but I wasn't about to start leafing through – Dad was the one with an interest in this place. Let him get his hands dirty. I stuck it on the window sill and began making myself a cup of coffee. The plug sparked as I flicked on the percolator and made me jump. God, I hated this house. You couldn't even make a cup of coffee without risking your life. The sooner Dad got this place rewired, the better.

Dad came through just as it finished percolating.

'Oh good, is there enough for me?'

I poured him out a cup and as he drank it he said, 'Did I tell you I need to go up to London tomorrow?'

A trip back to Notting Hill! Lauren – Suzie – all my old friends . . . I almost held my breath, but managed to stammer out, 'N-no, why?'

'I've got to get my crown refitted and we're not registered with a dentist down here yet. I thought I'd stay with James and Lorna while I'm up.'

Oh. James and Lorna were Dad's friends from way back; they had a one-bedroom flat in Bloomsbury. Dad would be sleeping on their sofa, and there'd be no room for me.

'Will you be all right while I'm gone?'

'Sure,' I said, trying to fight back disappointment.

'Honestly? Because this place can be pretty spooky at night, I know. I wondered if you'd like to invite some of your new friends over to stay, to keep you company.'

I suppressed the urge to snap that I didn't *have* any new friends and tried to keep a convincing smile on my face.

'I'll be fine, honestly. Don't worry, Dad. Have a good time.' Then I looked at my watch. 'Oh hell. I've got to run.'

8.44. I'd covered barely a third of the walk to school. It was starting to rain – oh, and I had a stone in my shoe. Could this morning get any better?

I knelt by the roadside and pulled off my shoe, scrabbling inside to try to find the damn stone. From far off came the roar of an engine, faint above the crashing waves. I was too busy lacing my shoe to look up, until a battered truck swept past, far too fast, its wheel clipping my school bag and sending it flying. Books flew up in the air and papers and pens rained down like bomb debris.

'You arse!' I screamed at the driver. 'You're driving like a maniac!'

I'd assumed he wouldn't hear over the roar of the engine but there was a squeal of brakes and the truck ground to a halt. The driver's door opened and I gulped – preparing for a road rage attack.

It was Seth Waters. He ran over, his face pale.

'Anna, I'm so, so sorry.'

Huh. Well at least he got my name right this time. I resisted the urge to say, 'It's fine, honestly, Sam,' and concentrated on picking up my belongings.

'I'm really sorry,' he repeated, kneeling beside me in the dust to gather up pens and sheets of A4. 'I didn't see you in the long grass. I didn't expect anyone along here – no one walks this way at this time of day. Not that that's an excuse.'

'We've just moved into the Witch's House. I mean, Wicker House,' I said crossly. 'So I'll be walking this way regularly from now on. It'd be nice if you could try not to run me over in future.'

'Let me give you a lift the rest of the way.'

'No thanks.' I was still shaking from the near miss, and too cross to trust myself to be polite on the journey.

'Hey.' He took my shoulder and turned me to look at

him. His face was full of remorse. 'I really am so, so sorry. Please, won't you let me give you a lift at least, to save you the walk?'

His eyes were pleading; I felt myself soften. The part of me that was still cross wanted to retort, 'What and risk my life all over again?' but instead I just shrugged. Caroline's icy countenance floated into my head.

'Please?' Seth held out my bag and the sheaf of crumpled homework pages. 'I promise I'll keep to the speed limit . . .' The warmth of his smile and his wheedling tone was impossible to resist. I reluctantly cracked a smile back. 'Go on, you know you want to. You're late anyway.'

'If you're sure—' I was going to say, 'If you're sure your girlfriend won't mind', but it suddenly sounded weird, presumptuous. I stopped, floundering.

'Course I'm sure! It's the least I can do after running over your bag. Come on, jump in.'

I nodded and climbed in, and Seth started the engine again with a roar.

'Sorry,' he called over the noise of the engine. 'It makes a bit of a racket I know. I inherited it off my dad; he was a plumber.'

'What does he do now?' I shouted back.

Seth gave a funny little apologetic smile and a shrug. 'Oh, well, he died. Pancreatic cancer.'

'Oh!' I flushed scarlet. 'I'm so sorry. I didn't know. Was it recent?'

'Four years ago this summer. Don't worry, you weren't to know. Anyway, it's nice to talk about him. No one does any more.'

'What was he like?'

'Great. I really miss him.'

We drove in silence for a bit, then Seth said, 'So what does your dad do?'

'Oh, he used to be a stockbroker. But he lost his job. That was why we had to move.' My face felt stiff with the effort of trying to say the words casually. Memories flashed into my head unbidden: Dad stumbling home from work, his face white and drawn; piles of red demands on the hall table; the *thump*, *thump* of a hammer as they nailed up the 'sold' sign outside our house.

'Oh, sorry.' He glanced at me with his intensely dark eyes. They seemed full of concern though I couldn't imagine why he'd give a toss about my dad's job. 'What happened?'

'He was made redundant and . . . well . . . he had a kind of breakdown,' I said reluctantly. 'So this is sort of a new start for him. For both of us.'

'What's he doing now?'

'Nothing. Just doing up our house. Well, he's got some

random idea about writing a book about the history of fishing on the south coast, but I can't see that happening any time soon.' I tried for a laugh.

'Sounds interesting,' Seth said. I looked at him sharply to see if he was being sarcastic, but he seemed to be serious. 'What does your mum do?'

'My mum's . . .' I hated this moment. 'Well, dead too, I guess.'

'Now I'm sorry again. Especially as I seem to have put my foot in it twice, with your dad's job and all.'

'No, it's really OK,' I tried to explain, not wanting to feel like a fake. 'It's not like your dad. I never knew her. She – oh God, it's all so difficult to explain.'

'How come?'

'Well . . .' Usually I brushed this conversation off with some stock responses and people backed away from intruding on grief, but I felt I couldn't do that in the face of Seth's honesty about his dad. 'She disappeared when I was a baby – I remember that she was declared legally dead when I was about seven, but that's pretty much all I know. I'm not really entitled to miss her or anything. I never knew her.'

'Of course you're entitled to miss her,' Seth said quietly. He shifted gear, his arm brushing mine. Heat rose up my cheeks. This was getting out of hand; OK the guy was

31

seriously good-looking and, in spite of what June had said about his reputation, he seemed pretty nice too, but he was also seriously taken. I wasn't about to start my life in Winter by stealing someone else's boyfriend – even in the unlikely event that he wanted me.

The atmosphere in the truck felt too charged for comfort so I tried for a laugh, which came out more wobbly than I would have liked.

'Sorry, this is a bit heavy for a Friday morning, isn't it? We should be talking about what we're doing over the weekend or something.'

'Hey, it's fine.' Seth stopped the truck and I suddenly realized we were in the school car park. He turned to face me and gave me an awkward half-hug across the seat. 'It's nice,' he said into my hair. 'I haven't talked about my dad for a long time. It's good to talk to someone else who knows what it's like.'

To my dismay I felt a sob begin to rise up inside me. It wasn't my mum – it couldn't be. I'd never known her enough to grieve for her. It was everything – the strain of starting at a new school, losing all my friends, being constantly alone. But mainly, it was how nice Seth was being. He must have felt the tremor of my chest because he hugged me harder, and I felt a complicated welter of emotion curl in the pit of my stomach. I was uncomfortably

32

aware of his arms, warm around me, and his unshaven cheekbone rough against mine. Outside there was a rumble of thunder and I jumped.

'Seth, I'm so sorry.' I pulled away and wiped my eyes in the wing mirror. 'I really don't know what's wrong with me – it must be PMT or something.' Yuck! I mentally smacked my forehead, what was I doing? Talking about PMT to an attractive bloke – I'm sure that wasn't in *The Rules*. Luckily he grinned.

'Well that's all right for you then. What's my excuse supposed to be?'

I laughed and got out of the truck awkwardly. It was higher off the ground than I was used to and I dropped my bag, spilling the papers all over the place once again. By the time I'd picked them up Seth had been swept off by his crowd, all shrieking and laughing and swapping plans for the weekend.

Only one person was left. Seth's girlfriend, Caroline, was standing in the car park with her arms folded, looking at me through narrowed blue eyes. As I straightened up she ground her cigarette out under her heel, staring at me all the while. Then she turned and, with a toss of her long, silky hair, disappeared inside the building after her friends.

* * *

'What are you doing this weekend, Liz?' June asked as we set out our books for Classics.

'Oh, trying to finish my essay on Greek vases, I expect. How about you?'

'I've got to do some serious mucking out up at the stables. What about you, Anna?'

'I'm not sure,' I said. 'My dad's off to London, but there's no room for me.' I didn't mean it to sound as forlorn as it came out.

'Oh my God, you're going to stay alone in that spooky house?' June shrieked. Mrs Finch gave her a meaningful look and she lowered her voice. 'Won't you be scared?'

I shrugged half-heartedly. 'Dad did suggest that I should get some people over to stay but . . .' I trailed off, then something about her friendly, open face made me ask, 'I don't suppose . . . would you two like to . . . ? I mean don't worry if you're busy but—'

'I'm not busy!' June said instantly. 'In fact it would work really well. I could go straight up to the stables on Sunday and it would save me a walk. Could I ask Prue too? Then we could both make an early start.'

'Sure!' I said, delighted at her enthusiasm. 'How about you, Liz?'

'Oooh, why not? I'm always up for a night in a haunted house.'

34

'Are you sure you'll be all right?' Dad asked for the millionth time as he hovered in the doorway, his bag on his shoulder. 'I know you'll be fine, but I really don't like you being here without any access to the phone.'

'I'll be *fine*,' I said firmly. 'I told you, I've got three girlfriends coming over and we'll have a great time.'

I stood in the doorway, waving him off as the car bumped down the rutted track. Soon I couldn't see him at all, just hear the crack and crunch of branches in the lane. Then the sound of the engine fading as he disappeared down the main road. Then . . . nothing. I was alone. Alone in Wicker House.

The heavy front door swung shut, and suddenly the house was full of small sounds, almost as if it was waking up, stretching, yawning. A clock ticked; pipes expanded, clunking and dinging; floorboards creaked; the wind shushed and moaned in the maze of cavernous chimneys. The house was coming to life.

'OK,' I said aloud, and my voice sounded small and lonely in my own ears. 'Better get started.'

I'd warned them about the state of the bathroom so I hoped they'd all remembered to shower before they left, but I tried to scrub the worst of the green slime off the tub anyway. Then I made a huge batch of brownies, changed

Dad's sheets so they'd have somewhere to sleep, and unrolled the futon on the floor of my room.

I was just adding extra logs to the living room fire when I heard the sound of tyres in the lane outside. Looking out I saw that dusk had fallen and Prue, June and Liz were bumping up the lane in Liz's battered Land Rover, waving cheerily out of the window as they saw me. I flicked the switch on the outside lamp, wincing as it fizzed and sputtered under my hand.

'O. M. G!' June said as they came into the hall, breathing frostily into the cold air. 'This place is amazing.' She peered into the living room. 'Your dad must have worked miracles. It's soooo beautiful, like something out of *Vogue Living*!'

Dad had packed a lot into his week of decorating. He'd painted the walls a kind of dark cream and the floor had been waxed and polished. Now it gleamed in the firelight, reflecting little flickers of light from the irregular panes of the leaded light window. The intricately carved fireplace had been scrubbed, and you could see the strange animals and plants that twined and coiled over the stone surround.

It still wasn't a patch on our lovely house in London but, seeing it through my friends' eyes, I realized again how hard my dad was working to try to make a home for us. Still, I only said, 'Well don't speak too soon – wait 'til you see the bits of the house he *hasn't* decorated.'

Liz and June wanted to go around the whole house straight away, but Prue said, 'We've got pizzas from the takeaway – they'll get cold. Shouldn't we eat first?'

So we sat around the kitchen table and ate slice after slice of pizza, swapping gossip about Winter and all its inhabitants.

'It's the kind of place that unless your grandparents were born within sight of Winter Castle they still refer to you as "the incomers",' Prue explained round a mouthful. 'Everyone pretty much knows everyone, and most of the people have roots in the fishing industry if you go back far enough.'

'How old is Winter, then?' I asked.

'Oh it goes right back to the Domesday book and beyond,' Liz said. She was very keen on history, I'd discovered, and her shyness disappeared as she began to talk. 'There was a settlement up on the cliffs in Roman times. But they didn't settle down in the harbour until the Middle Ages – I suppose because of the risk of attack from the sea, or perhaps because of the floods.'

'Does it ever flood these days?' I asked.

'Not any more. There's harbour defences.'

'There was a dreadful flood in the seventeenth century,'

Prue said with relish. 'Loads of people died. It was supposed to be caused by a witch and the villagers burned her for it.'

'They didn't burn her,' Liz corrected. 'They stoned her and drove her away, and she was caught in the flood and drowned.'

'Let's face it, it's all rubbish anyway.' June started to fold up the pizza boxes for recycling. 'She wasn't a witch, was she? Probably just some poor old biddy with a squint and nasty neighbours.'

'It was all drugs, according to this book I read.' Liz began to sweep crumbs off the table. 'They rubbed something on to their broomsticks – belladonna or something – and it gave them illusions they could fly.'

'Just goes to show there's nothing new under the sun,' said June. 'All Mr Harkaway's doom-monger predictions about the youth of the town wasting their education to drugs, and it turns out they were all at it back in the seventeenth century anyway.'

'Yes, you haven't had the treat of one of Mr Harkaway's assemblies on the Evil of Drink, have you?' said Prue.

'Oooh! Talking of which,' I suddenly remembered, 'Dad said we could drink one of the bottles in the fridge. Do you want to?'

* * *

38

In the end we drank all three, two of cava and one of rosé wine. We ate nearly the whole tray of brownies plus a tub of ice-cream, then swapped rude jokes and commiserated about each other's love lives. Liz and June were going to the Young Farmers' May Ball in a few weeks, and they were both very pessimistic about finding a partner.

'I went with Mark Pargiter last year,' Liz said, 'and it was *awful*. He just ignored me all night and spent the whole time talking to my brother and eating canapés. Then at the end he said "Are you going to let me do tongues or what?" Honestly. What. A. Tit.'

'Why don't you just not go?' I asked.

Prue rolled her eyes. 'You may well ask.'

'Look, it's just not that simple,' June moaned. 'Mum and Dad are on the committee so I can't just sod off for the night. And there's always the faint, faint hope that Philip Granger might get over himself and ask me.'

'Why don't you just ask him, woman?' Prue said, her words slurring slightly. 'The boy's got such a stiff upper lip it's become a medical condition. He'll never unbend enough to ask you – you'll have to ask him. It's no reflection on you, he's just constit . . .' She hicupped. 'Constit-tit . . . Consert . . .'

'Liz is no better with James,' June shoved in crossly. Liz went scarlet and shook her head violently.

'Completely different, June, and you know it.'

'I know he's going out with someone else, but personally I think you just pick these unattainable types to moon over so you don't actually *have* to do any asking.'

'I think I might be sick,' Prue said abruptly, at which point the lights went out.

'Oh arse, it must be a power cut.' June's voice was suddenly very sober in the darkness.

'Hang on, I think there's a torch on the window sill.' I groped my way over to the kitchen window and felt along it. It was all unfamiliar in the dark – strange lumps and bumps, dust under my fingernails. No torch. Just the intense darkness of the countryside pressing in on me, so thick it was almost palpable. Air so dark was hard to breathe somehow.

Then my fingers touched a bit of scrap paper, rough and thick, like a torn bit of wallpaper. I felt my way along the counter to the cooker and lit the edge of the paper on the gas ring. It flared into life, illuminating the room just long enough for me to see the torch, right where I had thought it was. I grabbed for it, just as the paper singed my fingers, and I dropped it. As soon as I had the torch safely lit I bent down and picked it up.

'I hope this wasn't anything important.' I peered at it in the torchlight.

Prue looked over my shoulder.

'Is it a letter or something?'

'I have no idea. Oh no!' I suddenly realized what it was. 'It's a piece of Dad's cookbook.'

'A cookbook?' Liz looked at it, the torchlight glinting off her glasses. 'It doesn't look like a cookbook. What does it say?'

'The rest of it's here.' I showed the bundle of charred scraps. 'Dad found it while he was redecorating. He thought it might be an old book of recipes but it's half burnt.'

'I don't think it's recipes,' Liz said slowly, leafing through the pages. 'It looks more like a spell book to me.'

Prue snorted.

'You've had too much cava, my dear. On top of all that talk about burning witches.'

'Oh shut up,' Liz said mildly. 'Look at this if you don't believe me.'

'I can't see anything by torchlight,' said Prue. 'Let's go into the living room – it'll be lighter by the fire.'

The fire had died down to embers but there was still enough light to see by. We all knelt around the hearth trying to make out the crabbed, spidery writing. It was headed '*Harm gainst the Fayling Gripe* and seemed to be a list of ingredients, most of them illegible or burned,

41

followed by an incantation in what looked like Old English.

'Wow!' Even Prue was impressed. 'It really *is* a spell book. Let's have a look at the rest of it, Liz. I can't say I'm particularly bothered by the Gripes so perhaps there's something more useful. Hey, Anna, does your dad have any more cava?'

I took the torch and went out to have a look. There was no more cava and I wasn't about to venture down into the cellar in the dark, but there was a bottle of whisky in the kitchen cupboard. The wind was howling in the chimney in a way that sent a shiver down my spine, and the torch made a shadowy cavern of the high kitchen ceiling. Something moved stealthily up in the rafters and I shuddered, longing to get back to the company of the others. I took the whisky, trying not to run as I made my way back.

'Sorry, only this.'

'Yuck,' said Prue. She gave a ladylike belch. 'Well, better than nothing I suppose. Pour away.'

'The book seems a bit too burned to be useful,' said Liz, 'but while you were occupied we did manage to find something a bit more to the point than the Gripes. Look at this!'

She held out the page slightly less charred than the

rest, and I saw the heading *Charm to Kepe A Hufband: to kepe a Hufband Faithfull both in Oath and Heart, let Þe wyfe take a little of her Blod and in secrette mix to his Wine. He will never quitte her.*

'Great,' I said. 'When I get married I'll be sure to do that. No doubt my huff-band will be thrilled.'

'And look at what Prue found – an incantation to bind an object of desire! You should try it on Philip, June.'

We all craned round to look at the page. Prue looked up, her broad face shining wickedly in the firelight.

'Go on, let's try it out! Listen.' She began to read haltingly, stumbling over the crabbed letters and unfamiliar spelling: 'To bind an object of desire, close as flesh to bone, as fish to sea, as flame to fire. When the moon waxeth, let the witch hold in her heart the beloved, even while she speak aloud the words of power.'

She held out the book and we bent our heads, silently reading through the short phrase. The strange words reminded me of doing *Beowulf* at school. *Tréowlufu* – I knew *lufu* was love, so perhaps *tréowlufu* was true love. *Ferhþ* I didn't recognize – I thought perhaps it was either faith or forever or something of that kind. *Sáwol* I had a feeling was something like soul. I couldn't suppress a shudder. What were we asking – or promising – with these words?

'Come on, let's do it!' Prue urged. Her face was shiny and scarlet with wine. I wondered if she had someone particular in mind. 'We'll all do it together.'

'Oooh . . . go on then!' Liz took another slosh of whisky.

'I'll do it if it'll make Philip ask me out!' June giggled, and then gave an almighty burp.

'Anna?'

I didn't want to. I really, really didn't want to. There was something sinister about the burnt-up book with its scratchy, spidery writing. I kept wondering who had last held it, and why they'd sealed it in the bread oven. Had they been trying to conceal it – or destroy it? Either way, someone had gone to a good deal of trouble to keep it away from prying eyes. And now we'd unburied it, opened its blackened pages, and read the words hidden and silent for so long. I had the strong feeling of meddling with something we shouldn't.

'I don't know,' I said. The fire flared up, casting tall wavering shadows on the walls and ceiling, and the flames reflected back at me from the window panes and the polished surface of the furniture, until it seemed as if Wicker House itself were burning.

'Oh come *ooooooooooon*,' begged June in an exaggerated tone of pleading. 'I thought you said you weren't superstitious?'

I had said that. And it did seem stupid to be afraid of a few words on a bit of charred paper. It wasn't like I was being asked to drink eye of newt. I looked around the ring of faces, their glittering eyes all urging me on, and that strange, tense feeling welled up inside me again. It felt like some creature inside me trying to get out, trying to escape.

'Scared?' Prue said, and her voice was taunting. I didn't want to, but I didn't want to be the prissy cry-baby from London either. The trapped thing rose inside me, suffocating me. There was no way out.

'Oh . . . OK,' I said. My voice sounded strange and hard in my ears and my face was hot.

'Hooray!' said June. 'I think we should join hands; circle of power and all that, you know.' We knelt on the hearth and joined hands in the flickering light of the fire. I was opposite Prue, her hair sticking up and tousled around her face. In the dim, shifting light she looked positively witchy, and I wouldn't have been surprised to hear a crack of thunder or the screech of an owl break across the quiet night.

'OK, can everyone see the page?' June asked. Everyone nodded.

'We're to hold in our minds the image of our beloved and say the incantation. Ready?'

I wasn't intending to think of anyone in particular. But as the strange, rolling words bubbled from my mouth an image came into my mind involuntarily. It was the face of Seth Waters.

After we all finished speaking there was a deep silence, broken only by the moan of the wind outside the window and the shift and crack of the logs in the grate. We loosed our sticky hands, and June bent and picked up the book.

'Well, that's that,' she said, and shut it with a clap. Something shaped like a leaf fluttered out and we all bent down simultaneously to pick it up.

It wasn't a leaf. It was a hand – the skin of the palm and fingers, dried and pressed flat between the pages of the book like a cruel, misshapen flower.

'Oh yuck, yuck!' shrieked June and kicked it violently towards the fire in a sickened panic. She caught a log with the toe of her boot and the whole mass shifted and crashed into the centre of the grate with a shower of sparks that flew out into the room. We beat them out with our hands and feet – and when the flames subsided the thing, whatever it was, had gone.

There was silence for a second then Prue vomited loudly into the coal scuttle, and the lights came on with a shocking suddenness.

* * *

I felt very glad not to be sleeping alone that night. The house creaked and groaned as if there was a strong wind outside, though the night was still. I listened to the slow rhythm of Prue's snores and tried not to hear the shrieks from the wood, or the rattling scratch of the things that stalked the attic.

Instead I lay in the darkness and tried to think of 'lovely things', just as Dad had told me when I was small and had a nightmare. I thought of Dad, Suzie, Lauren. I thought of seeing all my friends, having them to visit. Summer in the big garden . . . swimming in the sea . . .

My breathing slowed. I was almost asleep when my ear caught another sound, something fluttering against the window pane. The noise was stealthy, soft, persistent. I shut my eyes tighter and pulled the sheets to my chin, pushing away the vision of a dry, dead hand, pressed paper-thin, scrabbling against the window, trying to get in.

CHAPTER FOUR

On Monday morning I ran into Liz and Prue in the car park at school. They both looked a bit shamefaced. Prue was blushing.

'Sorry about being sick, Anna. I totally meant to clean it up but . . .'

'It's fine, honestly. I wasn't in such a bad shape as the rest of you, I think. Anyway I can't imagine mucking out the stable with a hangover was much more fun.'

'It wasn't,' Prue grimaced. 'Well, soz and all that. Oh – and surprise surprise, we saw Philip Granger on the way back from the stables and he ignored June as per usual. No short cuts in love, I guess. Oh look, there she is. Hi, June!'

June was sprinting across the car park. Her face was scarlet with exertion and she was wearing a very odd expression; a mixture of alarm and gleeful excitement.

'Hey girls,' she gasped. 'Anna – I came to warn you, get your flak jacket on.'

'What?' I said, puzzled.

June's chest was still heaving, but she managed, 'According to the grapevine—'

She broke off, her eyes fixed on something over my shoulder.

'Too late.'

Caroline was marching across the car park towards us. Her face was so bitter that I looked behind me involuntarily to see if someone else could be the object of her fury, but there was no one there. There was however a large crowd in front and more people were gathering every second. There was an electric buzz in the air.

When she reached us Caroline stopped. Her blue eyes were ice cold, and she leaned very close to me so that I could feel flecks of spit as she hissed into my face.

'Listen, you boyfriend-stealing bitch, I bet you're pleased with yourself at the moment, but I'm going to make sure that you don't have a single friend left in Winter by the end of today. Oh—' she paused in mock confusion and put a finger to her lips, 'I forgot. You didn't have any worth having to begin with. If you think some ugly skank can just swan down from London and start stealing the boyfriends of people who've lived here all their lives, you've got another think coming. We'd been going out for over a *year*, for God's sake.'

I saw with astonishment that there were tears in her eyes. One of her friends stepped forwards and said timidly, 'Caroline, just leave it.'

'Shut up!' Caroline shouted. Then she turned back to me. 'You are going to regret this for the rest of your life, bitch. In the meantime, here's something to be going on with.'

She drew her hand back and slapped me hard in the face.

It hurt. A lot. I staggered with the force of the blow, my ears hummed and I saw stars – just like in the movies. As the dizziness subsided I could feel my face begin to flame with a stinging pain. Then she spat at my feet and turned to stalk away.

'Stop it, Caroline!' someone shouted, and I looked to see Seth striding across the quad. His face was livid and for the first time I could see where some of his reputation came from – I'd had trouble believing the gossip June had passed on, but now, seeing his face dark with fury, the muscles in his shoulders taut and hard, I could imagine him hitting someone. Maybe even hitting them hard enough to cause considerable damage.

'Stop it.' His voice was quiet, but deadly angry. 'I

told you, it's not her fault.'

'Of course it's her fault,' Caroline spat. 'We were completely happy until *she* turned up. She's a total witch and I hate her.' She tried again to leave and Seth gripped her shoulder so hard I felt sympathetic, even in spite of the burning pain in my cheek.

'For God's sake,' Seth hissed through his teeth, 'just shut up, you're only embarrassing yourself. I suggest you apologize *now* for hitting her or *you're* going to be the one regretting this.'

'Get off me, Seth, you're hurting me!' She winced away from his grip on her shoulder and he released his hand, but shook his head.

'You hurt Anna first.'

'Good.'

She pushed past him without another word and was gone.

Seth turned to me and took my face tenderly in both his hands, turning my flaming cheek to the light.

'Oh, Anna, I'm so sorry.' He touched the swelling bruise gently. I winced, and his face reflected my pain like a mirror. 'I should have warned you. I knew she was on the war-path but I never guessed she'd stoop to this . . . Oh Christ.' He touched my lip. 'It's bleeding.'

'What's going on?' I said thickly. It was hard to speak

and the side of my mouth felt swollen. Seth looked strange – there were dark circles under his eyes as if he hadn't slept, and his clothes were even scruffier and more dishevelled than usual. 'Are you OK?' I asked, through the blood, but he ignored my question.

'We'd better get you to the nurse's office.'

He put an arm around my shoulder, leading me across the car park, through the throng of whispering, gawping spectators, who parted like the Red Sea to let us through. Their faces were alive with shock and, in more than a few cases, envy. I guessed many of them would have swapped with me, burning face and all, in order to be beside Seth's side. I'd rather have been almost anywhere else.

'What on earth!' exclaimed Mrs Carlisle as she unlocked the first aid cupboard. 'Who did this?'

Seth opened his mouth to speak, but I got there first.

'No one, I walked into a lamp-post.'

Mrs Carlisle turned back and raised one eyebrow sarcastically. 'Really.'

'Yes.' Except it came out more like 'yesh'.

'A hand-shaped lamp-post?'

I shrugged and she rolled her eyes.

'Well, I can't make you tell me, but there's a stringent

anti-bullying policy at this school and if I see you in this office again I'm going to be asking some questions – and I won't be asking *you*, Missy.'

I shrugged again, and then winced as she dabbed some TCP on to my split lip. Seth stood next to me holding my hand with his head bowed. He looked the picture of guilt and I got the impression that Mrs Carlisle thought he was probably responsible. It would have helped if I had the first idea what was going on, but I had no intention of dobbing on Caroline. There was obviously some major misunderstanding and I didn't really want to turn scab in my second week at Winter High.

When Mrs Carlisle had finished dressing the cut she gave me an icepack to hold to my cheek and said, 'I'm taking you to your first period, Anna. What is it?'

'Classhics,' I slurred.

'Right. Seth, where are you supposed to be?'

'Chemistry, but Mrs Carlisle, could I please walk Anna—'

'*No*,' said Mrs Carlisle so forcefully even Seth's obvious determination quailed a little. 'I want a word with Anna. Alone.'

As we walked across the quad she tried to get more information out of me by casual chit-chat, plainly not satisfied with the story she had so far. But I wasn't talking – for one thing it hurt too much – and my short yes-or-no answers weren't getting her anywhere. Eventually she had to leave it with my story of a lamp-post and a flat-out assertion that Seth was not involved in any way. She dropped me at the door of my Classics class, where June and Liz were goggling at me from their table, waiting for the story.

There was an audible hum as I slid into my place, and my cheeks began to burn again, not just with the sting of Caroline's slap. All heads turned to look at me until Mrs Finch barked, 'Back to the board, please.'

It was a class discussion of the homework essay, so we had no time to talk, but at the end of the lesson June dragged me aside.

'What did Seth say?'

'Nothing,' I said with difficulty, trying to move my mouth as little as possible. My lip had started to clot and every word cracked the scab painfully. 'What do you mean?'

'You mean he didn't ask you out?'

'No! What on earth do you mean?' I was so surprised I forgot to speak cautiously and winced as fresh blood came into my mouth.

'The story going round, and it's pretty convincing, is

54

that Seth dumped Caroline on Sunday. For you.'

'What!'

'So you don't know? You're not going out with him?'

'No! Of course not.' My cheeks flamed. 'It's complete rubbish; I'm telling you.'

'Well, rubbish or not, he really has dumped Caroline, and she obviously thinks you had something to do with it.'

'I didn't. There must be some misunderstanding.'

'Anna.' June narrowed her eyes. 'Who exactly did you think about when we did that spell?'

Fear curled in my stomach and I felt my face become hard.

'I didn't think of anyone. Anyway, what we did on Saturday had *nothing* to do with anything. It was just a silly schoolgirl game.'

'Hmm. Well, I hate to tell you, but your lip's bleeding on your shirt.'

'Oh crap.' I looked down and sure enough my shirt was stained with drops of blood.

I made my way to the loos, ignoring the stares of people in the corridor. It seemed that from being nobody at Winter High I was suddenly somebody, in a very big way indeed, and I was fast deciding that I'd much preferred being a nobody. I locked myself in a cubicle with a handful of wet loo paper and tried to dab off the worst of the blood, but I just ended up with a wet bloodstained shirt.

I hid in the loos for as long as I could but at last the third bell rang and I knew I had to get to Maths. The corridors were almost empty and I slipped into my seat at the back next to Seth, unnoticed by the rest of the class.

Except, of course, Seth. At my arrival his face lit with a mixture of fury and relief.

'Your face,' he said as I sat down. His expression was stricken and he reached out a hand to touch me. My heart started thudding, even as I flinched away. 'Sorry, sorry, is it very painful?'

'Pretty much, yes.'

'Anna, I'm so, so sorry. If I'd known—'

'Quiet everyone,' called Mr Henderson. 'Now, any problems with the homework?'

'Known what?' I whispered under cover of rustling papers. 'It's not your fault, Seth.'

'But it is,' Seth began.

'Silence!' roared Mr Henderson. 'Unless you have a comment about the homework, I don't want to hear from you.'

Seth waited until Mr Henderson was busy answering a question then carried on, under his breath. 'I wanted to speak to you before you saw Caroline; I didn't have the chance to explain, you see—'

'Seth Waters.' We both jumped. Mr Henderson stood an inch away from our desk, tapping his board ruler menacingly on his open palm. 'Do you, or do you not have a problem with the homework?'

'No, Mr Henderson.'

'Then if I hear from you again, you will be spending the rest of this lesson in the quad. Do you understand me?'

'Yes, Mr Henderson.'

He turned away, and Seth wrote on a piece of paper: *Meet me at the harbour at lunchtime?*

Reluctantly I nodded. I didn't really want to add fuel to whatever imaginary fire Caroline had concocted by sneaking off with Seth, but I very much wanted to know what was going on.

When I arrived at the harbour Seth was already there, sitting on a small sailing boat tethered to the quayside. He was looking down at something on his lap, and I watched him as I walked along the quay.

His profile was sharp against the grey of the water, his curly dark hair tousled by the sea wind gusting across the bay. Somehow he looked different from the boy I sat next to in Maths – older, more serious, more capable. He belonged with a crew of fishermen hauling oyster pots home in some Greek port, or gutting sardines on a

Portuguese quayside. Lots of things about him – his deep tan, his calloused hands, the lean strength of his arms and shoulders – suddenly made sense.

Then I tripped over a coil of rope and he looked up, and his expression changed to one of open delight.

'Anna! You came.'

'Of course.'

He folded up the chart he'd been reading and leapt easily off the boat onto the quay.

'Have you already got lunch? I should have warned you there aren't any cafés open yet, they don't open up until a bit later in the season.'

I shook my head.

'I'm not very hungry, I don't really want to eat much with my mouth like this.'

'Of course.' He looked stricken. 'Here.' He threw down a parcel of rolled up sails. 'Sit on this. It'll be a bit cleaner than the quay.'

'Seth, what's going on?'

Seth bit his lip and looked out to sea. For the first time I noticed that his eyes were not brown, as I'd thought, but very dark grey, like the chalky channel sea on a thundery day. There was silence for a while and then he sighed.

'Well, you know I broke up with Caroline.'

'I heard. I'm really sorry.'

58

'I'm not. But I am sorry that I said something stupid to her.'

I waited and he continued slowly, 'I said it was because of you.'

'I see,' I said. My throat suddenly closed and I found it impossible to say any more. I wanted to say, 'Don't be silly, it doesn't matter if you used me as an excuse, you don't have to apologize for anything, just set everything straight'. But I couldn't seem to get the words out.

'And Caroline got hold of the wrong end of the stick,' he continued heavily. 'She thought there was something going on between us.'

'Which there's not, obviously,' I said painfully. My lip had cracked again and I tasted blood.

Seth shook his head. 'No.' Then he reached and took both my hands in his. I felt the shocking warmth of his skin and the roughness of his fingers and palms. There was a deep welt, like a rope burn, along the underside of his wrist, and I had to fight the urge to run my thumb along the scar. His face was pale, in spite of his deep tan, and there were shadows under his eyes. He looked exhausted yet wired, and there was a frightening intensity in his expression that I couldn't understand. Then he took a breath. 'But I would like it if there was.'

'What?' I was so surprised that I stood up, pulling my

59

hands away. He stood too, his words tumbling over one another.

'I know, I know this is sudden and we've only just met, and I don't want to freak you out – but Anna, I've never met anyone like you. You're wonderful, and amazing, and clever and witty and beautiful. I woke up on Sunday and – I can't explain it – I suddenly realized that you were what's been missing in my life. I don't know how it took me so long.'

'So long!' I gasped. 'You've only known me a week!'

'I feel like I've known you all my life – I'm completely obsessed with you – with the way you look, the way you move, the way your skin smells, the way the sun brings out the little red glints in your hair. I've thought about nothing else since.' I was so shocked I couldn't speak, and he pressed on, 'I know this is probably all too much, too soon, but I couldn't carry on with Caroline feeling the way I do about you. Please, I'm not expecting anything in return, but I had to say something. I've never felt like this before. The girls in Winter – they're just so, so *ordinary*, and then you came along and it was like, like nothing else mattered any more.'

He stopped, touched my lip with his warm, calloused thumb, and swallowed.

'Anna, I know this sounds crazy but – I love you.'

For a minute I was mesmerized by it all – the sound of the sea crashing on the quay, the feel of his touch, the intensity of his slate-grey eyes. Then sanity broke through and I pushed his hand away violently.

'Seth, stop it! This is ridiculous.' My voice was shaking.

'I know.' He looked bewildered. 'I know it is, and I don't expect you to feel the way I do. I don't expect anything of you. I just want . . . I don't know. I want you to know I love you, and I always will.'

'Stop it!' I cried, putting my hands over my ears and closing my eyes. This was terrible – it was so right and yet so, so wrong.

'I'm sorry,' Seth said. There was a catch in his voice. 'I know this is ridiculously sudden. I won't say any more if it's upsetting you.'

A dreadful thought suddenly struck me and I opened my eyes.

'Is this a wind-up? Did June put you up to it?'

'What?' He looked horrified. 'No! What's June got to do with it? How could you think I would joke about something like this?'

For a moment I considered telling him about Saturday night and the incantation and the whole ridiculous childish business – then sanity returned. I couldn't. I couldn't possibly. And it couldn't possibly be true anyway. There

61

must be some other explanation – a rush of hormones – or some monumentally awful misunderstanding.

'I'm sorry,' I said at last. My voice shook. 'I can't do this. Please – please just forget it. Tomorrow you'll think better of all this and you'll be really embarrassed and so will I. Let's just pretend you never said any of this – it'll be better for both of us.'

'OK. But it won't change the way I feel. I love you. I'll feel the same way tomorrow, and the day after that, and the day after that. But I don't want to hurt you, Anna – I won't mention this again if it's making you unhappy.'

'It is,' I said, and felt tears rolling down my cheeks in spite of everything I could do to prevent them. And then I was in his arms, and he was stroking my hair.

'Please, please, Anna, don't cry. Oh love, please don't cry.'

I could feel the beat of his heart and the heat of his skin through the thin T-shirt. For a moment I considered staying there, resting my cheek against his chest and folding into his warmth. It would be so easy, so tempting, so right . . .

I stopped myself. This was wrong. However I felt about him, his feeling for me was nothing but some inexplicable mistake, a passing illusion. I was making a fool out of myself and, even if he didn't realize it, so was Seth.

'Please stop this,' I said as coldly as I could, trying to

struggle out of his arms. 'You don't love me, and I don't want to hear anything more about this. Just leave me alone, and we'll both be happier.'

'I don't believe you,' he said. His arms imprisoned me without effort, but it was the look in his intense dark eyes that made me stop fighting. 'I don't believe you. Tell me that you don't feel anything.'

But I couldn't. I couldn't speak. I only stood, trembling, my heart beating painfully, as he leaned down towards me. Then he kissed me.

For a long, long moment I did nothing, only melted into the kiss, my head spinning with desire, my arms twining up to his shoulders, feeling his muscles tremble and flex beneath the thin material of his T-shirt as he gripped me tighter. The sounds and scents of the port ebbed far away. The roar of the sea was drowned by the roar of blood in my head, the sound of Seth's heart, and our panting, gasping breaths as we locked closer and closer.

But even as I began to kiss him back, in the back of my mind a tiny voice was still insisting *This is wrong*.

'No!' I tore away and, not trusting myself any further, I ran. I ran up the quay, panting and blinded by tears, and on to the main road, where I half walked, half stumbled home, crying all the way.

CHAPTER FIVE

The whole business was obviously either a prank or some kind of mass hallucination – after a good night's sleep that much was obvious. I walked to school on Tuesday certain that Seth would have realized overnight what a tit he'd been – either that or there would be a massive sign at the school gates saying: 'ANNA WINTERSON – YOU JUST GOT PUNK'D!'

Whatever it was, no one could keep this up for two days. One way or another, everything had to be back to normal – didn't it?

The hope was dashed as soon as I entered the school grounds. Approximately three million eyes turned to stare at me – or at least that was what it felt like.

I walked slowly across the quad, trying to keep my gaze down, away from the curious faces, until a large group of girls barred the way. I stepped left, so did they.

I stepped right, so did they.

'Excuse me,' I said. The middle one, who I recognized as a friend of Caroline, folded her arms and put her head on one side, her long earrings jangling in the breeze.

'It looks like there's not enough room on this path for everyone, doesn't it? I suggest you go the long way round.'

I sighed. The long way round was a ten-minute walk.

'Isn't this a bit childish?'

'Look at it how you want. But this path is too small for all of us. And, frankly, so is this school. I don't know what they're like in *London*,' her voice dripped sarcasm, 'but in Winter we don't have much time for boyfriend-stealing bitches.'

I sighed again and turned away, and there was a snicker of satisfied laughter behind me. One of them called out a word I'd never heard used in school before, not even in London. My eyes blurred but I kept going even though I could barely see the path. I was not, I was *not* going to let them see me cry.

Suddenly I felt my arm seized.

'Listen,' hissed Seth's voice beside my ear, 'turn around, Anna. Those,' he choked, so angry he could barely speak, 'those *silly* little girls are going to beg your pardon and let you through before I'm done.'

'Seth, please don't. Please, just leave it.'

'No. You can't turn back; your life will be a misery at Winter if you give in now. You have to let me help you.'

He was right; I knew it. I turned wretchedly around and Seth spoke coolly to the leader.

'Hi, Jess.'

'Hi, Seth.' Her voice was guarded, as if she wasn't sure what she'd taken on.

'Anna would like to get through. I suggest you get out of her way.'

Indecision mixed with fury flickered across Jess's face and eventually she stood aside. But Seth didn't move.

'And perhaps you could say sorry for blocking the path so rudely.'

I cringed inside, but Seth had my arm in an iron grip. I could barely move, let alone slink away. Jess's face hardened.

'Perhaps. But I don't really want to.'

'I'm waiting.'

'Look, Seth, I've got no problem with you,' she said in a low voice.

'If you've got a problem with Anna, you've got a problem with me.' His voice was equally low, and full of menace. 'Beg. Her. Pardon.'

'Seth . . .' Jess looked over his shoulder at the large crowd that had gathered at the hint of a showdown.

I saw Caroline over the heads of the crowd, her face dark with fury.

I felt Seth come to a decision beside me. He put his arm around me and turned to face the crowd, raising his voice.

'OK, let's get one thing straight. Whatever happened with Caroline and me, Anna had nothing to do with it. But she's a good friend of mine and anyone who wants to be on speaking terms with me had better realize that. If you want to pick a fight with her, pick it with me first. Is that clear?'

I'd never felt so humiliated in my life. There was a murmur from the crowd and he turned back to Jess.

'Jess? I haven't got all day.'

She tossed her hair and muttered something under her breath. Seth leaned forward.

'I didn't catch that.'

'Sorry!' Jess practically shouted. 'All right?'

She turned and stormed away. As she left I saw her shrug her shoulders at Caroline.

I shrugged ungratefully out from under Seth's arm, trying my best to ignore the myriad students staring at me. Their expressions ranged from amusement (most of the boys) to green-eyed envy (at least half the girls – the more stupid half in my opinion). My cheeks were burning as I slipped as inconspicuously as possible into South Building. So much for things being back to normal.

I slunk into English and sat down next to Emmaline with my face still scarlet. To my surprise she was slinging books into her bag.

'Aren't you staying?' I asked.

'You've got a nerve,' she hissed. 'What the hell do you think you're playing at?'

'What?'

'Don't act innocent with me. Whatever you did on *Saturday*. You know what you've done to that poor boy and you should be ashamed of yourself. It's disgusting. It's cruel, it's fake and it's disgusting. And if you had any sense of shame you'd have *un*done it. I don't want to share a *town* with you, let alone a desk.'

And she swept out of the room, bumping into Ms Wright, who was just coming in.

'Not staying, Emmaline?' she asked in surprise.

'Sorry, Ms Wright, I'm going home. Something's made me feel horribly sick.' And with that Emmaline shot me a glance of pure hate and then walked out.

At break I cornered June.

'Have you talked to anyone about what we did on

Saturday?'

'No, of course not, why?'

'Because I just had a very strange run-in with Emmaline Peller and it certainly *sounded* like she knew what went on.'

'What – that snooty cow? Emmaline Peller won't give me the time of day, Anna. Frankly she's the last person I'm going to have a heart-to-heart with about drunken antics. Anyway, why do you care?'

I ignored the question and pursued, 'So you haven't told *anyone*?'

'For the last time, no! Why are you so bothered about this?'

'Because . . .' I said lamely. 'Because . . . It's just a bit embarrassing, especially now Seth's dumped Caroline.'

June gave me a very sharp look.

'I thought you said you didn't think about Seth on Saturday, that this whole business was nothing to do with you.'

'It's *not*.' I undermined my emphatic assertion by blushing a furious red. 'I didn't. But – but people might get the wrong idea.'

'Well, whatever. I certainly haven't told anyone. But I can't speak for Prue or Liz.'

But, when I questioned them, Prue and Liz both denied it too. I wasn't sure what to make of it. Most of Emmaline's words had been fairly ambiguous. But that spat out 'Whatever you did on *Saturday*' was pretty specific. It could only refer to one thing . . .

I worried at the question all the way home, barely noticing the climb as I trudged up the cliff road to the woods. My feelings swung back and forth like a pendulum, between a scoffing incredulity, and a stomach-churning acid fear that we really *had* set something off with the spell book.

Surely, *surely* this was ridiculous. This was the twenty-first century, not Cromwellian England. Burnings, bewitchments and spellbindings were things of the distant past.

And yet. Wasn't it a bit *too* much of a coincidence? Where had Seth's violent obsessive infatuation come from, if not from the spell book? I wasn't arrogant enough to think that Seth had gone crazy over me of his own accord. Guys like him just didn't fall for girls like me in the real world. Whatever I might want to believe.

Emmaline's angry words kept reverberating in my head: 'If you had any sense of shame you'd have *un*done it.' The realization came with a queasy mingling of relief and dread. If there was a spell in the book to bind someone, might there be a spell to *un*bind them . . . ?

* * *

My stomach was sick and churning as I climbed the creaking stairs to my room. I don't know why, but the first thing I did was to go to the window and draw the curtains, shutting out the brightness of the day. The last thing I saw as I pulled the curtains across was the spreading beech, crusted thicker than ever with hunched, beaked shadows, silent and watchful.

The book was hidden under my bed, wrapped in newspaper. Now I undid the bindings with the feeling of opening a Pandora's box – but the only thing that escaped was the smell of charred parchment as I leafed through the fragile pages. Every page felt like a sprung trap, hiding another pressed hand, or something worse, but I kept going, driven on by the memory of Seth's wild desperation and Emmaline's accusing eyes.

Many of the spells were completely burnt or illegible, and some called for ingredients I didn't recognize or couldn't possibly find, like the tongue of a manatee, or a handful of powdered mandragore, whatever that was. Others were very simple: an instruction to lay a broom across the door, so that *none with ille-intent may enter & harm thee*. Probably because they'd trip over the broom, jeered the sceptical voice in my head.

At last I came to a stop on a badly charred page. Flakes of ash smudged my fingers, but the words were more or less legible: *A Spelle to Releafe One Bewitched from a Charm.* I swallowed, and read on, trying to decipher the crabbed letters.

It instructed the reader to light a fire. Then to take a handful of salt and whisper the name of the charmed one to the salt. Then you had to throw the salt into the fire and say a short incantation *while the flammes burn brighte.* That looked OK; I had salt, I knew the name of the 'charmed one', and I could light a fire.

Feeling rather foolish, I lit the fire in my bedroom grate and waited for it to burn up a little. Then I took a handful of Dad's expensive Maldon salt flakes from the kitchen – it seemed somehow more witchy than the ordinary kind – and whispered Seth's name into my fist. When I threw the salt into the fire it flamed up impressively and I read aloud the incantation.

'Dóð swá ic bidde.' The words were thick and strange like treacle on my tongue, bitter and hard to speak. 'þone gehæftend álíese!'

My voice cracked – I swallowed, and cried the final line louder, defying my fear and the mocking voices in my head.

'Dóð swá ic bidde!'

My voice flung back at me from the rafters, harsh with determination, the strange words ringing long after the echoes died. What did it mean? Did I need to know? Did I *want* to know?

But as the flames subsided, only silence filled the room. I don't know what I expected to happen – some kind of sign perhaps. But nothing.

God. Who was I kidding with all this crap? I shut the book, with a feeling of sick disgust at myself, my gullibility, my desperation. But something coiled in my stomach, a clench of nerves at the thought of tomorrow.

The next morning I strode along the cliff path to school feeling half hopeful and half ridiculous. It was all so stupid – and I didn't believe it anyway. But how comforting if I turned up at the school gates to find Seth snogging Caroline behind the bike sheds and everything back to normal. I ignored the tiny twinge of pain that image provoked – Seth wasn't mine, it was stupid to feel sadness at the thought of losing what I didn't really have.

Suddenly a horn blasted out behind me. I jumped convulsively and turned to see Seth pulling up behind me in his dad's truck.

'Hi, Anna, can I give you a lift?' he called.

For a moment I hesitated – torn between wanting to accept and not wanting to enrage Caroline any further. Seth saw my indecision and sighed.

'Look, don't worry. I'm sorry I asked, and I'm really sorry about what happened down at the quay. I know I was out of line.' An expression of bewilderment crossed his face. 'I acted like . . . Well, anyway, I understand if you don't want to accept a lift from me.'

Guilt curdled in the pit of my stomach.

'Don't be silly, Seth. Of course I'd love a lift.' I hauled myself up into the truck and the engine roared into life. He sighed as he rebuckled his belt and gave me a wry look.

'I really am sorry, and I promise to keep my animal urges under control this time, if it's any consolation. I don't normally go around jumping on girls uninvited.'

'Seth, stop apologizing.' My face was scarlet and I felt like the worst person in the world. 'Let's change the subject. How are you?'

'Fine. How are you?'

'OK. Thanks.' I sneaked a look sideways, trying to work out if the spell had worked, but he was frowning over the steering wheel, his face unreadable.

'I hope you're not letting those girls at school get to you. I should never have said your name to Caroline in the first place; it wasn't fair on you. The sight of them laying into you like that—' His hands tightened on the steering wheel until the tendons stood out and his knuckles showed pale against the tanned skin. 'God, I could have cheerfully belted every last one of them, girls or not.'

'But you're not angry at Caroline are you?' I ventured. 'I mean, do you think you'll get back together?'

Seth turned a horrified face towards me.

'What? How can you ask that? Of course I'm not going to get back with her. I'm furious with her. If I ever was in love with her, which I'm not sure I was now, the way she's been treating you these past few days has been enough to put me off for good. I always knew she had a bitchy side but I never realized she was capable of being so downright cruel. I wouldn't be in the same room with her again, if I had the choice.'

Oh crap. This didn't sound good. I was cringing with embarrassment inside, but I had to know.

'Seth, listen, do you—' I swallowed. 'Do you still . . . like me?'

'*Like* you?' His expression was astonished. 'Of course I like you. What do you mean?'

I undid my seatbelt.

'Actually, Seth, I'm really sorry but I've just remembered something I forgot at home. Could you let me out?'

'I'll run you back,' he said, stopping at once and starting a three-point turn.

'No, please don't. I'd honestly rather you didn't.'

'It's no trouble. You can't trudge all the way back up that hill: you'll be late for school.'

'I – I'm not going to school,' I said desperately. 'I'm ill.'

'What?' He took his foot off the accelerator. 'Anna – are you OK?'

'No, please let me out.'

'But—' He reached out for my shoulder but I shook his hand off and fumbled for the door.

'Seth, please just – just leave me alone.'

I jumped down but again misjudged the height of the door and tripped, skinning my knee and ripping my jeans.

'Anna!' I could hear Seth grappling with his seatbelt as I started to walk, hobbling at first with the pain from my knee, then faster as I heard the slam of his door and his feet on the gravel behind me.

'Anna, stop! You're hurt!'

'No!' I shouted back, tears springing into my eyes out of a mixture of rage, frustration and pain.

'Anna!' He caught up to me, even though I was half running by now, and grabbed at my shoulder. 'For God's sake, let me take you home, Anna.'

'Stop it!' I screamed. He fell back at the sight of my tear-stained face. 'Seth, please just go away. I mean it. Go!'

'OK.' He held up a hand. His face was white with hurt,

and he half turned away. For a minute I thought he was going – but then something seemed to wrench at him, like a fish-hook in his flesh and he turned back. 'I'm sorry, Anna, but I can't just . . . Look, will you let me drive you home? I just want to—'

'No!' I couldn't bear a second more, just the sight of him twisted at my insides like a knife. A sob rose up inside me and I choked out, 'Please, Seth. Just – just leave me alone.'

He didn't say anything after that. He just stood and watched as I hobbled painfully up the long cliff road. After about twenty minutes I risked a glance back, and he was still there, his tall silhouette blurred with my tears. It began to rain and I hobbled on, feeling his steadfast gaze on my back, my tears mingling with the rain.

It started to thunder just as I got to the house. Dad's car was gone from the drive, so I knew he was out. I slammed the front door with relief and stripped off my wet shirt, shivering in my bra and jeans. There was a pile of laundry by the foot of the stairs and I grabbed a towel off the top of the heap and wrapped it round my shoulders, scrubbing my wet hair with it. In a flash of lightning I saw my face illuminated in the hall mirror. It gave me a start – I looked so gaunt and ghostly, with draggled rats' tails of sopping dark hair and eyes just pits of shadows. There was a smear of mud on my cheekbone. Then the thunder answered, making me jump again.

My teeth chattered uncontrollably as I retrieved the spell book from its hiding place. I crouched by the fireplace, trying to wipe my tears away enough to read the words. I wanted this *over*, as soon as possible. I wanted Seth back to normal and life back to normal and this whole twisted, bloody mess sorted out.

The thunder and lightning came again, closer together this time, and the ashes in the grate were being slowly pitted by raindrops from the chimney. As I turned the pages with numb fingers I heard a tap-tap at the window and leapt convulsively, expecting to see Seth's pale, rain-drenched face at the glass. I jumped up, ready to scream at him, to force him once and for all to leave me alone. I'd threaten to call the police if that was what it took.

But there was no one there, only the crow, hunched on the window sill. I stood, my hands shaking with cold and nerves while it watched me with expressionless eyes. It tapped on the glass again with its hooked black beak, as if asking for entry.

'Shoo!' I shouted, furious with myself for being scared. Then I beat on the glass so that the window shook in its frame and the leaded panes rattled. The crow rose, flapped its great wings, and wheeled away.

I watched it go, dissolving into the storm-wracked sky like a dot of black paint swirling into water, then returned to the book with a shudder. It had fallen open at the page I was looking for, and I smoothed out the instructions with trembling fingers.

To lift a Spelle – let this incantation be rede in the place of bewitchement.

Hagorúne.

Hagorún.

Hagorú.

Hagor.

Hago.

Hag.

Ha.

H.

This was it. The tingling rushed through me again, like pins and needles in my blood.

I drew a breath and then I said the words. My teeth were clenched with cold and I couldn't stop myself shivering convulsively as I spoke. My chattering teeth made the words sound even eerier, the last strangled 'H!' coming like a shuddering gasp of desire, or fear.

I finished, and there was silence for a few seconds. It was so quiet that I could hear the rush of blood in my ears and my own gasping breaths. Even the rain seemed to stop, and then came the most stupendous crack of thunder, accompanied by other noises from above – a roaring crash, like the roof was falling in, and what sounded like screams.

Something huge and heavy was coming down the chimney, sending great gusts of soot choking out into the room. Thuds and cracks sounded from the hearth, a mushroom cloud of ash spewed up from the grate. The room was filled with a sound like thunder and thick gouts of smoke and ash obscured my vision so that I was blinded as well as deafened. For a minute I thought I saw the crow's dark shadow, its wings beating at my face.

And then a searing pain in my head, a flashing brightness that tore across my vision, and a slide into darkness.

Everything was a jumble. My head was throbbing, and in time with the throbs a broken voice was saying, 'Anna, oh God, please wake up, Anna.' And then a gasped, 'Oh God!'

More thuds, rocks shaking the floor, making my head pound with each thump – something crouched over me, shielding me bodily. Then, as the dust settled again, strong arms reached around me, and there was a moment's agony as my head lolled and throbbed. Hands hot on the cold skin of my back . . . the sound of feet crunching on stone and a catch of breath as I was lowered carefully to the ground again. Pain like an electric shock rocked my body as my skull shifted against the hard ground and my muscles went weak and liquid.

Then I felt a rough hand stroking my cheek . . . and slowly my muscles relaxed from their tense agony into something nearing content. The cold abated slightly, kept at bay by the warm arms around me. I felt I could sleep . . . almost. If only my head would stop pounding.

I became aware that hot liquid was trickling down past my ear. It tickled unbearably, but my limbs were far too heavy to lift a hand to wipe it away. There was a low groaning sound and the voice said with a catch, 'Thank God! Anna, I know you can hear me. The ambulance is coming. There are people coming to help. Just hang on, please just hang on.'

The moan came again, and I wondered who was in so much pain. I felt very sorry for whoever it was. Then I realized it was me.

I woke to a confused babble of noise and a host of uncomfortable sensations – damp, gloved hands poking and prodding me, the chilly metallic kiss of a stethoscope on my bare chest, a strange, new voice insistently saying, 'Anna, Anna, Anna.'

'I had to move her,' said the voice. 'There were more rocks coming down.'

'You did the right thing; don't worry. You did really well to get hold of us so quick. If you hadn't been here it could have been a lot worse.'

'But will she be OK? All that blood, and she was so white when I found her, I thought . . .' His breath caught in his throat. 'I thought she was dead.'

Who was the voice? It was familiar and comforting but I couldn't place it. Not Dad . . .

'Anna, can you hear me?'

I was reluctantly yanked out of my introspection by two cold fingers pulling up my eyelids and a bright light searing my left eye.

'It's OK,' said the strange voice. 'She's coming to.' Then, over his shoulder to someone behind him, 'Breathing and circulation both good. BP a bit low but otherwise her obs are fine. Anna, Anna, can you hear me? Do you know where you are? Open your eyes please, Anna.'

'Owwww . . .' This time I recognized the husky moan for my own voice. My head was throbbing viciously. I opened my eyes to the blurry dazzle of the room and put a trembling hand up to the pain. It came away warm and sticky with crusted blood.

'Wh-what's happened?'

Someone bent over me and took my hand; my eyes were too dazzled to see properly but the familiar voice said, 'Anna, everything's OK. Don't worry, I've called your dad.'

'Anna, lie still please, don't try to move. You've just hit your head but you're fine,' the other voice said. 'There's an ambulance here waiting to take you to hospital.' I blinked. The blurry images shifted and resolved a little and I made out Seth, two paramedics behind him. I tried to sit up but found I was strapped to something, and the paramedic stepped in.

'Don't try to move, Anna. You've got a head injury. Can you tell me where you are?'

'H-home,' I managed.

'What's your full name?'

'Anna Winterson.' My voice was a thread and everything hurt.

'Very good, and what day is it?'

That was harder. I shut my eyes and moaned as the pain throbbed again.

'Anna, don't go back to sleep. Anna, do you know what day it is?'

'Tuesday,' I whispered. The paramedic nodded.

'Very good, good girl. We're going to lift you now, just stay relaxed.'

I found I was already strapped to a stretcher and one paramedic moved efficiently to each end, counting the lift. As I was being manoeuvred out of the door I heard Seth say, 'I want to come too.'

Oh God, couldn't the guy take a hint? I tried to shake my head but it seemed to be wedged in place by some kind of pillow and the first paramedic said, 'I'm sure that's fine. She'll do better with a familiar face around. What's your name, son?'

The second paramedic leaned over me and said slowly and clearly, 'Anna, we've called your dad, and in the meantime your boyfriend's going to come with you, so you won't be alone.'

'He's not . . .' I tried to say through thick lips, but the words were slurred.

'I'm just a friend,' I heard Seth say, but the paramedics weren't listening. They were speaking into their radios, discussing what route to take to the hospital.

In the ambulance they tucked a blanket around me. I shut my eyes, and everything, even the wail of the siren, began to take on an oddly distant quality. Even Seth's hand gripping mine wasn't enough to anchor me, and I slipped slowly into sleep.

When I woke up again Dad was sitting beside me, gently stroking my hair on the pillow, and Seth was nowhere to be seen. My throat was burningly dry and everything hurt, including my head.

'Thirsty,' I whispered, and Dad jumped.

'Anna! Oh sweetie, thank goodness.' He got up and reached for a jug of water, holding a paper cup to my lips. Most of it spilled down my front but I managed to sip enough to ease the hoarseness in my throat and I smiled up at Dad with weak relief.

'What happened?' I croaked. Dad gave a shaky laugh.

'I should be asking you that! All I know is what your friend Seth told me. You've got a lot to thank him for. Do you remember the thunderstorm?'

'Not sure,' I whispered.

'Seth said that you forgot something on the way to school and had to go back. He was waiting at the end of the lane and heard a clap of thunder followed by an almighty crash. When you didn't reappear he was worried enough to go after you. It looks like the living room chimney collapsed – God knows how – and some of the stones ricocheted down the flue. One of them hit you on the head and knocked you out. When Seth found you, you were unconscious in a pool of blood. He called the ambulance – and here we are.'

Memories were starting to come back. One of them was so unbearable I shut my eyes. Yes, I was lying in a pool of blood, *in my bra*. I moaned again and Dad put a concerned hand on my cheek.

'Oh, sweetie, is it very painful? I could ask for some more painkillers if you need them.'

'It's OK,' I whispered huskily. I felt surreptitiously under the sheets. I seemed to be wearing a hospital gown now, from what I could make out. Would I ever live this down at school?

'Well, they've done an X-ray and some other scans and it looks like you're fine, but they want to keep you in overnight in case there's concussion.'

At least it looked like I wouldn't have to face Caroline for another day or two. Every cloud, and all that.

'I'm furious with the surveyors,' Dad was saying. 'They said the house was perfectly structurally sound. I know there was a thunderstorm but there's no evidence of charring or anything to indicate a lightning hit, that I could see. From what I can make out, the tremors of the thunder just caused half the stack to collapse spontaneously. *And* there's a huge crack down the side of the house.'

'Will it cost a lot?'

'Probably, but it'll be covered by insurance. It's mainly the risk to you I'm angry about. The stack went right through your bedroom roof. If you'd been upstairs you'd almost certainly have been killed! As it was it's a miracle there's no skull fracture. You've got a lot to thank Seth for, you know. If he hadn't dragged you clear and called the paramedics when he did, things could have been a lot worse.'

'Has he gone?' I wasn't sure what answer I was hoping for.

'Yes, he stayed with you until I turned up and then left. But he must have been here a good five or six hours. I'll have to speak to the school to make sure he doesn't get into trouble for missing classes. He's been a very good friend to you, Anna.'

'I know,' I whispered.

It was almost a relief when Dad was gone. I asked the nurses to pull the curtains around my cubicle and lay on my unhurt side, letting my tears leak into the pillow.

Seth didn't deserve this. He deserved real love, not this unwilling, hypnotized, obsessive mockery – loving in spite of himself, loving against his true inclination. I might as well hold a gun to his head and force him to say the words, they would have had as much basis in reality.

87

I'd done protesting. I no longer believed it was coincidence. We *had* set something off with our meddling. No, that wasn't right. *I* had set something off with my meddling. Although the others had been there, although they'd said the words too, it seemed pretty plain that, for some reason, only I'd caused harm. Harm to poor, unsuspecting Seth. And now more harm with the collapse of the chimney – although at least the only person to suffer this time was myself.

I thought of the book with a shudder, the charred pages full of destructive, pent-up power. And I thought, too, of that other witch. The one who'd put the book there. The one who'd been stoned, burned, drowned, and driven away from Winter like a pariah. What good had her spells done her?

But I couldn't just leave matters as they were. I'd started this off, so I had to finish it somehow, I couldn't abandon Seth to his sentence of false love. Who knew when it would wear off. A month? A year? A lifetime?

As my tears dried, I made myself a promise. I would try one last spell to release Seth. And if that didn't work, I'd admit defeat. I'd burn the book and never meddle again. And somehow, *somehow*, I'd persuade Seth to leave me alone, even if that meant exercising a self-restraint I wasn't sure I possessed.

CHAPTER SIX

'Anna.' Dad put his head around the bedroom door. 'How are you feeling?'

I groaned and put down my book. 'For heaven's sake, Dad. It's been a week, nearly. Could we move on from the twice-hourly checks?'

'Well it's just I might need to go out for a bit – could you manage? I've hit a hitch with the bathroom and I need a new connector for the loo. It might take a while.'

'People have been known to survive several hours without fresh-pressed juice and cold flannels, you know.'

'Weeell . . . If you're sure.' He held me at arm's length and gave me a searching look as though he could detect brain swelling just with the power of his bifocal glasses. 'I feel a lot happier since we've had the phone line installed, I must admit. It really chilled me that Seth had to go to the main road to call 999 – you owe him your life, you know.'

'I know, I know. I could've bled to death, blah-di-blah.'

I didn't mean it to sound as petulant and teenagerish as it came out, but I was fed up of hearing for the millionth time how wonderful Seth had been and how much I owed him. Dad seemed to think I was being criminally ungrateful by refusing to return Seth's calls. And by any normal standards I was, but Dad had no idea how hard it was for me to keep Seth at bay, and how much harder he was making it by rubbing my ingratitude in my face.

'Well,' Dad said, 'I'll take my mobile, but if you need anything urgently you can call this number.' He passed me a post-it with a local number written on it, alongside the name *Elaine Waters*. I frowned.

'Who's this?'

'Oh, lovely lady. I met her at the Crown and Anchor. She owns it actually. She's offered to keep on standby in case there's any emergency or you don't feel well.'

'She's Seth's mum, isn't she?'

'I believe so.' Dad put up a feigned nonchalance.

'For God's sake, Dad, please don't meddle!'

'I'm not meddling!' He looked offended. 'Look, I met her well before all this business with the chimney. I do have a life while you're at school you know. Anyway,

I happened to ring her the other day, and she happened to volunteer to keep an eye out for you if I needed to go away.'

'Dad . . .' I said warningly. He put up a protesting hand.

'Yes, I admit it, part of the reason I contacted her to was to ask her to thank Seth for everything. I do think you should have returned his calls, but hey, what do I know? I'm just your dad.'

'Yes, you *don't* know, so please butt out.'

'I wasn't butting *in*, young lady. I'm entitled to thank him on my own account. He probably saved the life of my only child and, strange as it may seem, I *am* rather grateful for that fact.'

I said nothing, but only clenched my teeth. Dad sighed.

'Sometimes I think that chimney really did knock some of the sense out of your head. I'm sure you were never this difficult in London.'

'Oh, Dad, come on! That's not fair.'

Perhaps the hurt in my voice got through to him, even without knowing what was behind it, for his face softened and he patted my hand.

'Sorry, I know it's not really. And I know I shouldn't interfere in your life; you're old enough to make your own decisions. Whatever's going on with you and Seth, I promise I won't interfere. But I *do* like Elaine on her own account, so please be polite if she phones.'

'I'll be polite,' I promised. 'But nothing will come up, so please, just go, have a nice time, don't worry.'

'And *you*, take it easy and don't hesitate to ring if you need to, remember?'

An hour later I was standing by the living room window waving to Dad's car as it bumped down the rutted track to the main road, and out of sight.

He was gone. I was alone in the silent, watchful house. I'd been waiting for this moment for nearly a week – it was time to throw in my hand, sort this out once and for all.

As soon as I was sure Dad wasn't coming back, I took the book out from under my bed. I couldn't repress a shudder as I handled the heavy, crumbling mass of paper. It repelled me; the thick, curling pages like leathery skin, the crabbed scratchy writing, the lists of cruel necessities. As I leafed through the pages they sprang out at me; the tongue of a kitten, a child's tears, three hairs from an adulterous woman, blood from a virgin girl.

'To Brake of the Strongest Magick,' I read under my breath, 'a Darke Spell, onely to be Ufed in Great Need.'

Was this a case of great need? Nothing else had worked

and I couldn't condemn poor Seth to a lifetime of enchantment. The page was burned almost to ashes and in places the writing stood out silver against the blackened parchment. There were other marks: strange symbols in a witches' alphabet, and dark, rust-red blotches. I tried not to think about what they were. At the bottom of the page I made out a faint note in a different hand: *oh sisters Beware.*

I shuddered, then pulled myself together. I could do this. I could do this for Seth.

'Come on, Anna,' I whispered aloud, and felt a little courage return. But even so, the first line chilled me: *Take of the Bloode of a Witch.*

Well, there was no witch to hand, so I'd have to use the only blood available. Mine.

In the kitchen I took the sharpest knife I could find, shut my eyes and, steeling myself, I scraped my thumb down the blade. The rough metal bit into my flesh and when I opened my eyes a deep cut welled gore on to the kitchen table. It hurt, but I didn't have time to think about that. Instead I grabbed a teacup and caught as much blood as I could before the wound clotted. Then, binding a tea-towel tightly around my thumb, I went back to the living room and read on.

Mix her bloode with earth & ashes & eat thereof. While Þe

mouth still is thick with gore, speak the incantation.

Well, I had earth and I had ashes. I padded outside, ignoring the stones cutting into my bare feet and the heavy drops that were beginning to fall from the lowering sky. Purple clouds were racing in from the sea to join the ones already gathered on the mainland, and far off in the bay, white horses were whipping up. I shivered as the wind picked up, piercing my thin pyjama top, and quickly scooped up some earth from the path. Then I hurried inside, shutting the door against the wind and rain. On some superstitious instinct I shot the bolt as well.

There was plenty of soft white wood ash in all the grates in the house, so I took a handful from the study fireplace and added it to the mix. Then I went back to the living room hearth and stared down at the book.

Mix . . . & eat thereof.

I shuddered and stirred the cup with my finger. It squelched and ground and gritted, and a butcher's smell came up. Nausea rose in my throat and the cut on my hand throbbed painfully, but I'd come this far, I might as well get it over. I put it to my lips and took a mouthful.

It was indescribably disgusting; a thick mixture like wet clay; a foul, clotted mass of grit and gore. My stomach heaved, trying to spit it out – but I fought down the wave of revulsion and managed to swallow a little and keep it down. I was pretty sure that 'eat thereof' did not mean 'put in your mouth and sick right up again'.

While my mouth was still clotted, I spoke the words of the incantation.

'Hwat!' My tongue was clagged with grit, my throat closing and heaving against the trickling ooze.

'Hwat, storm-geboren.'

The taste was vile in my mouth.

'Hwat, loathéd lyftfloga.'

I choked, but forced myself on.

'Hwat, sceadu, Brimwolf.

Hwat, windræs.

Hwat, o Brimwolf.'

Nausea rose again, threatening to overwhelm me, and I gritted my teeth, drawing shuddering breaths in and out through my nose, trying to keep it together.

'Hwat, o Brimwolf!

Come!'

When I finished there was silence. I waited for a moment, fighting the urge to crouch and wrap my arms protectively around myself – but nothing happened.

I closed the book with a sigh. Probably I'd missed some vital step, or you needed the blood of a real witch. Probably I'd pronounced the incantations wrong. Let's face it – it was most likely all rubbish anyway.

Feeling flat and depressed, I washed out my mouth at the kitchen sink, then went up to my room to lie down. I put the spell book on the window sill. I'd return it to its hiding place later, I thought wearily, but right now I was more drained than I'd have thought possible. The wind shrieked and howled in the chimney as I climbed into bed, but I didn't care. My head hit the pillow, and I slipped into the cool abyss of sleep.

I awoke with a jump, to the sound of a crash in the meadow outside. Somewhere a gate had blown loose and banged with a ceaseless, monotonous rhythm. The wind was mounting, and there was something in its voice that made me shiver and huddle deeper into my duvet. It was a strange howling, a shrill booming roar. At last I gave up trying to ignore it and went to the window.

The forest stretched out, dark and lush, and beyond that the restless waters of the bay. Far out, over the water, a shadow was racing over the sea, darkening everything in its path. It looked like a great dark stormcloud, but I'd never seen a cloud move so fast. The shrieking grew louder, and the shadow spread and darkened until the whole bay was almost as dark as night, only the pathetic glint of the lighthouse piercing the murk. There was a terrible crash far away, like a rock fall into the bay, and a tearing, rending sound. I shivered, thinking of all the fishermen out in their boats in this dreadful weather.

The wind grew louder still, and its note had a wailing, keening sound, like children crying, or seagulls mewing, though there wasn't a single bird to be seen in the sky. Even the rooks had fled the great beech tree and the branches were clean and bare, for the first time since I'd come to Wicker House.

The dark cloud was coming closer and closer. First the forest was covered in its shadow, then the meadow, and now the windows of the house were darkening. I backed away, an inexplicable panic rising in me. I heard my own voice, thin and weak against the shrieking din, repeating, 'It's just a storm, it's just a storm, it's just a storm.' But finally I couldn't even hear my own voice, only the cacophonous wind, screaming at me: *Anna, Anna, Anna!*

A face – a face at the window, a terrifying, shapeless face that eddied and surged with the gale. An open, screaming mouth full of swirling storm-tossed debris, and sightless, empty eyes filled with leaves, dust and the feathers of birds. *Anna!* screamed the mouth. The voice was dreadful, it was all the voices of my nightmares rolled into one, it was shrill and deep and it entered my wounded skull, throbbing inside my head.

I tore the curtains shut and ran, blundering into doors

and furniture, not knowing where I was heading. Behind me I heard the crack and shriek of wood, smashing glass, and knew that the storm had broken through the window. I could hear the panes swinging to and fro, cracking against the walls with shocking violence. Shards of glass and storm debris scudded before me along the corridor and my breath tore in my throat.

When I reached the shelter of Dad's bedroom I slammed the door and leapt on to his big double bed, where I cowered beneath the covers in the foetal position, pressing thick wads of duvet to my ears and eyes, trying to shut out the terror and contain my trembling. There was blood running down my shin, but I couldn't feel the pain.

It was quieter now. The storm's violence was muffled by the thick stone walls of this part of the house and Dad's heavy oak bedroom door. The loudest sounds beneath the duvet were my tearing breaths, the thumping of my own heart, and the roar of blood in my ears.

Then the oak door began to creak. Peering out from under the duvet I saw the thick, ancient planks were bending, warping. Dead insects, stones and small bones began to skud under the doorway, tendrils of dust reaching across the floor like searching fingers.

I pulled the duvet back over my head, stifling a

whimper with its folds, and shut my eyes against the cotton darkness. The door rattled, shaking in its frame, and I heard the wind whistle through the gaps.

Nothing could keep it out. It was in the room. It was by the bed. *Something* was pressing on me, feeling for my shape beneath the duvet.

A wordless moan of terror came from my lips and I heard an answering scream from the storm-thing, so close the bed shook. Even through the covers I could smell its stench: bladderwrack and rotting driftwood. My stomach seemed to turn to water and the thing screamed again, ripping at the duvet.

'Go away!' The words were ripped from me, sobbed into my knees: 'Please, whatever you are, go away!'

'Noooooooooo!' it screamed, a long drawn-out howl of thwarted fury.

'G-go away! P-please go away!'

There was a dreadful sucking, hollow sound, the vortex of the storm drawing in on itself, and the thump and screech of furniture dragged across the wooden floor. And then . . . nothing.

I lay in Dad's bed with my forehead pressed to my knees, shivering and listening as the din slowly quietened to an ordinary storm. Then, with a suddenness that made me jump, I heard a battering from downstairs. Every bone in my body just wanted to huddle down and ignore the noise, but then I remembered the bolted front door. It might be Dad, trying to get in.

Stiffly, my limbs trembling with cramp, I got up, pulling the covers on the bed straight. There was a dead robin on the duvet and I picked it up sadly, wondering what to do with it. The battering came again.

I checked my face in the mirror, wiped a smear of earth-clotted blood off my chin, and tiptoed downstairs, holding the bird in my hand.

At the front door I drew the bolt, then belatedly remembered my London caution about answering the door to possible strangers.

'Who is it?' I shouted through the thick wood. The answer made me gape, then hastily pull back the lock.

Emmaline Peller and her mother stood on the doorstep, draggled and dripping, both with grim expressions. In the darkness I could dimly see broken branches and ripped-up trees strewn across the meadow.

'Come in!' I said, astonished at their appearance. I'd never met Mrs Peller but she looked exactly like Emmaline, only twenty years older. They had the same serious, angular face, the same long black hair, even similar glasses. Only the faint lines on her mother's face gave away her age. 'Are you OK? What happened?'

'We came to tell you, you have to stop,' Emmaline said, slamming the door shut behind her with a force that made the hallway mirror jump and rattle against the wall.

'Emmaline, that's enough, let me sort this,' her mother said with a look. She turned to me. 'Anna, I don't know why you're doing this, but Emmaline's right, you have to stop. What the hell were you doing with that storm? Do you realize you could have been killed? You're putting everyone in danger – including yourself. What are you trying to achieve?'

'I – I don't understand.' I quailed before her stern look.

'Please don't play games.' She looked very tired all of a sudden. 'We know what you are. We're admitting what we are. Let's just come out and call a spade a spade and we can discuss this properly.'

'W–what am I?' I asked, suddenly not sure if I wanted to hear the answer. Mrs Peller hesitated, as if a word hovered on the edge of her tongue, a word she was reluctant to use.

'A witch,' Emmaline spat into the silence. 'You're a witch, OK? We know. We know it's you doing this, we're not stupid. We've lived here all our lives; we've made peace with this community. How dare you waltz down from London and put us all in danger? You may be powerful but—'

'*Emmaline*,' said her mother with force. She turned back to me and studied my face, my trembling hands, the scab on my forehead. When she spoke her voice was soft. 'Child, is it possible . . . did you not know?'

Somehow I was seated at the kitchen table, Emmaline's mother plying me with tea, a worried little frownline etched between her narrow black brows.

'Well, you've clearly been in the wars, Anna. Why don't you tell us the whole story? Oh, and please stop calling me Mrs Peller. My name is Maya.'

I nodded, looking down into the steam of the mug, shame prickling at the back of my neck and heating my cheeks. It had been hard enough to justify my actions to myself; spelling it out in black and white to this lovely woman, especially with Emmaline's suspicious gaze at the other end of the table, was going to be excruciating. I had so many questions: how had this happened? How could I help Seth? Why me? But the first question I asked was none of these, it came to me with a shiver as the wind howled again in the chimney.

'What,' I shuddered slightly and wrapped my hands

more tightly round the scalding mug, 'what was that . . . that *thing*?'

Emmaline echoed my shudder involuntarily and Maya's face darkened.

'One of the forgotten powers. There are many out there, some roaming, some trapped, waiting to be called on. Some people call them elementals or demons. They're very old, very dark, and very powerful. Once they were worshipped – now they're ignored by men, and it angers them.'

'Did you send it away?'

'No.' She shook her head. 'I doubt we could have controlled it. It was summoned by you – did you command it?'

'I don't think so . . .' I tried to think back to the nightmare screaming wind and my sobs. 'I might have begged it to go away.'

'It was fortunate if that's what you did say. I think it was bound to your will and obeyed you. You were lucky, Anna. You might not be so lucky again. How did you come to summon it – why?'

I hardly knew how to answer that, but I tried.

'It all began when I found this book. I was with some other girls from school and we decided to try one of the spells, as a joke. We did a . . .'

I blushed and faltered and Emmaline said sarcastically, 'We know, a love spell. We saw the effects.'

'Yes. But I didn't think it would work – I mean, why would it? I don't believe in any of that r—' I stopped myself just in time from saying 'rubbish' and amended it to 'really'.

'But it did,' prompted Maya. I nodded unhappily, feeling the weight of it press down on me.

'Yes. I didn't know what to think – I hoped it was a joke, or that it would wear off. But it didn't, so I decided that I had to try something else.'

'And it didn't work?'

'No.'

'Did you check?'

'Yes! Of course. He was just as obsessed as ever. The first one, nothing happened. The second one our chimney collapsed and I got hit on the head.' My hand crept up to touch the scar on my head. 'I wanted to stop after that but I promised myself I'd give this last spell a try, and if it didn't work I would . . . I don't know. Accept defeat. Put Seth off some other way.'

Maya sighed and ran her hands through her hair.

'Well, so much for this. I can understand how it all came about. Although I don't know why you've failed to break the charm. You've power enough; you've proved that.'

'But *I* don't understand at all,' I said desperately. 'Why did it work for me but not the others? No one's following them around like love-lorn sheep.'

'Because,' Emmaline said with exaggerated patience, 'they have no powers. You do.'

I put my hand to my head. It was aching badly. Was this all real, or had I hit my head again in the storm? Surely I wasn't sitting around my kitchen table being accused of witchcraft by my school friend and her mum.

'So what are you?' I said at last.

'What do you mean?' Maya said.

'Well, at the door you said, "We know what you are, we're admitting what we are." What are you?'

'We're,' Maya bit her lip, 'well, witches too.' She rubbed at the bridge of her nose and suddenly looked very tired and very weary. 'But not, apparently, as powerful. After you showed your hand with that little love spell, Emmaline and I did everything we could to put a dampener on your magic. We were terrified of what you might do next. But clearly it didn't work.'

'Do you think that might be why my counter-spells didn't work?' I asked, knowing that I was clutching at straws, but trying anyway. 'Do you think you somehow stopped them working?'

'Oh no, they worked.' She looked grim. 'If you could

summon that storm demon then there's no way a simple little counter-charm would have failed. You've removed most of the protective enchantments on this house for a start – it was magic keeping the chimney up.'

'So it really is all my fault,' I said dully. 'Everything. Seth. The chimney. My head.'

'More than that,' Emmaline said acidly, but just then there was the sound of a key in the lock of the front door and Dad's voice called:

'Hi love, I'm back.' The front door slammed, and we all sat in silence, listening to him pulling off his boots. 'What's with all the branches in the lane and why's there a dead bird in the hall?'

He came into the kitchen and did a double-take, but was too polite to show his surprise. He only said mildly, 'Well, this is an unexpected pleasure. Who are your friends, Anna?'

For a long moment I was paralyzed with indecision, too spun out by the whole surreal situation to come up with a reply. What could I say: 'Hi, Dad, meet the local coven'?

Maya saved me. She stood, holding out her hand.

'Hello, you must be Anna's dad. Pleased to meet you. I'm Maya Peller and this is my daughter, Emmaline. She's in Anna's English class and promised to drop over the homework assignments so Anna doesn't get too far behind while she's sick. We called past to post them through the door but Anna was nice enough to ask us in for a cuppa – particularly as the weather was so appalling.'

'Yes – astonishing isn't it?' Dad looked out of the window at the branch-strewn meadow as if still unable to believe his eyes. 'Just blew out of nowhere! But coming all this way is *very* kind, I must say. People in Winter really are proving good neighbours. You must be very proud of your community.'

'We are,' Maya said with a smile. 'Thank you, Mr Winterson.'

'Please, call me Tom.'

'Well, it's lovely to meet you, Tom. Now I suppose we'd better be going.'

There was some to-ing and fro-ing with Dad politely trying to persuade Emmaline and her mother to stay for another cup, and both of them equally politely refusing. Then Maya somehow manoeuvred us all out of the door so that Emmaline and my father were in front. By the kitchen door she paused and grabbed my arm, forcing me to hang back for a moment.

'We don't have time for any more right now, but please will you come and see Emmaline and me as *soon* as you're back at school? And in the meantime, for God's sake, don't do anything more with that book. Will you promise me?'

I nodded, still half stunned but prepared to agree to anything that'd help solve this mess.

'Good girl.' She gave me a quick hug. 'I can see this has all been a big shock, but we'll sort it out.'

Then she moved on into the hall, calling after Emmaline and my dad as if nothing had happened.

While Dad was seeing them off I slipped upstairs to my room. The damage wasn't as bad as I'd expected, nothing I couldn't sort out with a hoover. I latched the broken window – that would need reglazing, but Dad could do that. I'd just have to tell him I'd left it open in the storm and it had banged shut and shattered.

Then I realized something. I looked around the room, under the bed, out of the window – but the only things disturbing the green sweep of meadow grass were branches and twigs. And something told me the search was hopeless anyway.

The book, which I'd left lying on the window sill, was gone, taken by the storm.

CHAPTER SEVEN

My return to school, complete with charming Harry Potter-style scar, caused something of a stir, but everyone was still bubbling over the news of the freak storm, so luckily I attracted less attention than I might otherwise have done.

No one could explain exactly how it had happened, but seemingly, during the storm, a chunk of cliff near the castle had fallen into the sea and a huge crack had appeared in the seawall which defended Winter from the full force of the winter storms. Everyone was worried that a major collapse was imminent.

Emmaline's walk home took us past the seawall and as we passed it we studied the crack, fenced round with workmen's tape and studded with markers for monitoring movement. It was pretty impressive – a long narrow crevasse in the solid bulk of the wall, as if the earth had torn itself apart. I pulled my coat around myself, the thin synthetic wool scant protection against the cold seawind, and shivered.

'Do they know what caused it yet?' I asked. Emmaline raised a single sardonic eyebrow at me, then when I did not respond, she sighed.

'Jesus, for an intelligent girl, Anna Winterson, you're remarkably dumb. *You*. You caused it.'

'No!' I was horrified.

'Or rather that – that dark *thing* you conjured.'

'Oh God.' It made what happened to Seth seem almost mild in comparison. 'Emmaline, I'm so, so sorry. I had no idea . . .' my voice trailed away. 'Will it be all right? The wall I mean – it won't crack any further, will it?'

She shrugged.

'Let's hope not or we might all be underwater at Christmas. Hold up, we're here.'

We were outside Winter Botanicals, a herbal shop that sold pot-pourri, essential oils and candles. I'd never been in but had often thought about it; the seductive smell lured you from yards up the high street.

'Turn up that alleyway,' Emmaline instructed and I saw a small opening to the side of the shop. Resisting the urge to duck my head, I turned into the narrow twittern, glad to be out of the chilly seawind that had chased us up the high street. There was a wooden door at the far end.

'Push.' Emmaline's voice came from behind me. I pushed, and found myself in the most beautiful garden I had ever seen – a lush, scented jungle of plants and trees, flowers and fruit. Vines curled overhead, stroking my cheeks as I passed underneath, and my nose tickled with the heady mix of pollens in the air.

There was a strange buzz in my ears and, as I looked around, I realized it was coming from the bees. There were bees everywhere; drowsy, friendly bees drifting slowly from flower to flower, heavy with sunshine-coloured dust. Their hum was a warm, audible backdrop to the garden that quite drowned out any trace of traffic noise. It felt as though we were in a little bubble all of our own – a tiny Eden Project right here in Winter.

'Sorry,' Emmaline said, with a hint of malice. 'Didn't I mention the bees? I hope you're not afraid of them.'

'Not at all,' I said truthfully. 'I like bees.'

Was it my imagination or did Emmaline look slightly disappointed? She pushed past me without another word and climbed the steps to the back door of the shop, calling, 'Ma, we're here.'

'Oh – hello, darling. Hello, Anna.' Maya appeared in the doorway wiping her hands on her shop apron. 'Just give me a sec to finish closing up and we'll go upstairs.'

We hovered by the stairs while Maya moved purposefully around closing drawers, turning keys in locks, and reordering the hundreds of apothecary jars filled with every kind of herb, flower petal and seed. Vials of essential oils gleamed and winked in the dim light from the windows as she moved about the shop. When every jar was back in place, Maya shot the bolt on the front door, removed her apron, and we climbed the stairs to the flat above the shop. My heart was thumping when we reached the top and though I tried to tell myself it was the climb, I knew that wasn't true. Something momentous was behind that door. I wasn't sure what – Seth's freedom maybe. Or perhaps the truth about myself.

I gulped, and crossed the threshold into the witches' lair.

I don't know what I expected, but the reality was pretty cool. The whole floor had been knocked through into one enormous, rambling cave crammed with books, plants and hangings. Prisms hung from each of the four windows, sending multi-coloured shards of light dancing around us, and in the centre of the high ceiling was a huge wrought-iron chandelier filled with dozens of beeswax candles. It was unlit, but I could imagine the blaze of light when they were all going, and the honeyed scent that would fill the room.

There were no crucibles or broomsticks that I could see – and the nearest thing to a cauldron was a huge kettle sitting on the cooker. In some weird way, the normality was unsettling. I'd been prepared for a stack of new-age tat: pentacles, crystals, and the like. The very lack of it somehow made the situation seem more real.

Maya turned on the gas and an eerie shriek filled the air as the kettle gusted out steam.

'I hope you don't mind.' She set out six cups and a pot. 'I've invited some other friends. We . . . consulted them, about the disturbances, before we knew what was going on, and I think they deserve to know the outcome. But they're not due for a while, so in the meantime let's have some cake and get to know each other.'

I sat at the table and Maya cut three thick slices of loaf-cake, sticky and scented with honey. Emmaline filled the teapot and poured us each a cup. A rich, strange smell filled the room and Maya curved her hands around her cup. Her eyes met mine across the curling tendrils of steam.

'Well, Anna. We have a lot of questions, but perhaps they should wait until our friends get here. And in the meantime, maybe it's fairer to let you ask your questions first. Is there anything Emmaline and I can tell you?'

All day I'd been full of questions, confusion – torn

113

between a desire to scoff the whole thing off as bullshit, and the uncomfortable conviction that it was anything but. Most of all I'd been bursting with the urge to pour out my troubles to someone older and wiser, finally get some answers. And now I found myself tongue-tied, helpless and confused. I put my cup against my forehead and the china burned my skin, but all I could think of to say was a petulant, childish, 'Why me?'

Maya shrugged.

'Why any of us? It's strongly hereditary. Usually through the female line. Your father seems unequivocally ungifted, so I'm guessing your mother? Where is she?'

'She's dead,' I said dully, not bothering with the nuances.

'Ah.' Maya's eyes softened. 'That explains a lot, although not everything.'

'How do you mean?'

'Well, obviously it explains why you know so little. But it doesn't explain this explosion of power – it doesn't normally manifest like this. Usually there's a slow build up from puberty onwards. There will be a few signs and family members will start to keep an eye out. What do your mother's family have to say about all this?'

'I don't know any of them. My father isn't in contact and he won't tell me anything about them. I've tried asking him, I even tried to trace them a few times, but nothing. I don't even know if any of them are alive.'

'I see. That does happen – although not often – we are a tough group, by and large, and extremely clannish. But if there's no family member around to help then usually someone else steps in. No one wants to see an accident like yours occur. Clearly no one stepped in, in your case. Do you remember any signs as you were growing up?'

'Signs? What kind of signs?'

'It's hard to say, it varies so much. Weather disturbances are common; freak storms, extreme unseasonal cold snaps or heatwaves. Electrical disturbances. Spontaneous fires. You don't remember anything like that when you were growing up?'

I shrugged helplessly.

'Not really. Of course there were storms – but I doubt they had anything to do with me. How would I know?'

'I think you would know. You knew something was wrong as soon as you'd bewitched Seth, didn't you?'

I nodded reluctantly. Yes, I had known, even if I hadn't wanted to admit it to myself. Part of me was kind of surprised that I wasn't totally freaking out here, calling the police to get Maya and Emmaline locked up. But perhaps that was why; they were only telling me stuff I already knew. Had always known.

'But that was different,' I said, 'that was a spell.'

Maya's brow furrowed.

'It's not so much a matter of spells, it's more about willpower, and exerting that will – you can cast your will without using any traditional spells or incantations. Spells are just a way of concentrating the mind. They have no power outside of the person saying the words.'

'You mean, you need to be a witch?' I said, confused. Maya winced and I stammered, 'S-sorry, is that the wrong word?'

'It's not wrong, exactly,' she said uncomfortably.

'It's pejorative,' Emmaline said flatly. 'It's not what we use to describe ourselves – or not usually.'

'It has so many negative associations,' Maya explained. 'It's associated with witch-hunts and burnings and so on, and it's usually the term used by outsiders to stigmatize. Some people like to use it, of course. There is a movement to reclaim it, and some feel that used by a member of the community it's acceptable. But it's not very usual in – in polite conversation.'

'What word do w– people use, then?'

Emmaline and her mother looked at each other and kind of laughed.

'Well, as to that, there are as many answers as there are ways of doing magic.' Maya shrugged. 'We are not a very united community. Well, apart from the Ealdwitan, who are united to a fault.' She pursed her lips as if in disapproval, but I didn't have time to pick apart her statement. There was something more important on my mind.

'How can I fix Seth?'

'Ah.' Both Emmaline and Maya stopped and looked at each other. Maya's brows furrowed again. She looked into her tea cup, then back up at me. 'To be honest, Anna, we don't know.'

'We already tried to take it off,' Emmaline said. 'That first day he turned up at school. But we didn't manage.'

'Our hope was that we could persuade you to do it,' Maya said. 'But clearly, you've already tried too.'

'Maybe I wasn't powerful enough?' I said hopefully, 'Maybe if we worked together?'

Maya took a bite of cake and shook her head as she swallowed.

'I really don't think that was the problem. Having seen what you did with that . . .' She shuddered. 'That *thing*, that came with the storm, I have no doubt that wherever the problem lies, it is not with your power. You stripped away charms that have surrounded the Wicker House since Tudor times. You removed protections that have sat on this village for hundreds of years – all without any focus or training. No, if brute force

117

could do it, that charm would be lifted by now.'

The disappointment was like a punch to the gut. I'd been so sure that Maya would have all the answers . . .

'You mean, I may never be able to undo the harm I've done?'

Maya saw my stricken expression and patted my hand.

'I'm not saying that. Just that for the moment, I can't quite see the way. And sorry though I am for your Seth, to be honest that's not the first priority. The most important thing is to reinstate some of the protections on the town, if we can. The last thing we want is a major disaster with loss of life. Compared to that, a love-lorn boy is the least of our worries.'

I put my head in my hands. I wasn't so sure. The possibility of a town collapse felt so remote and theoretical, whereas Seth's problems seemed very real and very near.

'But don't give up, the others may have an idea of why this charm is proving so stubborn,' Maya said, comfortingly. 'They're just coming up now.'

As she spoke I heard footsteps on the stairs, followed by a knock. Then a woman and two men were opening the door, coming in, stripping off coats, and the room was full of warmth and chatter. I hung back, trying to make sense of the group. The woman was young, in her teens or twenties, and obviously some relation to Maya and

Emmaline; she had the same dark eyes and long, clever face, although her hair was fair – a golden, sun-streaked mass. The two men looked like brothers – both tall with black hair and long, Roman noses. The older one wore a little pointed goatee, neatly trimmed. The younger – who looked to be in his early twenties – had at least a week's worth of stubble, but nothing organised enough to be called a beard. He was wearing a scruffy leather jacket.

'Ma!' The girl kissed Maya affectionately. 'How are you?'

'Sienna, darling.' Maya patted her back. 'My, it's good to see you again. It feels like much too long. Anna, this is Sienna, my older daughter.'

'So, this is the Anna we've heard so much about.' Sienna smiled at me with a tiny hint of equivocation. 'Anna, this is my husband, Simon Goldsmith.' She indicated the older man. 'And his younger brother, Abe.'

'Pleased to meet you.' Simon shook my hand formally. Abe only gave a slightly sardonic grin over Sienna's shoulder. He had a ring through his eyebrow.

'Do you mind?' Sienna said suddenly. She gestured towards the table. I shook my head, unsure what she meant, but not wanting to offend. Picking up my tea cup she swirled around the dregs and knocked out the last of the liquid into my saucer. Then she stared into the cup, her brows knitted in so exact a copy of Maya's characteristic

119

frown that it was almost comical. Suddenly her expression cleared and she smiled. 'Welcome to the family, Anna. I can see your path is going to be entwined with ours for a long time.'

I felt uncomfortable. This was too hokey, like a cheap pier-end fortuneteller without the scarf and bangles. But no one else seemed to find the action strange at all. I looked around the group.

'So are you all . . . ?' I stopped, not sure how to put it. They understood. Simon just nodded, but Abe closed his hand into a fist, then blew into his fingers as they unfurled. As he did, a handful of snow gusted out from between his fingers. The snowflakes fluttered towards me on his breath and one perfect crystal landed on the smooth table top. Before I could blink it had melted.

A shiver ran through me. It was the first piece of magic – real magic – that I had seen. The first thing that couldn't be dismissed as freaky coincidence, bad luck, or just plain weird. As Abe wiped his hand on his jeans and grinned, I knew; I'd crossed some invisible line. There was no going back now.

'Show-off!' Emmaline muttered under her breath.

'It's generally,' Sienna said sternly, 'considered unethical to expend power unnecessarily or affect the world more than we need to.' She raised her eyebrows reprovingly and Abe touched his forelock in a mockingly deferential way.

'As always, I'm happy to stand corrected by my dear sister-in-law. So, are we going to jabber all night at the poor girl, or actually let her see some magic?'

'More than that,' Maya said, with a touch of grimness to her voice. 'She's going to *do* some magic. If I'm right about Anna then she'll be doing most of the work.'

While Maya, Sienna, Simon and Abe cleared the decks for action, I took Emmaline aside.

'Emmaline, what do they expect of me? I don't know what to do!'

'Don't worry.' Her habitually acidic tone was softened slightly. 'Ma knows that. She'll lead you. You just have to trust her.'

'Emmaline,' Maya called from the other side of the room, 'could you open the windows?'

Emmaline threw them wide and Maya looked at each of the others in turn.

'Well, are we ready?'

They nodded and moved to form a circle in the centre of the room. I nodded myself, but couldn't stop my doubts creeping into my face.

'Anna.' Maya drew me into the circle beside her and looked at me, her dark eyes liquid and unreadable. 'I can't

121

really explain how this will work so will you trust me and lend me your strength when I ask?'

I had no idea what she meant but I nodded again. I did trust Maya. I couldn't put my finger on why, but I did.

'Thank you,' she said, and closed her eyes. The others followed suit – so I shut mine too.

For what seemed like a long time there was nothing. I felt like a fool standing there in Maya's kitchen with my hands dangling by my side, the clock ticking loudly over the cooker. I still couldn't shake a suspicion that I'd open my eyes and find them all holding their sides, cackling with laughter, unable to believe the gullibility of the girl from London. Certainly two weeks ago I'd have snorted, shouldered my rucksack and left the room after the first ten seconds.

But I'd seen too much to be completely sceptical. So I stood, shifting from one foot to the other and feeling more than faintly ridiculous, and waited, and waited.

After a while I became aware of a pressure, like a stress headache, a pushing, grinding sort of feeling at the base of my neck, in my temples and jaw. I put a hand up to massage the feeling and Maya took my other. She spoke very quietly. 'Anna, relax and let me in.'

It felt so, so wrong to open up my mind to a complete stranger, lower all my defences. But I closed my eyes tighter, consciously forcing the tense muscles in my neck and shoulders to relax. Suddenly there was a humming, a thrumming, a whirling buzz – and the magic flooded in.

I staggered with the force of it; it was like a river rushing through my mind, a whirlpool threatening to sweep me into its vortex. A feeling of huge power welled inside me – I felt the presence of the others, glowing with their own light: Sienna's golden aura, Emmaline's garnet red, Abe's dark brilliance, like onyx, each pulling me into the current of their will. For a minute I hung back, unsure. Then I let myself sweep into the flood, seeing how the others shaped and channelled it, forcing it into the paths of their choosing.

The shining, swelling torrent streamed out through the open window and into Winter's streets – a Winter at once familiar and strange. The everyday buildings were like shadows beneath a glowing, pulsing web of magic – spells holding up the buildings, charms on the harbour wall, bewitchments to calm the sea in the harbour, to keep the castle walls firm, to hold the river in its banks. A scarred black rupture through the centre of the web showed the path of the storm demon.

The magic ebbed and surged around us with terrifying, exhilarating force while Maya worked, knit, renewed, tirelessly, patiently. I tried to add my will to hers, feeling the power flowing out of me like blood draining from my arteries and flowing into the dark shredded wound.

And incredibly it was working; the threads were shining brighter and brighter, the black gash was closing, knitting. An invisible spider was repairing the ruptured web, coaxing it back into a semblance of its former beauty. It would never be the same, even I could see that. The scar would always be there. But Maya was closing the wound, and I could feel her using my strength to do it, the strangest sense of something unravelling out of me.

I don't know how long we stood, but suddenly the pulling, tugging ceased with a gust of release. I staggered backwards on shuddery legs, my eyes opening to a dark kitchen full of twilight shades. In front of me, Emmaline was rubbing her eyes dazedly. She sank to her knees and Abe bent over, his hands on his thighs, like a runner catching his breath after a fierce race. Only Maya was still standing straight, but her face was worn and drained. Still, she was smiling.

'Well done,' she said, the husky thread of her voice loud in the silent room. 'Well done, everyone. Now, I think we deserve something to eat.'

Two hours later, we'd stuffed ourselves with jacket potatoes running with butter, slatherings of cream cheese and handfuls of peppery rocket snatched from the dusky garden. The kitchen was full of candlelight, raucous laughter, and banter. I lay with my head on the sofa arm, enjoying the flow of conversation without trying to keep up. I was exhausted, my eyelids so heavy I felt like sleeping where I sat.

'You look shattered, Anna,' Maya said sympathetically as she took my plate. 'I keep forgetting that this is all new to you.'

'Did I – did we do OK?' I asked, stifling a yawn.

'Yes, you did more than OK.'

'But,' I felt like a broken record, but I had to know, 'what about Seth?'

They all looked at each other around the table, exchanging glances I couldn't read. Maya took my hand.

'I'm sorry, Anna, we don't know what's going on there. We can't find out what's still binding Seth. Simon has one theory although I'm not convinced . . .' She trailed off and Simon took over.

'You obviously have tremendous latent power, Anna, and as we were saying earlier, magic is largely a matter of exerting will, not of formal spells. It's possible that you've removed the actual enchantment but that your subconscious will is still having an effect on Seth.'

'You mean . . .' My tired mind struggled to disentangle

this. 'I don't really *want* him to go back to normal?'

'Effectively, yes. It's just a theory,' he hurried on, as he saw me looking affronted. 'I'm not saying you're doing this deliberately. Just that if there is a small part of your mind that still wants his – his regard, then that might be enough to keep him bound.'

'So what can I do?'

'Hmm. Not a lot really. Well, there is one thing I can think of – but it's not really a good idea.'

'I don't care!' I said desperately. 'I'll do *anything* to release him. Tell me, please.'

'Well . . . most people have quite effective inner protection against magical influence. It's usually quite hard to persuade them to act utterly against their inclination. So my idea was kind of based on that – but it's not actually practical. It's much too dangerous.'

'God, you're coyer than a bride on her wedding night,' Abe said. 'Just spit it out, whatever it is. You can't tease Anna with a solution and then get all mincy.'

'Tell him,' Simon said bluntly. 'Tell Seth what you did.'

'What?' Maya dropped the plate she was holding with a crash. 'That's a dreadful idea! It's far, *far* too dangerous. There's a massive risk of antagonizing the Ealdwitan. And it might not work anyway.'

'I agree!' Emmaline said hotly. 'It's all very well for you,

Simon, but we have to live here. The Ealdwitan would go *apeshit* if they found out. And what if word leaked back to the Malleus?'

'Well, obviously Anna wouldn't say anything about anyone else. The main risk would be to her. But I agree it's a pretty terrible idea – I was only theorizing really.'

'Simon.' For the first time since I'd seen her Maya looked truly pissed off. 'I suggest you think about your theories a bit more before you air them in future.' She turned to me and spoke seriously. 'Anna, listen to me, I *absolutely* veto this, do you understand? You're not to do this – the Ealdwitan would be furious. I'm sorry poor Seth is still entranced but on the scale of things it's not a big deal – you've undoubtedly removed the formal spell or we would have been able to see it, and any residual effect will wear off in time. Just ignore him. It will sort itself eventually – you'll all be off to uni in a year or two anyway.'

They argued back and forth but I heard little of the debate after that. The phrase 'a year or two' was ringing in my ears. A *year* or two? How could I condemn Seth to a year or more of enslavement?

CHAPTER EIGHT

A year or two. *A year or two?*

I was still obsessing over this idea in History the next day. It seemed so wrong that, after the amazing events of last night, life could still go on in the same mundane way, that school still had to be attended, homework completed. But the sight of Emmaline stumping down the hill on her way to lessons brought me back to reality. Witch or no witch, Emmaline still apparently needed A-levels, so presumably I did too.

I didn't sit near Seth in History – I had a desk over the far side of the classroom – but he watched me across the room as Mr Brereton ticked off the register, his eyes worried as he took in my scarred forehead and battered face. My heart twisted and I had to look away. I hadn't seen him since the accident and the sight of his concerned face brought the whole hideous mess rushing back. It was all very well for Maya to say ignore him. How could I ignore him when I'd forcibly shackled his heart to mine?

I was so lost in my thoughts that I barely heard the lesson, and jumped when Mr Brereton waved a basket full of scraps of paper under my nose.

'Anna Winterson, have you heard a word I've been saying?'

'Er, yes. No. I – I'm sorry, I was a bit distracted.'

The class snickered and Mr Brereton sighed with exaggerated patience.

'I was inviting you to pick a collaborator for the coming class project. And, as I have *already explained*, this time it will be randomly assigned by lot due to *some* people's—' He stared sternly round the class. '*Some* people's misapprehension that a collaboration apparently means one person's work adorned with two people's names.'

'Oh. Thank you.' I reached forward and took a slip.

'Name please?' Mr Brereton said crisply.

I unfolded the slip.

'Seth Waters,' I read aloud.

Across the classroom I saw Seth's worried face break into a smile.

Crap.

* * *

'So it's got to be a five-thousand word, collaborative project on an aspect of local history.' Seth bounded up beside me as we joined the flood of others making their way outside for first break. 'Any ideas?'

'Not really,' I said dully. Oh arse. How could I blank Seth if we were forced to do a project together?

I'd spent the rest of the lesson racing through increasingly impractical ideas for getting out of the project. My first thought had been to simply go to Mr Brereton and be reassigned, but what reason could I give? It seemed unlikely he would agree to my rather pathetic plea to swap because, er, well, just because really.

I don't know what was going across my face, but Seth suddenly stopped, pulling me into an alcove out of the flow of students.

'Look, Anna, I can see you're pissed at being paired with me—'

'I'm not pissed!' I interrupted wretchedly. 'Seth, please, that's not it at all, truly – it's just . . .'

For a minute I thought he was going to just stand there, watching me tie myself into knots, but then he closed his eyes wearily and put up a hand to rub his temple.

'Hey, it's fine. I was out of line – I know that. And I'm sorry, I really am. But I don't know what else to say –

we've got to do this project together somehow. How about you do your best to forget last week, and I do my best not to sexually harass you again. Deal?'

He held his strong, brown hand out towards me.

I wanted to put my head in my hands. I wanted to cry. I wanted to grab him and scream, 'You weren't sexually harassing me you idiot – I *wanted* you to kiss me – *I'm* the one who should be grovelling here.'

But I didn't. I didn't say any of that. Instead I took his large hand in my smaller one and nodded weakly.

'Deal.'

'I'm not doing the castle again,' Seth said, as we walked together towards Maths. 'I've done a project on that every sodding year since I was five. I had thought of local witchcraft, there's quite a bit in the town museum . . .' I shuddered involuntarily at that suggestion, but before my face could reveal my horror he continued, 'But I think James and Claire are doing that already and we don't want to compete, I guess. Can you think of anything different?'

'What about the local fishing industry?' I mumbled, thinking of Dad and his bloody book. Seth stopped dead and grabbed my shoulder.

'Anna, that's genius! My grandad is a fisherman – well, was – and I'm sure we could get some interesting stuff out of him. Well, at least . . .' He seemed to have a moment's doubt and then shook himself. 'No, I'm sure we could. Shall we go over this weekend and talk to him?'

'OK,' I was a little taken aback but prepared to go along with anything that didn't involve more witchcraft. 'Where does he live?'

'Out on Castle Spit.'

I'd never been to Castle Spit but had seen it often from the cliff-tops. A narrow strip of pebbly sand ran out to a small, barren island about quarter of a mile away. At extreme low tide you could walk out to the lighthouse there, but I'd been given many warnings about the treacherous speed of the tides.

'I didn't know anyone lived out there,' I said, surprised. 'It must be so lonely.'

'My grandad used to be the lighthouse keeper, before the light went automatic. He still lives in the keeper's cottage. It is lonely, but he's a bit of a loner so I don't think he minds too much.' He hesitated again, then added, 'He's . . . well, he's a bit odd.'

'Odd how?'

'Just . . . er . . . odd. He's disabled and doesn't get to the mainland much. But he knows a lot about the local fishing industry – he was a professional fisherman before he took on the lighthouse.'

'OK.' I was becoming quite enthusiastic about this, in spite of myself. 'What time do you want to meet? Will we walk over?'

Seth shook his head.

'Not unless you want to spend twelve hours there. It's either that or set back almost as soon as we get there.'

'Oh.' I hadn't thought of it like that. 'So how then?'

'In my boat, if you don't mind sailing?'

'I don't mind.' In fact I felt curiously excited about sailing with Seth. I wanted another glimpse of the stranger I'd seen in him that day at the quay.

'Good.' Seth looked pleased too. 'Saturday then, I'll meet you at the quay at noon.'

I had no idea what you wore sailing so I dressed in jeans and trainers, with Dad's Gore-tex jacket in my backpack in case of bad weather. It looked like it would be unnecessary though – the day had started out a blazing hot one, and I was pink and perspiring by the time I got to the cliff road, in spite of the breeze from the sea.

I was happy, I realized, as I walked along the cliff. Which meant I was officially a really bad person. I should have been taking Maya's advice, avoiding Seth, trying to keep my distance. Now Mr Brereton had made that impossible – and I couldn't stop something inside me unfurling and fizzing with joy, as hard as I tried to damp the feeling down.

Seth was already on the boat when I crested the hill. He was too absorbed to notice me as I approached, so I was free to watch him to my heart's content as I walked the last half mile down the road towards the harbour. He moved about the boat with swift efficient movements, tugging at ropes, tying knots, deftly threading up sails. By the time I got to the quay he seemed satisfied with the sails and their arrangement and was bent over, tinkering with the little engine, his back towards me.

He was stripped to the waist, his skin tanned the deep red-brown of someone who spends a lot of time in the open air, and he had a small tattoo at the base of his back. I couldn't see what it showed, but I remembered June's words that first day at Winter High, 'Seth's not exactly flavour of the month with authority . . . Drinks, smokes, got a tattoo against the rules . . . Smacked some guy's head against a wall . . .'

It was strange, none of her words fitted with the Seth I'd got to know since my arrival in Winter. I'd never seen him smoking, far less ever seen him violent, except if you counted his anger towards Caroline and Jess in my defence. Perhaps he drank – I wouldn't know. I didn't join what June derisively called 'the cool crowd' on their

Friday nights down at the harbour. But I did hear the Monday morning gossip, the stories of who'd got served, who'd been refused, who'd chucked up the best part of a bottle of Merrydown and who'd got off with who. Seth rarely ever featured in the gossip, except as a bystander. If he did drink, he wasn't one of the people throwing up over the seawall and engaging in drunken snogs.

And yet, here was that tattoo. Against the rules, as June had said. And illegal, as he was underage. I wondered who'd done it for him. There were places in London, I knew, that would tattoo anyone with the money to pay for it and the nerve to sit still for long enough – but I wouldn't have drunk a cup of tea in most of them, let alone let them stick a needle in me.

As I got closer I tried to see what it was. At first sight it looked like a circle, about a third of the way up his back, where the deep hollow of his spine started to flatten out with his ribs. The ink was dark blue-black against his tanned skin, and it stretched and shimmered in the sun as he moved, twisting a knob on the engine, then pulling the starter. He listened to the note for a few minutes then, seeming satisfied, he cut the engine and straightened, just as I reached the boat.

'Nice tattoo,' I said mischievously into the sudden silence. He jumped, grabbing his T-shirt reflexively and yanking it over his head.

'Hi, Anna,' he said. First his tousled hair, then his face appeared through the opening. He hadn't shaved and his cheeks rasped against the material as he forced it down. 'Glad you like it.'

'What is it?'

'Want to see?' He pulled up the back of the T-shirt a little, twisting round so I could look. I bent down, and there it was; a little fish, not blue-black, as I'd thought, but very dark blue-green. It was beautifully drawn, each scale individually shaded, the eye it cocked towards me bright and intelligent. Its body was twisted into a circle, the snub nose yearning towards the frisking tail, forever doomed to just miss the connection.

'So you like fish?' I said. I spoke more mockingly than I meant to, trying to cover up the way my fingers itched to reach out and touch the smooth tanned skin beneath.

He shrugged and dropped the T-shirt. There was a blush of self-consciousness under his deep tan.

'So what made you . . . ?'

'Get it done?' He shrugged again. 'Not sure really. I had a bad time a few years ago. It was not long after . . .' He didn't finish the sentence but I could guess. Not long after his dad. 'I did some silly things, getting a tat was probably one of the sillier ones at the time and I got a lot of grief about it, but I'm quite fond of it now.'

Suddenly I felt bad for teasing him.

'It's beautiful,' I said, and I meant it. 'I like it.'

'Thanks.' He smiled briefly. 'At least I had the sense to get it done below the neckline, eh?'

'You could have done worse.'

'Yeah. Well, I did, unfortunately.'

His voice was sombre and he turned away from me again, fiddling with the engine. I felt really bad now. He'd looked so tranquil, so truly happy as I walked down the cliff path. Now his head was bowed and there was a deep unhappiness in his voice. It seemed like I wasn't able to bring anything but unhappiness to Seth, one way and another.

'Do you want to . . . ?' I said uncertainly.

'Talk about it? Not really.' He looked up and smiled with forced jollity. 'I'd rather get sailing instead.' He held out his hand and suddenly the gap between the quay and the boat yawned very wide and constantly shifting. The drop looked about six feet, the boat dancing up and down in a terrifying manner.

'Don't worry,' Seth said, his smile real now. 'It's not as bad as it looks, I won't let you fall.'

I fought a temptation to shut my eyes and instead grasped his hand and lurched towards the void. The shifting, heaving deck tilted wildly at the first touch of my foot and I felt myself teetering back towards the slice of dark oily water between the concrete quay and the boat – but Seth's strong hand grasped me firmly, pulling me towards him.

For a minute there was nothing else – nothing but Seth's hard grip on my upper arm, his chest inches from mine, his breath warm on my face. But then he let me go, as quickly as if my touch had burned him.

Suddenly there I was, both feet on the wooden bottom of the boat, crouching and ducking under the flapping boom as it swung in the breeze.

'Do I need to do anything?' I asked, as Seth stuffed my rucksack into a stowage hole and did busy things with ropes and knots at the quayside. He shook his head, not looking at me.

'Nope. Just keep out of the way – oh, and put this on.' He flung a life jacket at me.

'You're not wearing one,' I said, feeling slightly sulky. The day was getting hotter and the prospect of sweltering in a massive, insulated jacket of yellow plastic wasn't enticing.

'How far can you swim?'

'I don't know. Twenty or thirty lengths?'

'In the sea.'

'I've never swum in the sea. Well, I mean I've paddled around, but not swum far.'

'Then I suggest you put it on. It's up to you, of course. I wear one if the sea's anything more than glassy smooth, and I'm a strong swimmer.'

I looked out at the choppy waves beyond the harbour. If this were Seth's idea of glassy smooth I'd hate to see a stiff breeze.

'Unless you just fancy another trip to A&E with me?' He was facing away from me, towards the quay, so I couldn't see his expression but there was something in his voice that made me suspect he was laughing at me.

'Tosser!' I aimed a kick at him but the boat shifted, spoiling my aim, and my foot whacked the bulkhead instead. 'Ow.'

'Serves you right.' Now he really *was* laughing and not troubling to hide it. 'Well, be it on your own head . . .'

He cast off and the boom whipped across my head, two inches from my skull. I hastily pulled the jacket over my head.

The trip was completely magical. Under Seth's hands the little boat seemed almost to fly across the scudding waves. Above our heads the bright sails billowed out, taut and full, and the air was filled with the ripping sound of the fluttering spinnaker, the slap, slap of waves against the wooden hull, the mew of seagulls and the salty clean smell of the waves.

Everything was perfect – the deep azure sky, the wind-whipped waves, the crisp cool breeze against my hot skin. But mostly I was entranced by Seth – at school he looked pretty competent but always slightly aloof, a bit too cool to care much. He got OK marks – but somehow gave the impression that this was chance, as much as anything, and that he was permanently thinking of something else, would rather be somewhere else.

Out on the water he was a totally different person; the craft, guided by his swift, sure hands, seemed almost a part of him. He crouched and stretched, using his strength to counter-balance the pull of the wind, leaning out across the water, his muscles taut against the force of a rope, all the time balancing the forces of the wind and the water with his own body. His face was completely concentrated and yet completely relaxed. He made sense, out here, in a way that he didn't at school. The phrase 'fish out of water' swam through my head and I smiled, thinking of his tattoo.

'What's the joke?' Seth called, above the noise of the waves and I blushed – I'd thought he was too absorbed to notice me.

'Nothing,' I called back, 'Just thinking about school.'

'I try not to,' he said, and grinned. 'But I'm glad someone's got the project on their mind. Actually that reminds me, just to warn you, I didn't manage to tell my grandad that we were coming. So I'm not sure if he knows or not.'

'What does that mean – he might be out?'

'No! He never leaves the island. But he might not be, er, very prepared. Very welcoming, I mean. It might be a false alarm,' he hastened as he saw me looking worried. 'I did leave quite a few messages, but he didn't return my calls, so I'm not sure if he got them.'

'Oh.' I digested this as the boat sped along. I wasn't sure what to make of Seth's grandfather. He wasn't painting a very reassuring portrait. 'If he never goes to the mainland how does he survive?' I asked at last.

'My mum drives over twice a week.'

'She drives over?' I was surprised. Seth nodded.

'Yes, in fine weather you can make it over in a four-by-four if you know the best route and pick your times. And he's got a lot of supplies – tins and stuff – so he can survive quite a while without a visit. In fact if civilization ever comes to an end, you'll probably find my grandad still out there ten years after they've dropped the bomb, living off tinned curry and irritably wondering where my mum is.

141

Watch your head – I'm going about.'

He pushed the tiller. There was a moment of flapping, whipping sails, and the wind suddenly dropped. I turned, and was surprised to see we were in the lee of the island – we seemed to have covered the distance from the harbour in no time at all, and were gliding towards a small jetty. There was a slight bump and a scrape, then Seth was out of the boat, tying the painter to a rusty iron ring.

'Welcome to Castle Spit,' he said, holding out his hand towards me. I grabbed it, he heaved me out of the boat, and there I was, on Seth's grandfather's island.

The overwhelming impression was of land barely holding out against the sea. It wasn't quite as barren as it looked from the mainland – a few stunted shrubs survived in pockets between the rocks – but they were twisted by the winds and crusted with salt. Huge rocks, like granite teeth, jutted up against the sky, and gulls crouched on top, crapping on everything, cawing in a way that sounded very much like mocking laughter.

Only here and there was a note of cheer – a pale purple flower blowing in the wind caught my eye. It seemed impossibly fragile to be growing in such a hostile environment.

I shivered, wrapping my arms around myself against the wind. One look back at Winter, bathed in sunshine and chocolate-box pretty, then I followed Seth up the path.

'Who's she?'

As openings go it wasn't encouraging. There'd been no answer to Seth's knock at the small granite cottage. We'd spent some ten minutes rapping our knuckles sore on the painted wood, until eventually Seth said, 'Well he can't be out,' and tried the door. It seemed to be locked. Seth rolled his eyes. 'Oh for crying out loud. Who's going to burgle him out here?'

The cottage only squatted, small and defiant beneath the shadow of the lighthouse tower. Then from behind us came a croaky, unused voice.

'Who's she?'

We turned around with a jump and behind us, on the path that led up from the rocks, was an old man in a yellow sou'wester, holding a rod in one hand and a brace of dead mackerel in the other. He had a grizzled white beard, pitch-black eyebrows, and eyes of the same slate grey as Seth, with deep-set wrinkles that spoke of years spent squinting against the sun and sea wind. As he stumped down the path towards us I saw his cruel limp and the battered crutch clamped under his right armpit.

'Oh hi, Grandad. This is Anna.'

'Huh.' He elbowed past us and gave the door a hefty kick. It opened with a screech of damp wood and he pushed through, kicking it shut in our faces. Seth, seemingly unperturbed by this welcome, caught the door with his foot and held it open for me, and we passed through into a low, beamed room that seemed to be everything: kitchen, living room, bedroom. There was even a chamber pot beneath the unmade bed in the corner of the room, so it looked like it might be a toilet as well, some of the time. The whole place stank of smoke, fish and paraffin. Oh, and unwashed old man. It made Wicker House look like a palace.

On the opposite side of the room from the fusty bed was a Rayburn. The old man hobbled across to it, threw open one of the covers, and banged an empty cast-iron skillet on the hot plate. Then he flung the fish down with a slap on the stone sink by the window and, taking up a knife that was lying on the counter, began to sharpen it on a whetstone.

'Anna, this is my grandfather, Bran Fisher.'

'Pleased to meet you,' I said. My voice sounded ridiculously faint and squeaky. I felt profoundly uncomfortable, but Seth was already kicking off his boots and opening the window to let some air into the room.

'Don't do that, you young oik, d'you want me to freeze?'

Bran grumbled. He stumped over and slammed the window shut, flipping the catch with the point of his knife. 'What are you doing here anyway? And *her.*' He stabbed with his knife in my direction before turning back to the fish.

'Didn't you get my message?' Seth flopped on to a threadbare armchair, setting the springs squeaking in protest.

'Message? What's wrong with speaking to a body, like a civilized human being?'

'Oh for Pete's sake, Grandad, what do you expect if you never check your phone? I asked if Anna and I could talk to you about the fishing industry.'

Bran didn't reply at first. Instead he set his knife to the fishes' gills and severed their heads with a sickening crunch. Dark blood trickled onto the stone drainer.

'Why?' he said at last.

'For a History project. We're doing an essay about the local fishing industry. It was Anna's idea,' he added. Bran snorted.

'What industry,' he said, rather bitterly. It was a statement, rather than a question. Seth shrugged.

'Well, I did say it was for History.'

The remark seemed to tickle Bran's sense of humour and he laughed; a rusty, creaking laugh that ended

145

on a wheezing coughing fit, leaving him red-eyed and spluttering.

'History is about right, eh young Seth,' he said, and with a swift, barely discernible movement of his knife he whipped up and down the backbone of the two mackerel, and flung four neat fillets on the sink. There was a sudden spitting crackle as he threw a knob of butter into the smoking skillet, then the mackerel fillets. The room filled with a deeply savoury smell that drove away the stench and made my mouth water. I suddenly realized I'd had no breakfast, and licked my lips involuntarily. Bran snorted again.

'Well, she likes fish anyway. And you.' He jerked his head at Seth. 'I never yet knew you to turn down a meal – you're a young streak of skin and bone like I was at your age.'

'If you're offering.' Seth grinned from the depths of the armchair. He seemed totally unfazed by his grandfather's hospitality, or rather lack of it.

'Oh, aye. Not come to see me for a month and then turn up when there's food on the table. That's the young for you.' He ground salt and pepper into the pan and then slapped the fish on to two chipped plates, setting them on the table with a crack.

'You must fight over this one.' He indicated one

plate with a nod as he started shovelling fish from the other into his mouth with a fork. 'I've no more clean plates to waste.'

'Clean' was pushing it. Both plates had visible traces of other meals, and oily thumbprints on the rim. But the fish smelled good and Seth jumped out of the armchair and pulled up a stool for each of us. Bran didn't offer us any cutlery, so we ate with our fingers, picking at the hot buttery fish and juggling it from hand to hand until it was cool enough to eat. Finally Bran wiped his mouth, rinsed his plate under the cold tap, and said, 'So it's fishing you want, is it?'

I nodded and Seth added, 'Whatever you can remember really, we can get the basic stuff from the library and the museum but anything you can tell us would be great.'

Bran made a noise somewhere between a laugh and a snort of disgust.

'Remember? There's precious few left that do remember. It's all pleasure boats and fiddling *line-caught scor-lops* now.' His gruff voice took on a mincing London twang. 'When I was a lad it was man's work, real man's work. There were plenty killed on the trawlers, and plenty more maimed, and it was a hard life with fish widows in most towns. But you could be rich in three days if you happened on the right shoal. That was

147

before all these quotas and fishing limits.' He spat into the fireplace.

'What about your grandad's day?' Seth asked.

'That was different again. Small boats mostly, more channel fishing and day fishing. Lobster, as well as fish, of course, then as well as now. My grandad was a great one for his lobster pots. Shellfish, too. The Victorians dearly loved a whelk.' He gave a crackling laugh and slapped his thigh. 'But Winter was a fishing port long before my grandad's day. They've been landing catches here since 1066 and before. There was even fishing families on Castle Spit, time was.'

'Here?' I said in surprise.

'Oh aye. I know the Spit isn't much to look at but it supported people for all that. There were three families here once. You can still see the ruins of their cottages.' He heaved himself out of his chair, clutching at his leg with a groan. But he shook off Seth's arm and hobbled over to the mantelpiece, where he took up a foul-smelling pipe and knocked out the ashes into the fire. 'But the Spit was a different animal then, before the sea levels rose. Time was, you could walk out most days and the causeway only submerged at the highest tides. Now it's under water twenty hours out of the twenty-four, and damn near impassable in winter.'

'What's causing the sea levels to rise?' I asked timidly. 'Is it global warming?'

'Some say. I've got my own notions.' He gave a derisive sniff and lit the pipe, puffing until the smoke filled the little room. Seth coughed.

'D'you know what, Grandad, I'm opening the window no matter what you say.'

'You can go outside if you don't like my pipe,' the old man said. 'Fresh air do you good, at your age. At mine it's as like to kill me as not.'

Seth snorted.

'If anything kills you it'll be that pipe, not an open window. I don't think a bit of a breeze is going to harm someone who spends eight hours a day fishing off the rocks. But I'm sure Anna would like to get some sunshine anyway.'

He led me outside and we sat in the sun on a little stone bench at the front of the cottage. The air was wonderfully crisp and fresh after the stench of the cottage and I breathed in great lungfuls as though I could store up a supply for our return. Seth saw me and smiled.

'Sorry, it is a bit close in there, isn't it? It's Grandad's disgusting pipe and his diet of fish, mainly. I don't mind the fish so much, but the smoke makes me want to retch.'

'I thought you smoked?'

'I do. Well, I did. I'm trying to give up, which makes it all the harder to have Grandad puffing away in my face. I gave up before, but then Caroline smokes like a chimney so I started again when I was going out with her. Now I'm trying to give up again.'

'Does he know?'

Seth shrugged. 'Possibly. Probably not. I doubt he cares much either way. You don't smoke, do you?'

'No.'

'I didn't think so.'

'How did you know?' I asked. Was it some good-girl stamp on my face? To my surprise Seth blushed and looked down at his bitten nails.

'What?' I prodded.

'Your hair,' he said, looking a little sheepish.

'My *hair*?' I said in surprise, flicking a lock of it forward over my shoulder for examination. It looked just like everyone else's – dark and ordinary in comparison to Caroline's spectacular blonde tresses.

'Not how it looks, you fool. The smell – it doesn't smell of smoke.' He gave my shoulder a friendly shove, but something in the movement, in our closeness, made me shiver and he looked away.

'Sorry, sorry, I keep telling myself not to—' He stopped and there was a moment's tense silence. To break it I

150

blurted out the first thing that came into my head.

'I was warned off you, you know. When I first came to Winter.'

'What!' It succeeded in changing the subject, that was for sure. Seth's incredulous expression hovered between annoyance and laughter. 'By who?'

'By . . .' It probably wasn't fair to drop June in it. 'By some girl, I forget her name. She told me you drank, smoked and had a tattoo, and . . .' I stumbled over the last. I'd been going to mention June's final comment, but then I remembered what she'd said, and Seth's reluctance to discuss his past this morning, and thought better of it. Seth raised an eyebrow.

'Oh, I see, that's why you noticed my tat! What was the other thing you were going to say?'

'Oh, just, some other thing . . . I can't quite remember.' I ended lamely. His face hardened.

'Let me guess; I got in trouble with the police for beating someone up, right?'

'Um.' I curled inside at his grim expression but there was no way out. 'Yes.'

'God, you do one stupid thing . . .' His face was bleak, defeated. 'I'm never going to live that down. Was that really the first thing they said about me?'

'They also said you were the school's official babe-magnet?' I offered up. It worked and he cracked a reluctant smile.

'Well, I suppose that's one step above a bare-knuckle thug.' He sighed and ran his hands through his hair in a gesture that looked weary and desperate. 'Shall I tell you what happened?'

'Not if you don't want to.' I felt horrible and wished I'd never brought the subject up.

'You're only going to wonder, if I don't.'

That was true, and I nodded.

'It was the year after my dad died – not that that excuses anything, I'm just explaining the context. I was fifteen and not – not coping very well, if you know what I mean. It was a Saturday and me and some mates went down to a fishermen's pub, down by the harbour. It's that one on the end of East Street.'

I nodded. I knew it, it was the kind of place where heads turned if you went in there, and piles of sick appeared outside on Sunday mornings.

'We'd drunk – a lot – and the landlord, Reg, called time. But this fisherman from up the coast was pissed off that he hadn't got his order in and started to go on a bit, you know, saying Reg was favouring locals – generally acting like a bit of a dick. I like Reg, he's a friend of my mum's, and I made some comment – I forget what – but

152

just basically saying this guy was being a tosser. It was stupid but I was drunk and . . . well, that was it basically; I was drunk. And of course this fisherman started in on me, threatening to rip my balls off and use them as lobster bait, all this crap. I was kind of laughing it off and he was getting more and more annoyed. And one of his mates said, "Steady on mate. His dad was Fred Waters." Meaning, I suppose, that this guy should cut me a break because of what happened to Dad, or something like that.'

He stopped and looked down at his bitten nails again. I waited for him to go on. The silence stretched, filled only with the crash of waves and the mew of gulls. Then Seth drew a breath.

'And then this guy said, "No he wasn't."' There was a catch in his voice and he bit down on one thumbnail before continuing. 'I didn't know what he meant at first, so he spelled it out, and said some other, other stuff about my mum. And then after that, well, I don't really remember much more. I remember when the police turned up though. And being hauled off down the cells. And my mum being rung up at three a.m. It dragged on for ages – for a long time it looked like they were going to prosecute and I'd probably have got a record. In the end I got let off with an official caution because there weren't enough witnesses.' I must have looked puzzled because Seth

153

added wryly, 'Selective amnesia. Not that I asked anyone to do me a favour, but I guess they all made their own decisions. I was very lucky not to end up in court, but I got suspended from school, and Reg got a pretty severe fine for letting me in the pub.'

He sighed again and stretched out his long legs.

'So I was not very popular with Reg, and not very popular at school and not very popular at home, for quite a while. It wasn't the best time, all in all.'

He trailed off and we sat in silence for a long time, listening to the crashing surf and feeling the sun on our limbs and faces. I don't know what Seth was thinking. I was turning his words over in my head, my heart aching with pity for him, for the troubled fifteen-year-old he'd been, and for the burden he now carried, and I felt my own secrets rise in my throat like gall. I thought of Simon's advice to tell Seth everything. Should I? Could I?

'Seth,' I said, hesitantly. He turned his head. And then there was a screech of damp-swollen wood and Bran limped out to stand over us.

'The wind's changing. You'd best go now, if you don't want to spend three hours tacking into harbour.'

Seth nodded and picked up my pack.

'Shall we come back next week?'

'If you like.' Bran gave a shrug with his good shoulder,

then struck Seth's foot with his crutch. 'Come on now, boy, this isn't the time for prattle.'

We hurried down the rocky path, Seth leading the way, and Bran limping after, grimacing with every step.

'I'll run on ahead and get the sails up,' Seth called over his shoulder. He disappeared round the corner, and Bran and I limped on towards the jetty.

We were in sight of the landing when the old man suddenly spoke, his voice terse with what I guessed was pain from his leg.

'What do you want?'

'Sorry?' I turned to him, startled at his blunt tone.

'You heard me.'

'You know what we want; it's a History project.'

'Not that.' He gave an impatient gesture. 'You know what I mean. Our kinds don't mix, you know that as well as I do. No good ever came of it. Oil and water.'

As we reached the jetty he grabbed my hand, stopping me from going any further.

'Whatever you want with him, no good will come of it. Leave him alone. Leave us be.'

'I don't know what you're talking about.' I shook my arm free and stumbled towards the boat, where Seth was obliviously shaking out sails and stowing our bags. 'Seth, are we ready?'

'Yup, let's get going.'

I jumped into the boat and Seth cast off. As I glanced back at the shore, Bran was standing there, leaning on his crutch, his hair wild in the wind.

'Remember what I said,' he called, his voice ripped and torn by the winds. 'Witch!'

CHAPTER NINE

The wind whipped across the bows, sending slops of cold surf and spray into the boat, and the sky to the north was turning an ugly bruised purple. Seth was crouched by the rudder, wiping salt water from his eyes. He wore an expression of fierce concentration, and every few minutes he changed course with a flurry of ropes and sails, forcing the little boat to tack yet again, weaving back and forth across the harbour mouth in the teeth of the wind. Waves slapped and smacked us from all sides. And all the time the dark clouds from the north loomed nearer.

I crouched at the other end of the boat with Dad's anorak hood pulled up, my eyes streaming with the stinging salt wind and my wet hair whipping in rats' tails across my face. I felt very glad of the life jacket strapped tightly around my chest. Seth was wearing his now, too. Mingled with the howls of the wind I seemed to hear Bran's voice following us. Had he really said what I'd heard?

At last Seth shouted something and I shook myself out of my thoughts.

'Sorry, what did you say?'

'I said, we're not making any headway. The wind's dead against us – we'll never get into the harbour at this rate. Can you hold the tiller while I drop the sails? I'm going to try the engine.'

I crawled over the rocking, bucking boat and took the tiller from his hand.

'Aim for that headland,' Seth shouted.

It trembled and strained like a live thing in my hand, buffeted by the waves. I hadn't realized, until I took it, what steady strength was needed to keep the course straight and how the little boat would resist my attempt to keep its head to the wind. I held on as best I could while Seth lowered the sails, then he elbowed me out of the way and dropped the outboard motor.

He pulled at the starter, once, twice. Nothing happened. The third time there was a grinding choke and he ripped desperately at the cord again and again, but nothing. After that there were no more engine sounds, only silence as he yanked at the cord and swore and the boat drifted before the wind, nearer and nearer to the rocky shore. Seth looked up at the cliffs and yanked again, the muscles on his arms taut with the effort. Then he pulled up the motor and beckoned me back. 'I'll row,' he called above the wind. 'But I can't row us into the harbour in this wind. I'll make for the beach. Can you steer?'

'I'll try.' I wiped the wet, salt-draggled hair out of my eyes. 'Where should I aim?'

'See that spot on the cliff, to the right of that rocky outcrop that looks like a nose? Aim for there. There's a path up the cliff.'

'OK.'

We shifted round the boat, which rocked wildly with every movement. It was impossible to keep a grip on the wet, heaving planks and I slipped and fell. Seth barely noticed, he was too busy manoeuvring the oars out from under the seat and fitting them into the rowlocks, trying not to lose them overboard in the sucking waves. At last they were fitted, and he began to row with steady, powerful strokes, patiently forcing us into the teeth of the gale. After a few minutes his gasps were audible even over the roaring of the wind.

The boat inched painfully across the waves. Above Seth's panting breaths and the crack and crunch of the oars in the rowlocks, I could hear the far-off crashing of the surf against the shingle beach, terrifyingly loud even at this remote distance. The sight of the white breakers tearing up the beach made my knees feel weak.

'Are we going to be able to land?' I called, trying not to let the fear show in my voice.

'I hope so,' Seth said tersely, but his strained face showed his doubts. 'I'm sorry, Anna—' he spoke in jerks between great heaves at the oars, 'I've never known a storm blow up so fast . . . I'd never have taken you out . . . if I'd known . . . There was no warning forecast though . . . It's like a complete freak of nature . . . a total freak storm.'

His words stirred an echo in my mind, and I tried to think where the memory had come from. Then it came to me – Maya's voice discussing manifestations of power: 'Weather disturbances are common, freak storms . . .'

It was as if something clicked in my mind, a sudden awareness that while the upper half of my mind was concentrating on steering the boat and desperately hoping the weather wouldn't worsen, down below some atavistic part of me was relishing the storm, releasing all my anger and confusion in the tearing winds and boiling clouds. The turmoil set off by Bran's words was finding an outlet in the violence of the weather. *I* was causing this. And if I didn't get a grip my emotions were going to kill us both.

Horror filled me and I dropped the tiller, causing the

boat to yaw and swing. Lightning split the sky – Seth swore again and I grabbed for the tiller as the rolling crash of thunder rumbled out.

'Sorry, sorry, I lost concentration,' I gabbled.

But he was barely listening, his whole being was concentrated on rowing, fighting the storm, fighting to get us to safety. Fighting *me*.

I forced myself to be calm.

If I was causing this, I could stop it. I shut my eyes and looked inside, into the rolling turmoil that was finding its echo in the turbulent weather. Be calm, I told myself desperately, feeling the thunder build inside. I breathed in through my nose, then exhaled. A tiny part of the confusion and anger subsided.

Be calm. Breathe. Inhale, exhale.

I repeated the words to myself like a mantra, and felt my breathing slow, and the roaring in my ears subside a little.

When I opened my eyes the sea had calmed slightly. There was a stiff breeze but nothing like the tearing gale of a few moments before. The waves were still racing along in great rollers, but the surf had subsided a little. On the horizon the dark clouds were shifting, parting. A thin stream of sunshine broke through.

Seth paused for a moment, looking at the small patch

of sunshine as if hardly daring to hope – and he resumed rowing, making progress now that he didn't have to battle the vicious wind. Then suddenly there was a crunching grind, and I felt shingle under the keel of the boat. Seth yanked off his life jacket and shoes, and pulled up first the rudder, then the keel. Then, before I'd fully realized what he was about to do, he leapt out, into the freezing, crashing surf. For a moment he was waist deep in the sucking back-draft, clinging on with his fingers to the stern, then the next second he was staggering forward, submerged to the neck in creamy, boiling surf. Without his weight the boat floated on the incoming wave, and he put his shoulder to the stern, heaving with all his might, thrusting the boat as far up the shingle as his strength would take it. Another wave, another thrust, up to the weedy belt halfway up the beach. Then he fell, panting, on to the sand, and just lay there, drenched from his head to his bare feet.

I climbed painfully out, stiff from my hunched vigil at the rudder, and knelt beside him. His curls were plastered to his skull, and his head looked like a wet seal. His chest rose and fell with painful gasps beneath the soaking fabric of his T-shirt. For a long moment he lay with his eyes closed and his head flung back, gasping for breath. I could see a vein beating furiously in his arched throat.

At last he spoke, his voice hoarse.

'Thank God that's over. I've never seen a storm blow up so fast, and I hope I never do again.'

'Are you OK?' I asked. My voice shook. He nodded, still gulping for breath.

'I'm so sorry, Anna, I should never have taken you out. Are you OK?'

'I'm fine,' I said. I felt incredibly guilty. 'Honestly. Please stop apologizing, it wasn't your fault.'

'It was; I should've double-checked the storm forecast for today. It was clear last night but these things can blow in from nowhere. You think you know a place, that's the thing. It's a trip I make ten times a month. You get complacent.'

'Will your boat be OK here?'

He nodded again, wearily.

'It'll be fine. I'll drag it above the high-water mark and come back for it tomorrow. I'm not sailing anywhere else tonight, my muscles feel like wet spaghetti.'

He was shivering. I took off Dad's anorak and put it around his shoulders, swallowing against the lump in my throat. He made a protest for a moment, but he was too tired to argue and we sat in silence for a while, watching the surf while he got his breath back. Then he put on his shoes, and we dragged the boat as far up the beach as

163

possible, and started on the climb up the cliff.

Seth led the way. He insisted on shouldering my backpack, but I could see that his legs were trembling with the effort of the climb and halfway up I made him give it back. We carried on, in silence. Seth was too exhausted and I was too guilt-ridden to make small talk. My throat felt as if I'd swallowed one of the flint pebbles on the beach – it stuck in my craw, cold and smooth and suffocating.

At last we reached the top of the cliff. The storm had completely cleared and the sky was a beautiful opalescent twilight. Only the hint of dark clouds at the horizon and the great waves still crashing on the beach below gave a clue that the day had been anything but calm.

We stood for a moment, catching our breath, then Seth wordlessly handed me Dad's anorak.

'Seth, thank you for everything. You were amazing,' I said, meaning it more sincerely than I could say. He shook his head.

'No, I was stupid. But luckily it turned out OK. Thank God you kept your head and kept calm. I couldn't have dealt with someone screaming and shouting on top of it all. I'm so, so sorry it turned out like that.'

Stop being so nice! It was my fault, you idiot! I wanted to shout. I felt like a traitor – Seth's apologies only adding to my guilt.

'I didn't do anything,' I muttered.

'That's the point.' He pressed his hand to his eyes. 'You kept calm and didn't panic, or do anything stupid, or ask silly questions. You were incredibly brave.'

This was appalling, worse than appalling. My insides curdled and suddenly I had to say something, anything, to stop him.

'Please, Seth,' I said desperately, 'please stop being so nice. You wouldn't say all this if you knew the truth. I'm not the person you think I am. This is all my fault.'

He'd been frowning as I spoke. Now he snorted and started to laugh in spite of his weariness.

'Don't be bloody stupid. What do you mean? The storm?'

'Yes – the storm – you being here – Caroline – everything.'

'Anna, you're talking crap.'

'I'm not!' I cried. I wanted to weep. 'Oh Seth, please believe me, I'm not a good person for you to know.'

'Anna.' He took my hand in his. 'I have no idea what you're on about, but whatever you've done, it can't be that bad, can it? Look at me. Lots of people in this town would write me off – lots of them *have* written me off already.

You know I've made mistakes; I've done things I'm not proud of. But I'm trying to be a better person, you make me *want* to be a better person.'

'No, no, no.' I shook my head, close to tears, 'Seth, you *are* a good person – you're a wonderful person. This is completely different. Oh please, won't you just trust me – forget you ever met me – go back to Caroline.'

'Why do you keep talking about Caroline? What's she got to do with anything? Anna, I am never, *never* going back to Caroline.'

I shook my head in mute misery and he gave an exclamation of frustration.

'How can I convince you? Look, I've told you more in one month of knowing you than I told her in a year of going out. You know why? Because she didn't give a toss about me or my feelings. Maybe she fancied me, but she didn't *care* about me, she never did. But you do. Or I feel like you do – don't you?'

'Yes.' My throat was tight and ached with the truth of this. 'Yes I do.'

But I knew that for this to be *really* true, I needed to be honest. I wanted to be the person Seth thought I was, and that meant destroying his illusions about me, destroying whatever friendship we'd built up. It meant telling the truth. I didn't care about Maya's warnings. There

166

couldn't be anything worse than this corrosive guilt.

I took a deep breath.

'Seth, do you remember that day, when you – when you decided that you *liked* me?'

He nodded, perplexed.

'And do you remember down at the quay when you—' I forced myself to continue, 'when you kissed me?'

He shut his eyes for a moment, and the expression that momentarily crossed his face made my heart wring. But he said nothing, only nodded again, reluctantly this time.

'Do you remember you said that it was totally out of character – like you were crazy, obsessed?'

Another nod. There was humiliation on his face now, as well as pain. He opened his mouth to say something, but I held out a hand, warding him off.

'Please, please don't. Let me finish. There – there was a reason, why you felt like that so suddenly. Why you woke up one morning obsessed with a girl from London you barely knew, and broke up with your gorgeous, long-term girlfriend, and fell for someone completely plain and ordinary and boring, in a totally inexplicable way.'

I swallowed. I couldn't think of a way to put it that didn't sound crazy.

'I – I enchanted you.'

He frowned, confused. I could see he didn't understand

the ambiguity of the phrase. Desperately, I spelled it out.

'I bewitched you. I made a spell. A love potion. Seth, you don't love me at all. I *made* you love me.' I stopped and gulped, then spat out the words like bitter stones. 'I'm a witch.'

Up until that point he had been silent, his expression flitting between perplexed and downright bewildered. Now he broke out into a shout of laughter.

'Anna! You had me worried there for a minute. Let me guess – you magicked gullible out of the dictionary as well?'

'It's true,' I said wretchedly. 'I wish it wasn't. I know you'll think it's mad. I thought so too at first. I never meant for it to happen – I just didn't know what I was doing.'

'Hmm, a witch with L-plates, eh?' He was still grinning, in spite of his tiredness.

'Seth, please don't make fun of me. I don't know what to do – how to convince you . . .' I broke off, thinking of Abe and his handful of snow. Could I do something similar? Something to *force* Seth to believe?

My eye fell on a stick beside the road and I had a sudden memory of a magician I'd seen at a party when I was a little girl. He'd made his wand blossom with paper flowers, a pretty hackneyed trick I suppose, but at the time I'd been incredibly impressed. I had no wand, but . . .

I picked up the stick and held it out to Seth.

'If you don't believe me, watch.'

I held the end in both hands and concentrated. Seth watched with polite but slightly sarcastic amusement. He didn't laugh again but I could tell there was a smile hovering at his lips.

This time I didn't shut my eyes, I didn't need to. I could feel the tendrils of power inside me rippling down my arms, into my hands, into the dry stick. I thought of sap rising, of leaves, buds, flowers. The wood grew warm and sweaty in my hands. It began to bud.

Tender swellings, furling leaves, blossom – it was like watching freeze-frame photography in real life. Within seconds the stick was heavy in my hands, too heavy to hold, and I dropped it, leaves, fruit and all. It fell to the ground with a thud, and an apple broke off and rolled towards Seth, landing at his feet.

He only stared, open-mouthed. Then he reached down and touched the apple – the lightest, most tentative of touches. He drew back immediately as if burned and, curious, I reached down to pick it up. It felt heavy, ordinary, unutterably real. It was slightly warm, but no warmer than an ordinary apple sitting in the sun. Its weight was the weight of a real apple. There was a slightly soft patch where it had hit the ground and had bruised, just as any other apple would. I sniffed it. It smelled of – apple. Delicious.

I held it out to Seth, with an attempt at a smile.

'Want to see what it tastes like?'

'No!' He recoiled, his face suddenly shocked out of its stupor into an expression of fear and something close to revulsion. 'No! Make it go away!'

I hung my head.

'I don't think I can – I mean, I don't know how. I seem to be good at magic, but not so good at undoing it.'

In truth I didn't want to try. Making a stick bud seemed comparatively harmless, but once I started wishing things into oblivion, where would it end? Might I accidentally obliterate the grass? Or the earth we were standing on? Or even Seth?

'My God, it's true,' he whispered, talking almost to himself. 'It's true. What else have you done? When you said the storm was your fault . . . ?'

I shut my eyes and only nodded, too shamed to find the words.

'And . . . me?'

I could not even nod, but a tear squeezed out from under my lashes. I felt it roll down my cheek.

'Why?' His voice was bewildered. 'What did I ever do to you?'

'Nothing,' I managed, though my throat was tight and sore. 'I'm so sorry . . .'

'Sorry? Sorry?'

It was as if the words had triggered something long suppressed.

'*Sorry!*' he shouted. Veins stood out on his neck and temples. I took a step back.

I'd seen his anger before, and it had been horrible, but at the same time exciting, because it had always been directed at others in my defence. Now his fury was directed at me. Bleak. Terrifying. Soul-destroying.

'I defended you to Caroline. I kissed you. I told you . . .' His face contorted as he remembered the things he'd said, and he tore his hands through his hair in an agony of self-reproach, 'Oh how could I, the things I said! How could *you*? I'll never trust anyone – I'll never even trust *myself* again.'

'Please, Seth . . .' I tried not to sob, but I'm not sure he even heard me.

'I said I *loved* you!' he yelled. His fingers clutched at his hair – he was almost sobbing himself. 'I bared my soul to you. You – you . . .' He stopped, unable, I thought, to think of a word vicious enough.

'Seth,' I sobbed, not caring now that tears were running down my face.

'Anna, just go,' he said stonily. 'Get away before I do something I regret.' His face made me quail, but I tried once more.

'Seth—'

'Just *go*!' He almost spat the words, but his voice was low. The red hot fury had vanished, replaced by a bleak calm that was even more terrifying. He spoke quite softly now, but the words were very clear.

'I never want to speak to you again. I never want to *see* you again. How could I ever have thought I loved you? You're the worst, most despicable person I've ever met.'

CHAPTER TEN

I opened the front door to the smell of cooking, and it made me feel sick. Dad was in the kitchen, stirring herbs into fragrant bubbling pots and humming tunelessly to himself. I couldn't face a fake-cheerful conversation and tried to sneak upstairs to my room unnoticed, but the wind caught the door, slamming it shut, and he called out, 'Anna, is that you?'

'Yes.' I swallowed the lump in my throat and managed to yell back, 'Just going upstairs to change.'

'Well come down and chat to me in a sec.' He put his head around the kitchen door, staring at me over steam-misted glasses. 'I feel like I haven't seen you for a week.'

'Yeah, OK,' I said wearily, but when I got upstairs I didn't change. I didn't do anything. I just lay on my front on my bed with my face buried in my pillow, feeling every bone in my body throb with tiredness.

I should have felt relieved that I'd done the right thing and told Seth. Judging by his anger I wouldn't have much to worry about in terms of unwanted affection. Problem solved – just like Simon had predicted. But I didn't feel any relief, only a deep, gnawing sadness.

If only I'd never started messing with that stupid spell. Without it, Seth would probably never have looked at me romantically, but perhaps I could have been his friend. Now I'd lost even that chance, and hurt Seth so badly he would never forgive me. And it was all my own stupid fault.

There was a perfunctory rap at the door, breaking in on my self-pity. Out of the corner of my eye I saw Dad standing in the doorway.

'I thought you were coming down?' he said, a touch of irritation in his voice.

I shook my head into the pillow and he sighed, and sat on the foot of the bed.

'What's up?'

'Nothing.' My voice was muffled by the pillow.

'How was Seth?'

'I don't really want to talk about it – sorry, Dad.'

'Well at least tell me how your trip out to Castle Spit went? I'm quite keen to hear what Mr Fisher had to say, it might be useful for my book.'

'Not much to tell.' I sat up wearily.

'Anna . . .' he said warningly, in the voice that meant: *You're trying my patience.*

'I don't. Want. To talk about it.' I didn't mean to sound so childish, but I felt close to tears, and I knew that if I started to discuss any of this with Dad it would all come spilling out, and I couldn't, I just couldn't bear it. My heart was too raw for Dad's blundering sympathy.

'For heaven's sake, Anna!' Dad exploded. 'I've really had enough of all these theatrics. What's got into you since we moved? You're secretive, you won't tell me about your friends, you won't answer simple questions about your day. I know that moving has been a big adjustment for you. It's been a big change for me too. But enough is enough. I don't expect you to tell me everything – you've a right to your privacy – but I do expect basic politeness and the bare facts about your life.'

The unfairness of this struck me dumb for a second. Then something snapped inside me.

'You're one to talk!' I screamed. 'How *dare* you lecture me about secrecy? You haven't told me *anything* about myself, about mum, about what happened between you. I was so desperate I even bloody *googled* her. Do you have any idea what that feels like? Don't I have a right to know about stuff too?'

'That's different.' Dad was shaking his head.

'Really? How? How is it different? Come on, if you're so big on the bare facts, what was her maiden name?'

'Anna . . .' His voice was warning.

'When did you get married? Were you even married at all?'

'Anna, stop this.'

'Is she alive or dead?' I pursued relentlessly. The sight of Dad's face tore at me but I had no sympathy to spare today and pressed on with an almost malicious delight in his pain. 'What happened? Come on, what happened? What *happened*?'

He stood for a moment, his face wrung with desperation. It was almost as if he *wanted* to speak but just couldn't. He opened his mouth and closed it again. Then he turned to leave, slamming the door behind him.

I didn't see him again that night, and at breakfast we discussed progress on the bathroom and pretended that nothing had happened. It was all very English. But Dad hadn't forgotten, I could see that, from the wariness in his eyes and the way he looked at me when he thought I wasn't watching.

* * *

My tiredness and the row with Dad had taken my mind off Seth for one night, but on Sunday I had nothing else to worry about, except some stupid essay I hadn't finished, and I spent a sleepless night, dreading seeing Seth in Maths the next morning. What would he say? Would we still sit together or would he find some way of getting out of it? The way he'd looked last night I wouldn't have put it past him to change his name to the opposite end of the alphabet by deed-poll, or drop the A-level altogether, if that was what it took to avoid me.

I needn't have worried. When I turned up, my mouth sour with too much coffee and too little breakfast, his seat was empty. It was empty in History too, and again the next day. I moved from class to class like an automaton, shunning conversation, sitting by myself at breaks, sleepwalking through the days, then tossing and turning at night.

First June, then Liz tried to talk to me, but my curt replies to their questions and my cold, closed face soon had them returning, baffled, to their crowd, shrugging their shoulders at my odd mood. No one tried again after that.

There'd been a coolness between us since the sleepover at my house anyway. Maybe it was embarrassment over what had happened. Maybe it was mystification or resentment at the way Seth had fallen at my feet. Whatever – they were still perfectly pleasant, but I got the sense that they'd let me do the running for a while, and while things had still been so complicated with Seth I'd let it slide, promising myself that I'd make it up to them afterwards, when things were sorted out. Now, my reserve seemed to be the last straw, and I was left alone.

They weren't the only people withdrawing from me. More and more I found myself alone in lessons. Sometimes the motive was obvious – all Caroline's friends avoided me studiously, which ruled out half the girls. But the reason behind the boys' aversion was more mysterious. Very often there was a seat free beside me and some boy would hasten over, only to think better of it and back away. Once I was even talking to some guy in the dinner line when his friend walked up and nudged him. He seemed to recall something he'd forgotten and with a muffled, 'Oh,' made poor excuses and melted away. I tried not to care – but it was impossible not to feel hurt. Invisibility, I could have coped with. I didn't mind being overlooked, in fact there would have been a sort of restfulness to it, compared to all the whispering and gossip over what had happened with Seth and Caroline. But being shunned was harder to cope with. In vain I tried to think what I might be doing wrong. But the only answers were things I couldn't change: Caroline, Seth, me.

Luckily the fatwa didn't seem to affect Emmaline, and on Thursday she sought me out at lunch.

'What the hell is going on?' she demanded with her usual lack of tact, banging her tray down next to mine in the canteen.

'What do you mean?' I said, dully.

'Well, where's Seth?'

'How should I know?' I countered, but I said it with less than complete conviction. Emmaline put her hands on her hips.

'Oh pur-lease, Anna. You go out in his boat, a freak storm blows up, then he disappears for a week? And this is all supposed to be nothing to do with you?'

'Oh for crying out loud! Does everyone know everything in this bloody village?'

'More or less, yes. So come clean and fess up. His mum's giving out some rubbish about him being suddenly called away to visit an ill relative. Who apparently has no name, isn't on the phone, and doesn't require Seth's mother's presence. Forgive me for being a little sceptical.' She raised one narrow eyebrow and I caved.

'OK, I'll tell you, but not here. After school, OK?'

'OK,' she agreed. 'We'll meet at the south gate, shall we?'

That afternoon we met at the gate and walked slowly up the hill. After the rush of students had passed us I told her in a low voice everything that had happened. I included everything, even Seth's grandfather's parting remark. The only thing I left out was what Seth had told me about his fight in the bar. I felt that was his secret, not mine.

'So he knows.' Emmaline's face was set in lines I could not read. I nodded.

'Well you've got balls, Anna. I'll give you that.'

There was a long silence. I wasn't sure how to respond to this and eventually said, 'Er, thanks. What do you think I should do now?'

'Do?' She shrugged. 'What can you do? Nothing. Sit tight and hope to hell he doesn't spill the beans.'

'Spill the beans? What, tell someone you mean? Why would he?'

'More to the point, why wouldn't he? He doesn't owe you anything. And he's bloody angry, by the sound of it.'

'But who'd believe him? Everyone would think he was mad.'

'Not everyone.'

'Oh come on!'

'I wouldn't think he was mad, would I? If he came to me.'

'But you're a w— you know.'

'Exactly.'

'What – you mean other people, other people like us, they might disapprove?'

She gave a tight nod.

'But why?' I asked. 'What's it to them?'

'A lot, Anna. Remember how angry Mum was about the storm demon and stuff? It's not in our interests to have people blundering about, telling our secrets.'

A chill ran through me.

'What might happen?' I asked in a small voice. Emmaline took a deep breath and looked over her shoulder.

'Look, we shouldn't be talking like this in public. Can you come over to mine?'

'Yes, of course,' I said, really worried now.

'OK, let's go. I'll explain when we get there.'

Maya was busy in the shop and only waved as we made our way up the back stairs to the flat. I sat hunched on a stool in the kitchen while Emmaline put on the kettle and stuffed some scones into the toaster. Then she sat down opposite me at the kitchen table, unpacking her school

181

bag. She didn't seem in a hurry to get back to the topic of Seth, so at last, when we'd both had tea and buttered scones, I said, 'So, what were you going to tell me, out on the street?'

Emmaline swallowed and looked down at her hands, holding the mug of tea.

'Look, please don't repeat any of this, OK? Mum didn't want to tell you – she said we weren't necessarily the best judges and that you had to make up your own mind when the time came. I think she knows something – or perhaps Sienna's seen something in the future, I don't know. Whatever it is, they're not telling me. But I think if you're going to have a run in with the Ealdwitan you deserve to know as much as possible in advance.'

'The Ee-ald what?' I stumbled. It wasn't the first time I'd heard the word, but somehow I'd never caught it properly, they seemed to skip over it, almost uneasily.

'The Ealdwitan.' Emmaline had lowered her voice, though surely it was impossible anyone would overhear us up here. 'They're kind of like . . . a council. They set laws and ensure they're not broken, and they band together against foreign forces if necessary.'

'Like a government?' I said, confused. 'Or like police, do you mean?'

'Not like either, really,' Emmaline said slowly. 'And

yet . . . I suppose they do have an element of both those things. Imagine the House of Lords, crossed with the Skull and Bones – does that makes any sense?'

'Not really. What kind of council? Who elects them?'

'No one. The key posts are supposed to be hereditary – drawn from four or five of the key Families and the rest are appointed. Oh—' she gave an exclamation of annoyance, 'I'm not explaining this very well. Look, to understand you need to know a bit about our society – it's very clannish, and there are a handful of Families who wield a lot of power. Most people have links to one or other of them and they run the Ealdwitan between them. The council seats go to Family heads, and the boring administrative positions are appointed to people who show the right "qualities" – you get tapped on the shoulder at university and invited off for an interview at some secret, backstreet address in London.'

'If it's so secret, how do you know all this?' I asked. Emmaline shrugged.

'Everyone knows about the Ealdwitan, to some extent. It's in their interests to make their power talked about – just not the specifics. There are rumours – there are supposed to be members of the Ealdwitan in the Cabinet and the House of Lords, and at least two of the Law Lords are apparently Ealdwitan members. Some of the Oxbridge colleges are allegedly bristling with them. But most of what I know comes from Abe – he got in trouble with them a while back and found himself on the sharp end of their supposed justice.'

'What happened?'

Emmaline shook her head.

'It's not fair for me to tell you – you'll have to ask Abe yourself some time.'

'So . . .' I was staggering under the weight of all this new information, desperately trying to process it. 'So where do I come into all this?'

'One of their major tenets is secrecy, and not interfering with the outwith . . . Non-magical people,' she added, seeing my blank look. 'The edict is supposed to protect us from being persecuted, and them from exploitation.'

'OK,' I said slowly, 'that seems fair enough. I can see that you could do a lot of harm to someone if you had power and they didn't.'

'Yes,' said Emmaline patiently, 'it does seem fair enough, as laws go, but you broke it with your spell on Seth.'

'Oh.' Coldness stirred in the pit of my stomach.

'And like most of the Ealdwitan's laws, they're mainly concerned about the ones protecting their own cushy nests. So as long as you don't make too many ripples, you're fine. You could, for example, quite easily get away with a discreet little love potion and even if they found out, you'd be unlikely to get anything more than a telling off. But what will be harder for them to swallow is what you did next.'

'You mean – I told him?'

'Precisely. Anything that rocks the boat is deeply unpopular. And if you *seriously* rock the boat, you're up the creek without a paddle.'

'So . . . how would they know? That I told him, I mean?'

'They won't. Unless Seth passes on your little nugget of info to someone who passes it back to them. That's why you're in his hands now. That's why you'd better hope he keeps his pretty mouth shut.'

I swore and Emmaline raised that sardonic eyebrow again.

'Nice language, Anna.'

'Sorry, sorry.'

'Oh for Pete's sake, I'm joking! I'm not the boss of you. You can turn the air blue for all I care. You've got reason enough.'

'But I didn't know!' I said. 'Surely they'll realize I didn't do it deliberately. Why didn't Simon say something when he suggested telling Seth?'

'Well he didn't exactly *suggest* it, did he, Anna? He said he'd had an idea but it wasn't practical because it was too dangerous, if you remember.'

Now she said it, I did remember. But I'd been so focussed on the idea of freeing Seth . . .

'In fact, if I recall correctly, Mum actually *vetoed* it, and specifically mentioned the Ealdwitan as one of the reasons she thought it was a dreadful idea. I think the word "apeshit" was bandied about.'

'Oh help.' I put my head in my hands. I felt like banging my forehead on the wooden table. 'I've really screwed up again, haven't I?'

'Mmm, well, I wouldn't say you're exactly wrong there.' Then she saw my distraught expression and softened a little. 'Look on the bright side, you've mainly dropped yourself in it this time. At least you haven't dragged anyone else down with you.'

'Huh, thanks,' I said. Oddly enough though, it *was* a comfort. If the Ealdwitan were after anyone over this, it would be me. And, after all, I deserved it.

'Anna.' Emmaline put her hand on my arm. 'Look, don't worry too much. I shouldn't have been so dramatic. Seth's not likely to tell anyone, is he? And anyway, I'll be the first to admit – I'm a bit biassed over the Ealdwitan. I think Abe's opinion of them has probably rubbed off on me. They're not out to get you – not really. They're just not very nice people to cross, even by accident.'

I couldn't think of anything to reply. I could only hope that Seth was even nicer than I thought he was, and even more forgiving.

CHAPTER ELEVEN

It took a long time for me to fall asleep that night, in spite of my exhaustion. I lay and read until my eyes scratched with tiredness and the radio had finished the Shipping Forecast and Sailing By. When the reader announced close-down I knew it was time to turn out the lights and – hopefully – to sleep. It was still school the next day, in spite of everything.

So I turned out the lights, turned my pillow to the cool side, and lay staring into the blackness, my eyes playing tricks on me with small twinkling lights that existed only in my mind, or as an echo of my reading lamp.

I'd never get used to the darkness of Winter, I thought. In London there'd always been a faint orange glow around my window where the street-lights filtered through, no matter how dense the blackout blind. But here, night was dark. Completely dark, unless there was a moon. I could hear sounds though – not the muted roar of traffic that had always filled my room in London, but the sound of Dad snoring through the wall and the movement of small animals in the woods outside. The screech of an owl and the scream of the small creature it had just caught. The rustle of leaves, the crack of a twig, a gate swinging in the wind, very faint and far away.

I lay and dozed, not quite sleeping, but not far off.

Crack.

My heart thudded, loud in the silence. What was that? A crack, a definite loud crack, like someone stepping on a stick. Then, a scraping, stealthy rustle. My heart was pounding so hard that I put my hand up, as if to press it into silence.

Was it the crow again? There were so many of them around the house, more every day it seemed. They stalked across the lawn like hunched old men in mourning weeds, tapped on the windows, threw bones and shells down the chimneys in the middle of the night. I'd developed an irrational hatred of them and their bold, watchful malevolence.

Please, let it not be a crow, scrabbling into my room in the darkness of the night and stealthily creeping around, with its sharp beak and malignant black eyes.

I was still paralyzed when there was a knock, not at the

door, but at the window. I leapt, stifling an involuntary scream with my sheets. For a long moment I sat, completely still apart from my trembling hands. But the next noise I heard stirred me into movement. The window, which I'd left ajar, was opening. I knew its distinctive creak anywhere. With shaking fingers I fumbled for the lamp and turned it on expecting, I don't know – dark wings, black eyes, a cold black beak.

The room blazed. A bare foot and a leg, covered in blue denim, was appearing from under the curtain. I drew breath, ready to scream the scream of my life – and knocked over the lamp. I heard the bulb smash. The room went pitch black again. Then, very loud in the silence:

'Anna – it's me.'

It was Seth.

My heart was thumping so hard I wasn't sure whether to run over and hug him, or push him back outside. He stumbled into the room in the pitch black, knocking over a pile of books by the window. At that I jumped out of bed, blindly heading for the reading lamp on my desk, and we blundered into each other in the dark. His frozen fingers clutched at me – I could hear his breath tearing in his throat as though he'd run a mile, or more likely swum it, judging by his shivers and his damp T-shirt.

'Are you mad?' I whispered. He stumbled again, and I wrapped my arms around him, trying to steady him. He leaned against me, pulling me into him, shuddering with cold. We both staggered and he dropped to his knees, pulling me with him. I put my hand up to his face in the dark; it was wet, though I could not remember it raining. I felt him shake his head.

'Perhaps. I don't think so. But I'm drunk.' He laughed bitterly. 'Not very drunk, just drunk enough.'

'Seth, what are you doing? You'll wake my dad.' Although I knew that wasn't true. Dad was still snoring, and if the clatter of Seth's entrance hadn't woken him, nothing would.

'I don't care.' His voice was hoarse, and I could smell whisky and smoke on his breath, on his skin.

'Where have you been all week?'

'Were you worried?' I could hear a smile in his voice.

'Yes! But not as worried as I am now. Seth, please, this is crazy, let go of me.'

'No.' His fingers clutched me tighter, painfully tight through my thin pyjamas.

'Yes.' I began to gently disengage his grip. 'I just want to put on the light.'

'No, wait.' He held me still, and I could feel his heart

pounding even faster than mine. 'Wait, Anna, it wasn't true, what you said.'

'What? What wasn't true?'

'All that—' He shook his head angrily, like a swimmer trying to get the water out of their ears. 'All that crap, about bewitching me, enchanting me.'

'Oh please no – Seth, not this again.' I felt desperation rise up. 'It's true. I swear, it's all true. You saw the apple.'

'It's *not*,' he hissed, with frightening vehemence. 'It's not true. I don't care – I don't care what you did, or what you thought, or what you said, d'you hear me? I don't care. I know what I feel. I *know*. And I love you, Anna. It's nothing to do with any stupid bloody schoolgirl potions. I love *you*. Can't you understand? I love your skin, your lips, the little line between your eyebrows when you frown, the way you catch your breath before you speak, the way you smile when you think no one's looking. You can't *enchant* that.' His hands were in my hair, on my cheek, gripping me with painful intensity in the darkness.

'I did,' I said wretchedly. 'I wish I could pretend not, but I did. Seth, please believe me—'

'Anna, just shut up! I know what I know. I know what I feel. Yes, those stupid first days when I kissed you and acted like a twat, none of that was me. I know that. You and your silly potions did that, you can have that. But you can't change someone's soul with a spell, Anna – you can't make them *love*, not real love, not like this. How can I make you believe me? For God's sake – I don't *want* to love you – can't you see that? I want to hate you. But I can't.'

He stopped, his forehead resting on mine in the darkness, his hands twined in my hair. I felt his breath on my face, his lips so close to mine that I could feel the heat of his mouth, and my knees went weak. I knew in a minute I would do something very, very stupid. Every part of my body wanted to believe Seth, but wasn't I just hearing what I wanted to hear? Whatever Seth thought, whatever his feelings now, it all rested on a lie. The truth was that I had started all this, with the spell book. And I had to finish it.

I shut my eyes, drawing up all the strength I possessed.

'No.' I tore his hands away and stood for a minute, trembling with the effort of will. Then I felt my way across the room and groped for the reading lamp. 'Seth, please go.'

He looked awful in the lamplight. His T-shirt was wet and torn, his jeans ripped and muddied up to the knees. But he seemed not even to hear me. Instead, he stumbled to the foot of my bed and half slumped, half knelt at the foot, his head resting on the bedspread. He was cut about the face and hands with brambles, the slashes shocking even in the soft half-light.

'How did you get here?' I whispered.

'Walked, climbed . . .'

'Up the sheer side of my *house*?'

'It's not so hard . . .' His voice was faint and he shuddered. 'Anna, I'm so cold.'

'You're wet.' I laid my hand on his back and felt his T-shirt. 'Did you swim too?'

He didn't answer, his only response was the rise and fall of his ribs beneath my hand, and the occasional tremors from his cold, exhausted muscles. My heart seemed to hurt inside me. I wanted so much to hold him.

I gathered together all my resolve, all my willpower, for one final attempt.

'Seth,' I said softly, holding his shoulder, 'Seth, you need to go. Please go, you can't be here. It'll be morning in a few hours, my dad will be up.'

He raised his head with a great effort and looked at me with exhausted, bleak grey eyes. The cuts on his face stood out, sharp and beaded with blood where he must have caught twigs and brambles in the dark.

'Please don't send me away, Anna,' he whispered. 'I'm so tired . . .'

He'd never make it home, I realized. Even if I managed

to smuggle him past Dad's room, downstairs and out the front door, he looked as if he could barely walk from one side of the room to the other, let alone the two miles into Winter through the dark, treacherous wood, then another mile or so across town to the Crown and Anchor.

'OK,' I said, defeated by his vulnerability. 'I won't make you go.'

I turned out the light and he crawled into bed beside me, pulling off his wet T-shirt. I wrapped my arms around him and he huddled into me, his head on my shoulder, the harsh stubble of his cheek grazing my bare neck. Gradually his shivering subsided. His shuddering breaths grew regular, and he slept.

I lay awake, listening to his quiet breathing, and feeling his cold skin begin to grow warm, absorbing the heat of my own. I had no right to feel so happy, so content, yet I did. I lay there, hardly daring to breathe, feeling the weight of his head on my shoulder and the slow, dreamy thud of his heart. When I was sure he was completely asleep I risked a small movement, pulling my dead arm out from under his head, and turning to face him. It was too dark to see much, but I could sense his face just inches from mine. I imagined his dark lashes sweeping his bruised cheeks, his lips, slack and peaceful in sleep.

I closed my eyes and slept, deeply and completely relaxed.

When I woke it was early morning, the birds were singing the dawn chorus, the sun was filtering through the curtains, and I stretched, wondering why I felt so happy.

Then I turned my head and he was there, beside me, his tousled head on my pillow, his eyes still closed in complete contentment. I couldn't help it – I broke into a huge smile. He was here. Everything was right.

I let my toes explore beneath the sheets, feeling Seth's long legs and the roughness of his jeans. When I raised my head I could see his bare feet and half a foot of shin sticking out over the end of the bed. He'd thrown the duvet partly off in the night, and lay with one arm outflung, his naked back golden in the muted, rose-coloured sunshine, perfectly at peace. Only the little fish was awake, still endlessly circling in the small of his back. But then Seth stirred, and suddenly I was aware of the narrowness of my bed and the way my body was curved into his. I jumped up and scrambled out of bed, turning to the window to hide my fiery blush, pretending I was admiring the view and had been there for ages.

'Morning,' Seth said sleepily, as sunlight flooded the room. I turned back to him. His eyes were open, crinkled against the sun, and he gave a huge smile as wide as my own. I hoped it was just general contentment and that he would put my pink cheeks down to the dawn sun streaming through the window. 'Did you sleep well?'

'Very, thanks. Did you?'

'Oooooooooohhhh.' He stretched luxuriously, so hard that I heard his joints click. 'Soooo well, the best I've slept in ages. What's the time?'

'Still early – it's only five – but you have to be out before my dad wakes up.'

'Five! Come on, there's not really any huge hurry, is there?' Seth coaxed. He held out his arms. 'Come back to bed. It's so cold, and my clothes are still wet. And we wasted all that time last night sleeping . . . Besides, you wouldn't be so cruel as to throw me out in the middle of the night, would you?'

'It's not the middle of the night.' I tried to look stern but his grin was infectious. He looked so endearing, lying there with his hair all tousled against the pillow, his cheeks flushed with sleep. 'It's morning.'

'It's too cold.' He stretched again and held out a hand. 'Anyway, I think I'm feverish. I should stay in bed.'

I took his hand and sat on the side of the bed. Now that I'd adjusted I could feel that his skin *was* very hot. I touched his forehead with the back of my hand, as Dad used to when I was small and running a temperature. It was burning.

'I think you *are* feverish,' I said. 'Though why I'm surprised I don't know – running around in wet clothes in the middle of the night . . . What were you thinking?'

'I wasn't thinking.' He rubbed the sleep out of his eyes. 'I was acting . . .'

'Enchanted?' I finished.

'Drunk,' he amended defiantly.

'Let's just say, "under the influence", and agree that you were talking a lot of rubbish.'

Seth gave a groan and propped himself on his elbow.

'Anna, please, not this again. Don't spoil today. I thought I'd convinced you last night.'

'You'll never convince me. I know what I know.'

'You don't know *me*.' He shook his head. 'And I do. Ugh, for a rational person you're remarkably stubborn, Anna Winterson.'

I had to laugh in spite of my frustration – I'd just been thinking the same thing about him.

'What's so funny?' he asked. I shook my head.

'Nothing. Nothing important. Oh Seth, what are we going to do?'

'I don't see what the problem is. I love you – and are you going to tell me that you don't feel anything at all for me? Because I just won't believe you. I'm no more arrogant than the next bloke, but after last night I just can't believe you don't feel something. Can you honestly say you don't feel anything for me? Can you swear it?'

My heart swelled in my throat. I just couldn't do it – I couldn't lie yet again, adding yet more hurt and deception to the mountain of complexities in my life.

'No, I can't swear it.'

'So you do? Feel something?' In spite of his supposed certainty he looked jubilant, exalted in comparison to my broken defeat.

'I . . . Seth . . .'

He sprang upright, holding my hands, gazing at me with open delight.

'Then what's the problem? Anna—' he touched my face with astonishment. 'You're crying! What's wrong? Oh Anna, Anna, please don't cry.'

'You can say it all you like,' I gulped, 'but I will never, never believe that you love me.'

'Ugh!' He broke away, his fists clenched with frustration, and began to pace the room. 'You're mad! This is so infuriating. I love you and whatever you say, I *know* you love me – isn't that worth *anything*? For crying out loud – this should be so easy, and you're making it so hard. How have I managed to fall in love with the most stubborn, crazy person in existence?'

I could only shrug, trying to smile through my tears.

'I'm special, I guess.'

'You are.' He sat down beside me, tracing the tears on my cheeks with one finger. 'You most definitely are.' Then he seemed to come to a decision and squared his shoulders. 'Well, you know what? I don't care. I don't care what you think. I know the truth. Once we've been going out for a few years you're bound to come round – you'll end up believing me after the third child or so. Definitely by the time we're drawing our pensions.'

I snorted in spite of my tears at that, and hit his shoulder.

'Shut up.'

He smiled and wiped at my cheek with a corner of the sheets. 'Why is it so hard for you to believe me?'

I seized his arm and pulled him off the bed, dragging him over to my dressing-table mirror.

'Look,' I said. A boy and a girl stared back at us from the mirror; serious, wide-eyed, and so patently incompatible that it answered my point.

'What? Look at what?' Seth asked. I stared at him in the mirror – not sure if he was being wilfully stupid or really didn't get my point.

'At what? At us! At you and me, Seth. How could we

ever be a couple? Look at me – I barely come up to your shoulder, I'm never going to make *FHM*'s hot totty, I'm just the drab girl next-door. I'm so – so *ordinary*. Can't you see that?'

Seth turned away from the mirror to stare at me.

'Anna, what's wrong with you? Are you even looking at yourself or just some figment of your imagination? There is nothing, *nothing* ordinary about you, Anna. You're the most extraordinary person I've ever met. In fact—'

But he never finished what he was going to say, for unmistakeably we heard the noise of Dad's door opening.

We both froze, Seth gripping my arm so hard that I winced. There were footsteps in the corridor. Then a door opening – the toilet door, I recognized the distinctive squeak.

'*Go!*' I hissed. Seth nodded and pulled his damp T-shirt back on with a shudder.

'OK, I'll see you in school.'

'Yes, yes, just . . . Will you be OK climbing out?'

He opened the window and gave me a look.

'I think if I can do it drunk in the dark, I'll be OK in daylight in full possession of my senses, don't you?'

'All right, but just – just be careful, OK?'

'I'll be careful.'

He hooked one leg over the sill, then said, 'Anna?'

'Yes?'

'I love you.'

My heart twisted. I so much wanted to say it back.

'I . . .'

He pulled me towards him, half in and half out the window, and kissed me fiercely, his mouth burning on mine. For a moment dizziness enveloped me and I staggered, then my instincts took over. I clutched him, kissing him back with a desperation I didn't even try to conceal.

Then we both heard the sound of a toilet flushing and Seth pulled away.

'Goodbye.'

'Goodbye – be careful.'

I watched him as he scaled down the old pitted brickwork, fitting his toes and fingers into the crevices so dexterously it almost looked easy. He jumped the last foot or two, picked his shoes up from where he'd left them under a bush then, with a wave, he sprinted off into the woods.

Far off, in the forest, something cawed, disturbed by his flight.

I shivered and shut the window.

CHAPTER TWELVE

James slid into the empty seat beside me in History and looked around with exaggerated caution.

'Am I safe?' he asked.

'What do you mean?' I said, surprised.

'To sit here? Waters is still off, I take it?'

'Well, yes, he's ill. But what's that got to do with anything?'

'Well, you know. Private property and all that. We had rather got the message. Hands off.'

Damn Seth. So that was why people – especially boys – had been behaving so weirdly around me for the past few weeks.

'I'm most certainly not private property – whatever that means. And yes, please, sit down.'

James unpacked his books, taking up what seemed like an unnecessary amount of desk.

'So what's up with Waters?'

'Man flu,' I said acidly, 'contracted while acting like a tit.' Man flu was unfair, as Seth's mother had barred him in his room when his temperature topped a hundred and four. But I was burning over the 'private property' comment and if I couldn't punish Seth in person, I'd do it in his absence.

James raised a ginger eyebrow.

'Oo la la. Lovers' tiff?'

'Oh shut up,' I snapped. I was beginning to seriously regret letting him sit down at all. To change the subject I said, 'So how are you getting along with the project?'

'Done,' he said smugly. 'How's yours?'

'Not done.' I fought off a wave of dismay. 'When's the deadline again?'

'Next week. Didn't you hand the abstract in last week?'

'No.'

Oh great.

I was packing up my books at the end of class when Mr Brereton said, 'Anna, could I speak to you for a moment?'

Oh, really really great.

I took a deep breath and began my excuses as the rest of the class filed out.

'I'm so sorry about the abstract, Mr Brereton. Seth's

204

been sick, as you know. Do you think we might be able to get an extension? I know the deadline was fixed but . . .'

He let me speak until I trailed to a halt, then gave an amused smile that had me doubting my ground.

'Wasn't that what you wanted to speak to me about?' I ventured.

'Actually no, though now you mention it, you're quite right, your abstract was due in last week. I will give you until the middle of next week for the abstract, and an additional one week extension on the full project in view of Seth's absence, but after that I'll expect it in – without his co-operation if necessary, and I'll mark it as a solo project. Does that sound fair?'

'Oh, yes. Thank you.'

So what did he want to speak to me about?

'However, I expect you're wondering what I was actually wanting to discuss.'

'Er, yes.'

'Perhaps I could I offer you a lift home?'

I blinked at the apparent change of subject. Warning bells rang in my head about inappropriate offers from male teachers – but Mr Brereton must have been sixty if he was a day, and extremely proper. I simply couldn't imagine him groping my leg in the car park.

'A lift?'

'Yes, I'd like to discuss it on the way.'

'Um. OK.'

'Good, I'll see you at the staff car park at three-thirty p.m. Goodbye, Miss Winterson.'

And I somehow found myself outside the classroom, no wiser as to what was going on.

At three-thirty I was hanging awkwardly around the staff car park, certain that at any moment someone was going to ask me what I was doing and whether I shouldn't be cutting along home. But no one came out, until I saw the stiff figure of Mr Brereton in his tweed jacket making his slow way across the car park.

'Over here, Anna,' he called, gesturing to a Morris Minor parked against the far wall. I hurried to join him.

He made pleasant conversation as we exited the car park and drove up the road. At the roundabout I ventured the information that I lived out in Wicker Wood and he inclined his head.

'Thank you, I'm quite well aware of that. We'll take the sea road, if you don't mind?'

'Not at all,' I said faintly, still wondering what on earth this was all about. The Morris climbed slowly up the cliff road, but just as I was expecting it to swing right, following the main road round the headland, Mr Brereton took a left turn down the rutted track that led to the beach, the track Seth and I had used only the other day. I was just wondering if I should have bought my rape alarm after all, when he stopped and turned off the engine.

'Well, Miss Winterson. Perhaps you'd like to explain that.' He gestured out of the window towards the verge.

For a second I had no idea what he meant. Then horror washed over me. By the side of the track was a majestic, spreading apple tree, heavy with fruit. It looked at least thirty or forty years old. The gnarled trunk was a couple of feet around and the branches twisted high into the air, seeming oblivious to the searing sea wind that came over the cliff.

'It's an apple tree,' I said in a small voice.

'Quite. A Cox's Orange Pippin, I believe. Not a very hardy variety. And yet it is growing in a location where no other tree has managed to root, let alone bear fruit. Talking of the fruit, it is currently June. Coxes do not normally bear mature fruit until about September. Finally – and this is the key point, Anna, my dear – it was not there last week.'

'Oh?' I said faintly.

'No. Have you any light to shed on this conundrum?'

'N-not really.'

Mr Brereton sighed, lowering his glasses down his

nose. He stared at me over the lenses until I felt my insides jellify. I've never been a good liar. But how did he *know*?

'Try again, Miss Winterson. You can do better than that.'

'Who are you? What do you want?' I said desperately.

'Who am I? I am one of the community, my dear. One of *our* community. Yours and mine. As for what I want, well, a little common sense would not go amiss. For heaven's sake, my good girl,' he looked exasperated now, 'don't you know what danger you're putting yourself in? I realize you probably wanted to impress your young man, but this kind of tomfoolery is not acceptable.'

'I'm sorry,' I whispered. My head was reeling. Were there witches *everywhere*? Maya and Emmaline had been shock enough, but now my school teacher? My first thought, ridiculously, was to wonder if Ofsted knew about this.

My second thought was more to the point: what else did he know about, apart from the tree? I couldn't tell. The reference to 'my young man' might have been benign, or not.

'You have great power,' he was saying, 'and you are young. It's a heady combination, I do realize that. But there are people who can help you contain and direct that power into more appropriate avenues.'

'There are?'

'Yes. I have . . . friends, who would like to help you. They realize you need tuition. And they think you have great gifts and that those gifts might accomplish great things, given the right help and training. Anna, you have a great deal of power, that is something to be proud of.' He smiled at me, full of warmth now. 'But it is also a danger – a danger to yourself and others. We all make mistakes without the help and support of friends, particularly friends who are older and wiser than we. Will you let my friends help you? They can show you the marvels that a mind like yours could accomplish. You could do great good, Anna. My friends would like to help you accomplish that good.'

I stared at him, my mind spinning with wonderful visions. No more blundering in the dark, no more trial and error, no more hideous mistakes. Instead – what? Answers would have been enough to tempt me. But greatness as well? Was that really possible? He was silent, seeming to read my mind, content to let me finish without hurry.

'Who are your friends?' I asked at last.

'Just a little group of academics – with certain gifts of their own. Teachers, if you like.' He paused, and I was just trying to think of what to say when he added, almost absently, 'Some call us the Ealdwitan.'

Shock paralyzed me for a moment then, trying not to let my reactions show in my voice, I said carefully, 'I see.'

'Do you?' He peered at me over his glasses. There was a slight suspicion in his face. Had I betrayed my feelings somehow? I gulped against my suddenly racing heart, and tried to speak coolly.

'And what would they want in return, your friends?'

'In return?'

'For all this help and tuition.'

He spread his hands, the picture of deprecation. 'No return, Anna. Apart, that is, from the privilege of helping to form a young and brilliant mind. Does the teacher ask for return, other than the knowledge that his pupil progresses?'

His words reeked with falseness, every instinct I possessed was screaming *There must be a catch!* but I kept my face neutral and asked, 'May I think it over?'

'Of course.' If he was disappointed or vexed, he didn't show it. 'Perhaps you could give me your answer on Monday?'

'I can walk from here.' I said, evading the question, as he started up the motor. 'Thank you very much for the lift Mr Brereton.'

'Not at all.' He inclined his head in a quaint, old-fashioned gesture. 'Well, until Monday, my dear.'

'Until Monday,' I echoed, and watched his car bump up the chalky track.

By the time I got home I'd left three messages on Emmaline's phone, plus a text, and as I opened the front door I heard the landline going.

'Anna?' Emmaline said, as I picked up the phone.

'Yes, did you get my messages?'

'Yes, all forty-five of them.'

I mentally stuck out my tongue at her, but there were more important things at stake than Emmaline's sarcasm.

'Listen, the Ealdwitan—'

'I know,' she cut in. 'Don't talk about it on the phone. Can you come here?'

'OK. I'll see if I can get Dad to give me a lift.'

'You need to learn how to drive, woman,' Emmaline said severely. Then she hung up.

She was waiting for me in the passage when Dad dropped me off, her face grim.

'How did you know?' I gasped, chasing after her as she took the stairs two at a time. She looked over her shoulder at me.

'What do you mean?'

211

'You said,' I panted, 'when I mentioned the Ealdwitan on the phone, you said, "I know".'

'Oh.' Emmaline shrugged. 'Part of my, you know. My "power".' She managed to put the words in ironic quote marks with her tone. 'I see things. It's not like Sienna, I can't control it very well or ask specific questions. I just get flashes sometimes.'

'Of the future?'

'More often the present, or else just a second or two in the future. It's not very useful – I never see anything helpful like an exam paper.' Then she shook her head with impatience. 'Look, anyway, this is more important. What did he say? I only caught a glimpse.'

I relayed the conversation and she frowned.

'Well, I'm not altogether surprised he's one of them – Mr Brereton, I mean. I've always thought he was deeply creepy. He's half the reason I took Philosophy instead of History. Leather elbow patches just seemed like someone trying a bit too hard to act the part of a History teacher.'

'What do you think he wants?' I asked. Emmaline's brow furrowed.

'I don't know. Sienna saw that they were thinking about contacting you and Mum was worried because she thought you'd be getting a telling off about Seth but this

– well, it's weird, to be honest. It almost sounds like they're trying to *recruit* you.'

'Recruit me? But why on earth would they want me?' I said, astonished.

'I'm not sure. They tend to want people with very specific powers, from what I've heard. They must think you have something that would be useful to them. Are you *sure* you've not got some secret ability you've never noticed?'

'Apart from my beauty and charm, you mean?' Hey, I could be sarcastic too. Emmaline rolled her eyes.

'Well it can't be your rapier wit. Come on, Anna, this is serious. What are you going to tell Mr Brereton? You should be bricking it about Monday, not cracking jokes.'

'I *am* bricking it about Monday. Why do you think I'm here? What am I going to say?'

'We can't make up your mind for you.' Her face was serious now. 'You have to decide that for yourself. All I can say is, I wouldn't be in your shoes for a lot.'

'Great, thanks, Emmaline. Very constructive. I know you can't tell me what to say – but you can tell me about *them*. Can't you?'

'Not really, no. I've never met any of them. Well, apart from Mr Brereton, as we now know.'

'Well what about Abe?'

213

'What about him?'

'He's met them, hasn't he?'

'He doesn't talk about it.'

'What – ever?'

'Not really, no.'

'But this is an emergency – I'm not wanting to gossip about their taste in wallpaper for goodness' sake.'

Emmaline sighed.

'OK, I'll text him. But don't be surprised if he's washing his hair.'

While she was tapping at her phone Maya came up the stairs, yawning and stretching.

'Oooo, another day grinds to an end. Is something going on? The hives were full of something or other but I didn't have time to check on them. I'll go down in a sec when I've had a cup of tea.' Then she saw me over Emmaline's shoulder and looked mildly surprised. 'Hello, Anna. I didn't know you were here.'

'Hello, Maya,' I said. My worries must have shown in my face because she sat beside me with a concerned look.

'What's happened?'

'Anna's received the black spot,' Emmaline said, still tapping.

'What?'

'Mr Brereton at school is one of the Ealdwitan,' I said

miserably, 'and he's trying to *groom* me. Or something.'

I repeated the conversation for the second time. Maya sat down heavily and put her hand to her head.

'I knew I should have listened to the bees, if only that blasted woman had bought her herbs a bit quicker. Well. What are you going to say?'

'I don't know. That's why I came here.'

'What do you think they want with her, Ma?' Emmaline asked. 'Is it her power?'

'I don't know.' Maya looked worried. 'It could be but somehow . . . I don't know. I doubt it could be only that – it's a bit too crude for the way they normally work. They've got power enough of their own. Perhaps something in your background, Anna?'

'But what?' I asked desperately. Maya only spread her hands in mute sympathy. I put my head in my own hands and groaned. 'They want an answer on Monday. What am I going to say?'

'We can't tell you, Anna.' Her face was full of sympathetic concern. 'I wish I had the answers but I don't. There's a lot about the Ealdwitan that isn't pretty – all the spying and closed ranks and secrecy. But you can't police a community like ours without doing some unpleasant things – many would say they're just doing a difficult job in difficult circumstances. All I know is

215

I'd rather be under their radar and, failing that, I'd prefer to be on their good side. It's very cold being on the wrong side of the Ealdwitan.'

'She wants to talk to Abe.' Emmaline closed her phone. Maya looked thoughtful.

'It's not a bad idea. Just remember, Anna, he's got his own agenda.'

Emmaline's phone bleeped and she glanced down.

'He's coming.' She sounded surprised.

It was nearly seven when Abe finally turned up. Maya was cooking supper, Emmaline was chopping salad, and I was looking at my watch worrying about Dad. Then we heard the door downstairs slam and someone shouted up from the foot of the stairs, 'It's only me.'

'Hi Abe,' Maya called down. There were feet on the stairs and Abe's hand came round the door and rapped on the wood.

'Knock, knock.'

'Come in, you fool,' Emmaline grumbled.

'Hello, my second favourite sister-in-law. Hello Maya, Anna.'

'Can you stop for supper?' Maya asked. Abe shook his head.

'No, sorry. I'm just passing through. I only came by to

216

give Anna the benefit of my jaundiced opinion en route.'

'Are you staying, Anna?' Maya paused with a fistful of spaghetti over the pot.

I shook my head.

'No, I'd love to but Dad'll have made supper. I'm already late.'

'Tell you what,' Abe said. 'I'll drop you. It's not out of my way and we can talk on the way. Are you ready to leave?'

I nodded. 'Thanks for all the advice, Maya. See you Monday, Emmaline.'

'Goodbye,' said Maya.

'And good luck,' Emmaline added drily. 'Let me know what to expect on Monday . . .'

I nodded again and made my way down the stairs behind Abe.

Abe's car was parked around the corner: a disreputable thing, too old even to have seatbelts. I raised an eyebrow at the state of it and he shrugged.

'What? You're a witch – if there's a crash you'll take care of yourself.'

'First of all, I don't know the first thing about how to do any magic. And second, I thought that word wasn't polite?'

'What word – witch? Neither are a lot of the other words I use, but I don't let it stop me.' He opened the car door and bowed. 'Your chariot, milady.'

I got in. He put the car into gear with a dreadful crunch, and we set off. Given Emmaline's dark hints about Abe's sensitivity towards the Ealdwitan I didn't quite know how to bring the subject up, but he introduced it quite baldly as soon as the car pulled away from the kerb.

'So you wanted to talk to me about the Ealdwitan?'

'Yes. Did Emmaline explain?'

'She said that some old guy at your school had thrown off his false beard and fake leather elbow patches and revealed himself as spy-master general, recruiting for his dark army of minions.'

'More or less. They want an answer by Monday.'

He snorted.

'Typically high-handed. And have they said what will happen if you give the wrong response?'

'What is the wrong response?'

'Well "no", obviously. They've bothered to approach you, they must want you onside. Whether they trust you or just want you where they can see you, I'm not sure. But they obviously know something.' He looked at me sideways in an appraising way that contained a new note of interest. 'Any idea what they're after?'

'None!' I said, feeling the desperation rise again. 'Literally none! Emmaline kept asking me that – all they said was I had "a brilliant mind".'

'Hmm. Very original,' Abe said with a twisted smile. 'And do you? Have a brilliant mind, I mean.'

'No one else seems to think so.'

'Well, you must be reasonably powerful, given what you've accomplished without any training. But if they want brute force there're plenty of other people out there who could supply it. What makes them so interested in you?' He pondered the question for a moment as we waited at the traffic lights, then shrugged and seemed to dismiss it from his mind.

'So what brought you to their attention?' I asked, more as a way to divert the conversation from my less-than-brilliant mind. His face darkened and from a clear sky hail suddenly spattered the windscreen. Then he seemed to bring himself under control with an effort and the evening sun appeared again through the clouds.

'Oh, usual nonsense. Betting on the weather, among other things.'

'Betting on the weather?'

'Mmm, you know you can bet on things like snow falling on Broadcasting House on Christmas Day – all that crap. Well, I did a series of, er, rather successful bets.

Spectacularly successful, some of them were.' He grinned wolfishly. 'Anyway, my form was a bit *too* good, so the bookmakers got a little suspicious. Which brought the Ealdwitan down on me. As you may have already heard, as far as they're concerned the first, second and third commandment is Thou Shalt Not Get Found Out. The fourth is Thou Shalt Not Draw Attention to Thyself.'

'And where does Thou Shalt Not Kill come in?' I asked, in a low voice, not sure if I wanted to know the answer.

'I doubt it even makes the list,' Abe said, looking grim.

'What happened? With the Ealdwitan, I mean.'

'Fine.' Abe said. I blinked.

'Sorry, you were fine?'

'No, *a* fine. I got fined.'

It was not the answer I'd been expecting. Somehow I'd expected the rack, or amputation of a minor extremity at least.

'Huh! Well, that doesn't sound so bad,' I said thoughtlessly. Abe's face went hard.

'It was bad enough,' he said coldly, and I felt the subject invisibly closed. Then he smiled, 'So what do you think of old Sienna, Maya and Emmaline, then?'

'They're really nice. Although I'm not sure "old" is quite the word I'd use to describe them.'

'No?' He gave me a wicked sideways look. 'How old

would you say Sienna was then?'

'I don't know.' I felt uncomfortably put on the spot. 'Twenty-two? Twenty-three?'

'Try thirty-five.'

'*No!*' I was genuinely shocked. 'Are you joking? She can't be.'

'She's a witch, she can do what she likes with the bloody wrinkles. C'mon, don't tell me you won't be giving your crows' feet a little lift in ten years?'

'How old are you then?'

'Guess.'

'Twelve,' I said sulkily.

'Very good. Just for that, Miss Cheeky, I won't tell you. Only that I'm younger than Simon. And *much* younger than Maya.'

'How old's Emmaline?'

'She's seventeen, genius. School entry is based on your birth certificate, not your crows' feet, in case you hadn't noticed. It's all cosmetic of course – if there's one thing witchcraft can't do, it's make you immortal. Or raise the dead. So it's all pretty bloody useless at the end of the day.'

There was a curious bitterness in his voice, but I felt I didn't know him well enough to probe. He turned the car up the cliff road, and I suddenly realized I had very little time left to ask him about the Ealdwitan.

'Look, this isn't what I wanted to ask you. Abe, what would you do? In my shoes, I mean?'

We drove in silence for a while, then on the cliff top he pulled to one side and stopped.

'I can't drive and think at the same time. What would I do? Run. Run until they stopped the hunt – or they caught me.'

I felt cold.

'Don't say that.'

'Why?'

'Because I can't run – it's not an option.'

'You've got legs haven't you? Why not?'

'Because.' Lots of answers he would probably discount or think stupid. A-levels. Money. Dad. Seth. 'Because I'm seventeen, Abe.'

'I left home at seventeen,' he said mildly. 'I survived. Well, barring the fact I had to sell my virtue and some of my organs.' Then, suddenly serious, 'Look, Anna, the way I see it, they've got you in a cleft stick. They want you. They know where you are. In your shoes, I wouldn't be wanting to say either yes *or* no. They aren't very nice people to know, trust me. They make better friends than enemies, but they're the kind of people you don't want as either.'

'Oh. So you don't think they'll let me walk away?'

'I don't know. I hope so, Anna. It depends what their agenda is. They may just want to know where you are, keep an eye on you. In which case they'll probably accept a polite "no thanks" and an assurance that you'll be a good girl. But without knowing what they want of you, I don't know.'

'Great,' I said bitterly. 'Just great. Being a witch isn't very bloody magical so far.'

'You want magic?' He smiled at me in the darkening car. I shrugged. Then I shivered – the balmy June night had grown almost chilly.

'Are you cold?' I asked. Abe said nothing, only continued to smile. I frowned, waiting for him to say something, then I realized the car was *really* cold.

I looked around and gasped.

The most beautiful frost flowers were creeping across the windows, starting from the corners of the windscreen and spreading, fern-like, across the glass. As I sat, holding my breath, Abe painted the car with patterns so exquisite I could only sit and marvel, forgetting my cold fingers, forgetting the Ealdwitan, forgetting everything. Finally, we were in a white cave, each glass panel etched with patterns so lovely I hardly dared exhale for fear of melting them.

Then Abe let his breath go and warm air flooded through the car. Condensation formed on the glass, then little runnels of water, and within minutes the windows were clear, the car just an ordinary piece of junk again.

'Abe,' I whispered, 'how did you do that? It was so beautiful.'

'So useless, you mean.' He smiled and turned the key in the engine. 'We'd better get you home.'

CHAPTER THIRTEEN

Monday morning. Double whammy. Maths – where I would probably see Seth for the first time in a week. And after that History – with Mr Brereton.

But when I got to Maths, Seth's side of the desk was still empty. I sat down with a strange feeling of mingled relief and regret.

Mr Henderson began ticking off the register while we got out our homework, his eyes darting from student to student as he ran down the list. At last he closed the file and asked, 'Can anyone enlighten me as to Seth Water's whereabouts? Is he still off sick?'

'Nope,' said a voice from the doorway, 'just late. Sorry, Mr Henderson.'

And Seth walked into the room.

My pulse speeded up to a sickening race as he sat down beside me. He looked thinner, paler, but it suited him. Even sick, he looked better than every other guy in the room. I watched him hungrily as Mr Henderson ran through the homework questions. Then, as Mr Henderson turned towards the board, Seth looked at me and smiled. My heart flipped over – and he leaned towards me, twined his hand in my hair, and kissed me, hard and fierce.

There was a gasp from the rest of the class and I yanked away, my cheeks flaming. Just in time, as Mr Henderson turned back to the class, frowning crossly at the interruption.

'Is there something someone would like to share with us?' His eyes swept the room, stopping at our desk, where he took in my furious scarlet blush and Seth's open, grinning delight. 'Anna, Seth? Something to contribute?'

'Sorry, Mr Henderson, just something I wanted to give Anna.' Seth's grin was wide and infectious, and so good-natured that Mr Henderson just sighed and turned back to his problem.

Seth said nothing for the rest of the hour, but every bone exuded his triumph. At the end of class I turned to him furiously.

'If you ever do that again, Seth Waters, I will do more than enchant you,' I hissed under my breath. 'I'll make you regret you were ever born.'

'Go on, don't stop. You're even more beautiful

when you're angry,' he said teasingly.

'I mean it,' I said severely, fighting to maintain my crossness. 'I'll – I'll turn you into a frog.'

'I thought it was supposed to be the other way around.' He grinned. 'The kiss transforms the frog into the handsome prince. But feel free to practise, I like the way your other spells have turned out so far.'

'Seth, please. I'm not joking. I'm not a safe person for you to be around, you know that. What happened – that night, last week – it didn't change anything.'

'No,' he agreed defiantly. 'It didn't change anything. You can talk all you like, Anna, but we both know how you feel and how I feel. And you're right. That's not going to change.'

Damn him. I swung round and stalked away. The last thing I heard was his mocking voice following me down the corridor.

'You've still got to see me in History . . .'

Oh God, Mr Brereton. For once I had more on my mind than just Seth. It should have been a relief to be worrying about something else, but it wasn't.

The lesson passed in a grim blur of dread and stumbling answers, until at last the bell went with teeth-jarring abruptness. Mr Brereton dismissed the class and then added, as if as an afterthought, 'Oh, Anna, there was something you wanted to discuss I think. The rest of you may go.'

I waited submissively by my desk as the rest of the class filed out, my stomach churning and turning, still not certain what I was going to tell him. Because in spite of what Maya, Emmaline and Abe had told me, the lure of the Ealdwitan's offer was tempting. Knowledge. Guidance. And surely, surely with all that power, *they* would be able to put right what had gone wrong with Seth?

Wasn't it possible that the Ealdwitan weren't as bad as they'd been painted? I only had the Pellers' side of the picture, and even though I liked and trusted Maya, I wasn't naïve enough to accept her word completely without question.

But there was something about Mr Brereton's smooth, ultra-reassuring manner that freaked me out. Why was he so eager to persuade me? What did he want? I had the strong feeling of being backed into a corner – and it brought out every ounce of stubbornness in my character.

Now he softly closed the classroom door, smiling his terrifying, cosy smile, and something inside me clicked into place. In that instant, I knew what I was going to say. I just didn't know what would happen next.

'There. Now we can chat, uninterrupted. Not that we

don't have ways of securing privacy from the outwith, but the simplest methods are usually the best, I find. How are you my dear? Did you enjoy the discussion today? Henry VIII is such a fascinating subject, I always think.'

The charade made me feel sick.

'If we can't be overheard, Mr Brereton, please, let's drop all the pretence.'

'Very well. My, my, like most of the young these days you are distressingly abrupt. What is your answer then, my dear?'

I swallowed. Was I about to make the second biggest mistake of my life? Of Seth's life? I felt something biting into my palms, and realized that my hands were clenched so hard that my fingernails were cutting my skin.

'I'm sorry, but it's no.' I said. Mr Brereton inclined his head and I felt compelled to add, 'Thank you.'

He sighed.

'Well, my dear, I won't pretend that my friends won't be disappointed. They have great admiration for your talents and were looking forward to helping you control and explore them. But of course we respect your decision.'

I blinked. This seemed almost too easy.

'Really?'

'But of course! We have no use for unwilling students. However, in view of the somewhat, well, *unfortunate* consequences that have attended your previous experiments, my friends have a little advice.'

I waited.

'They merely ask – or perhaps that's too strong a word – let's say they merely *suggest* that if you prefer to keep a lone path, that you do not interfere with the outwith, you do not practise magic upon them, and you keep secret your talents from them. We all have a responsibility to safeguard our community, and equally to protect those who cannot protect themselves. Does this seem reasonable?'

'*More* than reasonable!' I said with heartfelt relief. I never wanted to cast another spell on another ordinary person ever again. Seth had certainly cured me of that.

'You absolutely undertake not to cast a spell on, or to do any magic in the presence of, an outwith then? You do understand what I mean by this term, by the way?'

Frankly, I would have promised not to cast any spell, ever again, ever. Agreeing not to interfere with ordinary people seemed like mere common sense.

'Yes, I understand,' I said happily. 'Yes, I agree completely.'

'Otherwise my friends may have to intervene,' Mr Brereton warned.

I nodded again.

'I quite understand. And don't worry, I promise I'll keep in line.'

Mr Brereton smiled.

'Very well then, let us part friends, Miss Winterson. I wish you well upon your magical path in life. Your more prosaic academic path, however, leads you back here to my classroom tomorrow, which brings me to ask whether you have completed the abstract for your project with Seth Waters yet?'

'No,' I said guiltily. 'But I will, I truly promise I will, Mr Brereton.'

'Hmm, well I appreciate you may have had a lot on your mind.'

Was it my imagination or was there a twinkle in his eye?

'Let us say Wednesday for the abstract?'

'Wednesday,' I echoed. I'd better tell Seth . . .

In English I joyously filled in Emmaline – my words tumbling over each other with relief.

'It was totally, totally fine. All that worry over nothing – I don't think they're half as sinister as Abe made out. Honestly, he was just like: OK, it's fine either way, just don't enchant any more students.'

'What did he actually *say*?' Emmaline asked, sceptically.

I repeated the conversation as accurately as I could remember. She looked dissatisfied but then Ms Wright called on her for a question and we had to turn our attention to the board. When the discussion was finished, we were able to talk again and Emmaline turned back to me.

'A bit of a change of tone, don't you think?' she hissed.

'What?' I whispered back.

'Over the course of the conversation. I mean, first of all it's "we merely suggest" and then he gets around to an *absolute undertaking* not to do it under *any* circumstances. And finally it's "my friends will have to intervene". He kind of led you into a noose, don't you think?'

'Well . . .' I floundered, 'but it's so totally reasonable . . .'

'Exactly.' There was still that strange dissatisfied look on her face. 'It's *entirely* reasonable. No sane person could disagree. Which is what makes me think there's another agenda there.'

'Oh, you've been listening to Abe for too long,' I scoffed. 'I think they're just not as sinister as Abe wants us to believe.'

'Did he tell you about his run-in with them?' Emmaline said.

'Yes, all about betting on the weather too many times in a row?'

'What?' She looked taken aback and then snorted. 'Huh! Is that what he said?'

'Yes – why? Is that not what happened?'

'Well that happened, yes.'

'But something else happened – right?'

'Yes, but if Abe didn't want to tell you, I certainly can't.'

'Oh come on!' I hissed. 'At least give me a clue.'

'Anna, it's his business. I'm not spilling his secrets, he'd kill me.' Then she relented a little. 'It was to do with a girl he liked . . . It ended dreadfully. Really dreadfully.'

'Yes?' I pressed. 'Dreadfully how?' Emmaline shook her head and I grabbed her wrist. 'Em please, this isn't just gossip. I need to know.'

Em bit her lip – but she seemed to realize she'd said too much to stop now. 'Oh crap. Look – she died. It was awful. But that's *all* I'm saying. You want more, you have to ask him.'

Oh, Abe. I closed my eyes. Now I felt like a bitch for wringing it out of Emmaline. But I had to know the worst.

'Em, I promise I won't ask any more but . . . her death – it wasn't anything to do with *them*, was it?'

'The Ealdwitan?' Her voice was almost inaudible. 'No – not really. No. Natural causes.'

'So . . . in the end, all Abe got was a fine? That's not so dreadful, it is?'

233

'You don't know what you're talking about,' Em said curtly. 'They didn't fine *him*. They fined his family. They lost their business, their house, everything. The Ealdwitan broke them, and Abe's family have never forgiven him. He was seventeen, and they threw him out without a penny, without anything except the clothes on his back, and cut him off for dead. Simon's the only one who even acknowledges his existence now.'

'Emmaline!' broke in Ms Wright. 'Would you and Anna like to share this chat with the rest of the class?'

'Sorry, Ms Wright.'

We put our heads down after that and got on with the work, but at the end of the lesson, while we were gathering up our books, Emmaline turned to me.

'Look, I hope I'm being paranoid – maybe I am. But just be very, very careful what you do around the outwith from now on. It's all too easy to slip up, especially in times of stress. I don't think you realize what you've committed yourself to.'

I shook my head vehemently. 'It's not just a question of the Ealdwitan, Emmaline. I've promised myself never to do magic around ordinary people ever again. Can't you understand – after what happened with Seth I'm *pleased* they've put this condition on. I'm never meddling again.'

'Oh I *see*,' Emmaline said, 'so this is all for Seth, is it?'

'If you want to put it like that,' I said stiffly. Emmaline rolled her eyes. 'What?' I demanded.

'Look – I really don't think Seth's enchanted any more, Anna. In fact if anyone's besotted, I'd say it's you.'

'What do you mean?'

'He just . . .' She shrugged. 'I don't know. Yes, for sure, you had him under a spell at first. But now . . . well, he just doesn't act like he's bewitched. There's no diagnostic test you know – you can't pee on a stick and get one line for fine or two lines for enchanted. But taking my best guess, I'd say Seth's under the influence of plenty of hormones – but that's probably it.'

'Yeah right,' I said. 'Guys like Seth don't fall for girls like me in the real world. What could he possibly see in me?'

'I don't know, do I? I'm not a guy. Why does anyone fall for anyone?

'You can think what you like, but what I did to Seth was unforgivable. No; I've had it with magic. I'm never casting a spell again, as long as I live.'

Emmaline only looked at me over her glasses with an expression I couldn't quite read. Then she sighed and turned to leave.

'Well, Anna, for your sake,' she said over her shoulder, 'I truly hope you never have to.'

* * *

I went to bed happier than I'd been for a long time, and even the sight of the watchful crow crouched at my window the next day didn't dispel my mood. 'Oh sod off!' I told it, grinning. It shifted from foot to foot and hunched its head into its shoulders, like an angry old man. Then it lifted its wings and flapped away. A moment later something came shushing down the chimney, landing with a soft thud on the hearth. It was a dead dormouse, its eyes bloody holes in its head. I shuddered and picked it up by the soft tail. Its body was still warm, its paws curled beneath it as if it were sleeping.

Bloody hateful vicious crows. Tears sprang into my eyes as I wrapped the little corpse gently in tissues. Then I slung on jeans and a top, and went slowly downstairs to put the poor thing in the bin. Dad was already seated at the kitchen table, nibbling a piece of toast and reading a book about Icelandic fishing quotas.

The smell of coffee and toast revived my mood a little, and I took a piece from his plate and bit into it.

'Morning.'

'Excuse me, my dear, there's bread by the Aga if you want toast. No need to pinch mine.'

'Sorry, I'll put some more on.' I fiddled around with the toast griddle and then looked in the cupboard.

'We're out of Marmite. Can you add it to the list?'

'Fine, fine.' Dad nodded, and took another bite.

He was about to chew when he broke off, looking at the open kitchen window. A crow was hunched in the frame. It bobbed its head, letting a stream of guano fall on to the sill. Then it flapped onto the sideboard and began to peck at the bread.

'Those bloody things!' Dad said indistinctly around his mouthful. 'Oy! Shoo! SH—'

He stopped, coughed, coughed again. His face turned puce and his breath rattled in his throat, then stopped altogether.

'Dad? Are you OK?' I said, alarmed. He shook his head desperately and mimed patting himself on the back. I thumped his back, but nothing happened. As I watched, horrified, his face turned from pink, to red, and finally to dark purple. His eyes bulged and the veins in his forehead stood out. Sweat broke out on his forehead, his fingers alternately clutched at the table and clawed at his throat.

'Dad! Dad! Help, oh God! What should I do?'

He only shook his head, tears springing from his eyes with the effort of trying to choke up the piece of toast lodged in his throat. I felt terror and power build inside me like a spring trying to force its way through the earth – but with a huge effort I shoved the magic back down,

237

frantically searching my memory for ways of dealing with a choking fit.

OK. Five back slaps first – I slapped him hard between the shoulder blades, and he flung forward like a rag doll, limp and blue.

Next, five abdominal thrusts. I heaved him out of his chair and put my arms under his sternum, heaving back and up with all my force.

Dad buckled against my arms. I heaved again. Still nothing. His huge weight was limp and my arms felt like they were tearing out of their sockets. Fighting back tears, I heaved for a third time.

There was a sound like vomiting and a mangled piece of toast flew out of Dad's mouth and hit the table. I let go and Dad collapsed forward, gasping and choking. His gasps were terrible to hear, like sandpaper rasping in his windpipe, but I didn't care. Just hearing the air coming in and out of his lungs was incredible. After a moment he pulled himself upright and back into his chair, and I watched as the pink began to come back into his cheeks and lips.

When I was sure he was OK I ran to get a glass of water and helped him drink it, wiping the sweat from his forehead with a tea-towel.

'Anna,' Dad croaked, 'I thought my number was

up.' He stopped and coughed piteously. There was blood mixed with the spit on his lips. I put a hand on his shoulder.

'Dad, don't talk! Drink some water.'

He took a sip and coughed again. Then he said, more easily, 'Thank goodness you were here. You were brilliant, sweetheart. I think you just saved my life!'

I gave a shaky laugh and hugged his shoulder. He put an arm around me, hugging me back very hard.

'Well done, sweetie. Who taught you to do that?'

'Telly,' I said.

Dad laughed too, then broke into a coughing fit. When he'd finished he said, 'I'll never complain about you watching the goggly-box too much again.'

'Oh, Dad!' It felt like something was stuck in my own throat. 'You might have . . . You could have . . .' I couldn't finish. He squeezed my shoulders.

'There, there. Don't go on. I could have but I didn't. You were here – all's well that ends well.' He gave a final hoarse cough and looked down at his plate, at the remains of the toast. 'Do you know, I think perhaps I'm not very hungry for breakfast any more. I might just have a yoghurt.'

He laughed. I laughed too, more shakily.

'Do I dare go to school?'

239

'Do you dare *not* go to school, you mean.' He gave me a mock stern look. 'I think your old dad can manage from here, thank you. I'm not quite senile and I promise I'll have soup for lunch.'

'OK. No solid foods until I get home!' I said, trying for another tremulous laugh. He smiled back.

'OK. It's a deal. Now get going, you'll be late.'

I looked at the clock on the wall. I was late already, but I could hardly bear to leave Dad – just the thought . . .

'Anna . . .' he said, realizing my reluctance. I nodded, and he opened the door and held out my bag, jerking his head towards the forest with a meaningful look.

'All right, all right. Take care.' I kissed him and then set off.

As I crossed the drive the hateful, bloody crows lifted into the air, a cloud of black against the achingly blue sky, and I thought, with a shudder, of Emmaline's *I hope you never have to*. What if the thrusts hadn't worked?

I was late, I realized as I came out of the wood on to the road. I was really late. And there was a Maths test this morning. I should have asked Dad for a lift. Even at this painful half-walk, half-trot I wasn't going to make it.

I was starting to think up excuses when there was the sound of an engine behind me and I turned to see

Seth pulling onto the verge.

'You're late,' he yelled out the window. 'Want a lift?'

'Oh! Yes please.' I ran back along the tarmac and yanked at the truck handle. 'Thanks.'

'You're lucky I've just been to drop off some shopping for Grandad.' Seth put the truck into gear and swung back onto the road. 'What happened to you – over-slept?'

I told him about Dad's choking fit.

'It terrified me,' I admitted. 'I didn't really realize how much until afterwards. I don't think Dad was that frightened but – well, *you* know what it's like when you only have one parent. You constantly worry; what if something happens to them?'

Seth nodded, his face full of sympathy, and we drove in silence for a while. I watched the sea out of the truck window. You could see it crashing at the foot of the cliff at this part of the road, for the track led very close to the cliff edge. Some people went round by the inland route to avoid it, but I wasn't bothered by heights and Seth presumably drove this stretch every time he visited his grandad. It was a calming, cooling sound on a hot day like today.

I should have felt relieved that it had all turned out OK – that Dad was fine. But something was fretting at the corner of my mind, like a sore tooth niggling away. And I couldn't put my finger on what it was. I only knew that Emmaline's words kept nagging away at me: *I hope you never have to.*

Was that what was bothering me – how close I'd come to breaking my promise? Except that I hadn't, had I? It was all fine. But it had been very close. Too close maybe. Too close for . . . coincidence.

A huge black crow, the largest I'd ever seen, swooped suddenly across the windscreen like the shadow of death and the answer came to me like a cold hand clutching around my heart.

It wasn't coincidence. Of course it wasn't. It was engineered, engineered to try to get me to break my promise. It had failed – but that only meant there would be another attempt.

Who else did I care for more than anything in the world? Who else did I love? Who else would I break any promise to save?

'Seth, you have to let me out of the car.' I struggled with the door lock of the moving van.

'Anna!' He stared at me in frank disbelief. 'Are you nuts?'

My mind was buzzing with one, obsessive thought: I had to get away from him. If I wasn't around him, then I couldn't use magic to save him, so therefore there would be no attack. That was logical, surely? It was my presence that was dangerous to Seth – without me there, the Ealdwitan wouldn't waste time on him. I had to get away from Seth at all costs.

'Stop the car and let me out!'

'You can't go back – you'll be late for the test!'

'Let me *out!*'

I yanked at the handbrake and we jackknifed across the road, Seth fighting wildly to retain control of the steering. As we struggled the speed dropped, and I saw my chance. I tore open the door and leapt, feeling the gravel rip into my skin as I hit the ground in a flurry of grit and flapping textbooks.

I lay for a moment, stunned by the impact with the tarmac, then saw to my horror that Seth had stopped the truck at the edge of the road. He sat, his head thrown back and his chest heaving with spent adrenaline. Then he looked straight at me and his eyes were furious.

'You lunatic!' he yelled. 'What were you . . . ?'

He stopped. Looked down at the foot pedals. When he looked back up there was panic in his face. The truck was moving – rolling backwards towards the cliff.

I saw him stamp furiously at the foot brake, then heave at the handbrake in a desperate attempt to stop the truck's inexorable slide. Again and again he yanked the lever. But

243

it was no use. Neither brake had any effect at all. The truck was picking up speed.

I began to run towards him.

'Anna, get back,' he yelled, fear in his eyes. 'Oh God, if I can just get it into gear . . .'

I raced across the grass, feeling the terror rise in my gut, threatening to choke me. If only I could reach him in time . . .

But I knew it was futile.

As the truck shot off the edge of the cliff I exerted every ounce of power I possessed – and stopped it.

For a long moment, the truck hovered in mid-air, about three feet away from the cliff edge. It was incredibly heavy, but if I could just pull it back – inch it back towards the cliff edge . . .

Sweat broke out on my forehead and I fell to my knees on the short turf, every muscle, every bone in my body straining to keep the truck in mid-air and edge it backwards. The leaden weight tore at my guts. But it was working, incredibly it was working . . . The truck stayed level with the cliff, then trembled and jerked an inch or two towards safety.

My breath sobbed between my teeth and I let out a whimper of exertion. Sweat trickled down my nose. I was so tired. It wasn't just the truck, there was something else, a huge, inexorable weight bearing down on my shoulders, crushing me to the ground. *Something* was fighting me.

I shut my eyes and bowed my head, summoning power from every cell of my body. I could do this. Then I opened my eyes.

A huge crow crouched just inches away from me on the turf, watching me with its glittering black gaze. As my eyes widened in shock it leapt, snapping with its curved beak, scratching for my eyes.

I scrambled back and my concentration slipped, just for an instant, but it was enough. The truck jerked, hung vertically by one wheel for a split second, and then fell.

What I did next, I did purely on instinct. I had no thought for anything except Seth.

I dived.

I fell, perhaps a hundred feet. I had barely time to notice the air tearing in my throat and ripping at my clothes and hair, before I hit the surface of the sea with a smack that sent my head ringing. The salt water forced its way into every pore of my skin with excruciating pressure, stinging my nose and eyes, and the momentum of my fall thrust me deep, deep into the sea, down into the murky storm-torn depths at the foot of the cliff. It was so cold I thought I'd die from the chill alone, but then I saw Seth's truck, upended on the seabed, shaken by the waves that reached even to these depths.

I fell the last few feet in slow motion, all the air long since crushed from my lungs, only my witchcraft keeping me alive now.

Seth was in the truck, slumped over the steering wheel just a few yards away in the murk. Grabbing a rock from the seabed I flung it at the windscreen, but it was like throwing in treacle, and my strength, in this depth of water, was piteous. The rock fell yards short, drifting softly to the seabed with a little flurry of murk. Wearily I half waded, half crawled to the cab and tried again, pounding at the glass on the driver's side window again and again. Inside I could see Seth, terrifyingly motionless, blood trickling from his nose and mouth.

At last – at last there was a crack. After that the pressure of the water did the work. A web of splinters swiftly spread across the pane, then, with a roar, the water entered, buffeting Seth sideways with its force. It didn't take long – first Seth's legs were wet, then his chest, and finally his head was submerged, the blood drifting away in the sluggish water like red smoke. I watched in an agony of impatience and as soon as the cab was pretty much full I yanked at the door latch with numb and trembling hands. It opened and I crawled into the rocking, unstable cab, tearing at Seth's seatbelt catch.

It seemed like forever, but at last the belt came free and I ripped and heaved and tore Seth out of his seat, his head lolling. A silver stream of precious air bubbled from his mouth and nose, spelling out the fact that his life was slipping away with every passing second.

Now I only needed to get us both to the surface, but with little air in Seth's lungs, and none in mine, we were both dead weights with no buoyancy to help me as I struck for the surface. I could barely support my own weight, let alone Seth's twelve stone alongside me. Tiredness and chill were striking into my bones. I would have sobbed, but I had no oxygen to make a sound, and the tears just mingled with the salt of the sea. I couldn't do it. I couldn't do it. We were both going to die here, in the cold of the sea, just another car accident, another black statistic of young people too young to drive, but not too young to die.

Maybe it wouldn't be so bad. It would be rest at least. I wouldn't have to go on, fighting my way through the cold murk. My muscles tore with a fiery pain and my poor heart beat, oxygenless, with panicked bird-like flutters. My eyes stung and my lungs choked against the salt water. Wouldn't it be easier just to give up? Seth and I could rest here, together.

I hugged Seth to me, threading my hands in his dark curls, running my fingertips over his closed lids, bruised and dark, and the contours of his throat. His beautiful face was blue, blood drifting in scarlet feathers from his mouth. It looked like this would be my last memory. A cold embrace, from the boy I'd loved – and had killed. His last memory would be of my betrayal – of my leaping from the truck, letting it drop. He would never know the truth, because I'd never be able to explain. He'd always think I'd run away when he needed me most.

No! The searing agony of that thought tore through me, bringing heat to my numb, frozen limbs. Damn the Ealdwitan. I would *not* let us die here. Seth had saved me, twice. It was my turn to save him.

I struck out, fighting for the surface, fighting for Seth's life.

Pain, pain in my chest, someone beating on it with a hammer, crushing me. Plastic at my mouth, light in my eyes. More pounding pain. Leave me alone. Leave me alone.

'The boy's breathing by himself. I think he'll make it, but looks to me like the girl's a goner,' I heard through a haze.

'Well that's for them to call at the hospital. Let's get her

248

intubated and we can start getting them up that cliff.'

Who were these people? What were they talking about? I tried to speak but there was something hard in my mouth and my lungs felt like they were clagged with some gross, sticky substance. The effort was too much. I let the darkness close over my head.

Sounds: a roaring in my ears, and the scream of a siren, very close, incredibly loud. The insistent beeping of medical machines, and – most heart-breaking – the sound of tearing, heaving sobs from someone very near.

'Calm down, Seth. Calm down.' A male voice, calm, official, comforting.

But the sobs continued.

Bumping, rattling, the screech of trolley wheels and a bang as the footrest hit a swinging door. A flurry of medical stats shouted to and fro.

'CPR commenced at the scene by a passerby . . . intubated at ten thirty-eight . . . ten rounds of adrenaline and warm saline by IV . . . asystole throughout . . .'

I heard the other trolley rattle away down the corridor, and then a far off cry,

'Anna, no! No! I won't leave her! *No!*' The sound receded . . .

Needles, tubes, pushing, shouting – everything hurt. I just wanted it to stop. I wanted everything to stop. And then I heard, 'Sorry everyone, I'm going to have to call this one. Is everyone agreed? OK, stop resuscitation, time of death is . . .'

At last there was silence.

I lay, completely at peace, feeling the warmth of the lights on my cold skin. Someone had pulled a sheet over my face, and the harsh, starched fabric rasped at my cheeks and nose. It was wonderful simply to lie still, not to fight any more, in this quiet corner of the hospital. I felt so tired, more tired than I had ever felt in my life before. I could have slept forever.

But there was the memory of those dreadful, tearing sobs . . . I had to get up. Seth. I couldn't leave him in some far corner of the hospital. I had to go and find him.

My hand shook with exhaustion, but I reached up and pulled the sheet from my face. Then, tilting my head to one side, I vomited and choked all the phlegm, foam and seawater out of my lungs. There was an astonishing amount. It flooded the lino, a tide of gross pinkish foam.

Ripping air back into my lungs hurt far worse than drowning. Every inch was raw and scoured with salt, and the air cut like knives. I sat up, choking and sobbing and gasping. A monitor at my side flickered into life and began a slow *pip*, *pip*, in time with my reluctant pulse.

There was a scream.

'The girl! She's – she's – she's—'

My quiet corner was no longer quiet. Curtains were ripped back, feet came running, panicked shouts echoed down the corridor, hands pushed me back on to the trolley.

'Christ, who called this? Why didn't someone check her?'

'We did! Dr Mahmood – the paramedics . . .'

'Blankets! Get me a drip, quick! Where's her chart?'

'What's her name? Quick, quick! What's her *name*?'

'Hell, where's the chart?'

'Somebody find the damn chart!'

'Here it is . . . Anna – Anna Winterson.'

'Anna, Anna, listen to me, you're OK. You're going to be OK.'

But I knew that already.

For what seemed like hours it was all tests and drips and cannulas and muttered, indignant conferences in corners about who'd missed what, who'd failed to check what, which protocols had been adhered to, or not.

But eventually the panic and shock subsided and – rather reluctantly, or so it seemed – the doctors were forced to admit that I was here, alive, with astonishingly few side effects from my long immersion.

'I want to see Seth,' I said, when they eventually unhooked me from the monitor. A man in a white coat shook his head.

'I'm sorry; he's under sedation.'

Oh my poor Seth.

'I have to see him,' I said. 'I can get hysterical if you like, but wouldn't it be simpler just to let me see him now?'

There was a hurried conference and eventually a female doctor said, 'You can see him, of course, Anna. But just for a few minutes. Don't be alarmed when you see him – he's fine. It's just the effect of the sedative they gave him to calm him down.'

They wouldn't let me walk, so I was wheeled in a wheelchair down endless corridors, the doctor pushing and a nurse following with my drip bag on a little stand. Doors opened and closed, more doors, a keypad, then a long ward full of cubicles.

'Here he is,' said the doctor, drawing aside a curtain. I got out of the wheelchair, ignoring the nurse's protests, and knelt beside the bed.

His face was very pale, and he lay like a child who'd cried himself to sleep, with one hand under his cheek. Traces of tears were still visible on his face.

The doctor spoke in a whisper.

'He was very distressed. Your condition initially looked much more serious and . . .' She trailed off. I suppose there's no easy way to say, *We told him you were dead.*

I touched his cheek, very gently, and he stirred.

'Seth,' I said softly, 'Seth, it's OK, I'm here. I'm alive and well. It's all OK.'

He didn't wake, but he moved under the covers to face me, and his expression softened, relaxed. When I took his free hand, still bruised with the marks of the IV drip inserted into the back, his fingers closed reflexively on mine – his grip, even in sleep, surprisingly strong.

'Please can't I stay?' I said pleadingly to the doctor. She looked sympathetic but shook her head.

'I'm very sorry, Anna, but this is a male ward. Also the effect of the sedative won't wear off for several hours. But we'll come and get you as soon as he wakes up.'

'Do you *promise*?' I said fiercely. 'Even if it's the middle of the night? Even if I'm asleep?'

'I promise,' she said, and nodded.

* * *

A couple of hours later I was woken from deep sleep, by the same doctor shaking my shoulder gently.

'Anna, Anna,' she was saying insistently. I opened my eyes painfully and blinked, and she whispered, 'I'm so sorry to wake you up, but your friend is awake and asking for you. Also your dad's on his way. We finally managed to get hold of his phone.'

I struggled up and out of bed, ignoring the swooning dizziness in my head, and pulled the cannula painfully out of the back of my hand. The drip bag was empty anyway.

The doctor persuaded me into a wheelchair again and we set off, infuriatingly slowly, with pauses at every security door for her to fumble for her key fob, and a maddening wait at the lift.

Corridors, more security, then at last Seth's ward, Seth's cubicle, with the curtains open, and Seth sitting up in bed, wild-eyed and furious.

'I don't care.' I heard forcefully down the corridor. 'I'm going to see her. I'll sign whatever you want, just get this bloody thing out of my arm.'

'Seth!' I called. I shoved the brake on the wheelchair and levered myself out, hobbling down the corridor as fast as my weak legs could go.

The doctor's protests came as if from a long way off,

her words a senseless jumble. All I could hear was Seth's cry of 'Anna!' as he struggled off the sheets and limped out of bed, into my arms.

'Oh Seth, oh Seth!'

A tangle of bruised limbs and IV tubing, and our rushing, sobbing words tumbling over each other:

'They told me—' 'I thought—' 'I knew that you'd never—' 'You saved my life—' 'I'll never leave you again . . .'

Sometime later, as we sat, curled together on Seth's bed:

'Nice dress, Anna.'

'What do you mean?' I looked down at the hospital gown and then behind at my naked back.

'Shut up!'

Later still:

'Anna . . .'

'Mmm?'

'How did you do it? My van – it must have been in fifty feet of water. The doctors all assumed you must've been in the truck when it fell, but I know what really happened. I didn't say anything but . . .'

I sighed. There didn't seem much point in pretending any more – not now.

'You know, Seth. You know what I am.'

'What? A witch?' He spoke the words with shocking loudness and I winced. 'Sorry.' He lowered his voice. 'But are you really?'

'You saw what I did.'

'I half thought . . . The apple tree – I mean, I began to think I must have dreamed it, or had some kind of post-traumatic stress episode.'

'Well, you didn't dream it,' I said shortly. 'I am a . . .' It was extraordinarily hard to say the word, and suddenly I understood Maya and Emmaline's reluctance to use it. I took a deep breath. 'I *am* a witch. That's why I'm not a safe person for you to know.'

'And that's why you ran off, right before the accident?'

I nodded. My heart hurt.

'Seth, I'm so sorry. I'm so, so sorry. Can you ever forgive me?'

'Forgive you?' He shook his head, and for a minute I went cold all over; so this was it . . . But then he carried on, his voice slow, full of incredulity. '*Forgive* you? Shouldn't you be asking how I can ever repay you? Anna, you saved me. You gave your *life* for me.'

'Don't be silly,' I said shortly, trying to hide the tears rising inside me. He shook his head violently.

'I saw what happened on the beach. You were dead. Your heart had stopped – your lungs were completely saturated. You don't come back from that.'

'But I came back,' I said.

'But you came back,' he said softly. I nodded, and a tear escaped, running hot down my cheek.

'Seth, I don't know what to do. There are people out there – people who want to hurt everyone I care about. They're trying to persuade me to do something – and unless I do it, everyone I love is in danger. It's better if you just forget me, don't see me. I can't bear for them to hurt you because of me.'

'If I disappear, will you forget me?' he asked quietly.

'No!' My shocked response burst from me before I had time to think what it meant. Suddenly I saw. How could I have been so stupid?

'Then what's the point?' Seth spelled it out. 'It doesn't matter where I am – whether we're together or apart. As long as you care about me, I'll be a target. Can you make your feelings disappear too?'

'I'm sorry,' I whispered. 'I wish I could.'

'If you'd go out with me I'd have a witch for a girlfriend,' he said, his voice teasing. 'What could be safer than that?'

I looked up to see him smiling at me.

'Seth, please, I'm serious. These are scary, scary people. I don't know how to protect you.'

'We'll think of a way. It'll all be fine, as long as we're together.'

In that short moment everything changed, shifted, reassembled in a new pattern. It was true. Seth wasn't better off without me. Keeping away would do nothing to save him from the Ealdwitan – he was in danger wherever he was; in fact I could protect him much better by his side. The realization brought me elation – and despair. I had the perfect excuse to be with him at last – but it might cost him his life.

I don't know what I would have said next, because there was a rustle at the edge of the cubicle and a disembodied voice said: 'Knock, knock – I've got Mum and Dad here.'

We sprang apart and our parents came through the curtains, their faces wearing twin masks of anxiety – changing to a sort of cross jubilation as they saw us both alive and well.

'Oh, Seth!' Elaine grabbed Seth and hugged him furiously. 'Never, never do that to me again. When I got that call . . .'

'Anna, thank God you're OK – thank God you're *both* OK.' Dad crushed me to his chest. 'What on earth happened? The hospital made it sound like a near-death experience. You had a *car* accident, is that right?'

'It was my fault,' Seth said, at the exact same time as I said, 'It wasn't his fault.' We shot each other a look, and I suddenly wished we'd had time to get our stories straight. The only thing we'd agreed on, and that fairly hurriedly, was not to tell my dad, if at all possible, the true severity of what had happened to me. I didn't think the phrase 'pronounced dead on arrival' would be exactly music to his ears, and I hoped the hospital wouldn't be in a hurry to bring it up either.

'Please, ladies first,' Seth said at last, and waved his hand.

'Well,' I started, 'we, er, we were driving to school, and Seth needed to stop the truck for a sec, so he parked on the edge of the road, where it comes quite close to the cliff, and the brakes failed. Seth kept his head and tried everything – the handbrake as well as the foot brake, and then he tried to get it into gear, but the truck had too much momentum.'

'How could the brakes fail? You only had it serviced last month!' Elaine exclaimed. Seth shrugged.

'I know, but it's old, isn't it? Anyway there wasn't time to get out. It fell off the cliff, into the sea.'

Both Elaine and my dad flinched visibly at this so I hurried in.

'But we were fine – both fine. We just swallowed a lot

of water and got rather cold.'

'Anna was amazing,' Seth said proudly. 'I hit my head on the steering wheel so I was pretty useless, but she got me out and dragged us both on to the rocks.'

'And then a passer-by found us and called the ambulance,' I finished brightly, trying to make it sound like your average stroll in the country.

Dad blenched and I wondered if I was going to be allowed near the sea or a moving vehicle ever again. Thank goodness he hadn't heard the full unexpurgated version.

'Well,' Elaine said, almost as shaken, 'all I can say is, it's a miracle you're both alive.'

'Yes,' said Seth solemnly. 'Quite magical in fact.' I resisted the urge to kick him, hard.

'And of course the police want to talk to you both,' she added.

That wiped the smile off Seth's face. For myself, I couldn't have cared less about a police interview. Our story would probably sound fairly convincing – well, on one level it was the truth. Any evidence to the contrary lay fifty feet down in stormy salt water, being quickly battered into so much scrap metal. No, I was worried about a quite different interview, the one with Mr Brereton when I got back to school.

CHAPTER FOURTEEN

The police turned out to be politely sceptical that both brakes on the truck could fail at the same time, and it definitely didn't help that Seth was already known to them. They never came right out and said it, but I knew what they thought – that either Seth had been driving too fast and had taken the bend recklessly, or that we'd had an argument and he'd deliberately driven off in some bizarre double suicide/murder pact.

Their disbelief made me furious – but all I could do was keep stubbornly repeating the story we'd given to our parents and hope that Seth – being interviewed in a separate cell – was doing the same. After all, the evidence was on our side. The tyre marks on the cliff-top showed that the truck had been doing five miles per hour, not fifty, when it went over.

At last, plainly dissatisfied but unable to shake my

story, they let me go. I waited outside for Seth, who emerged pale and cross. He made a face as he saw me.

'That was vile, were you OK?'

'Fine – were they horrible to you? They kept trying to make me say that you were driving too fast.'

'It was fairly unpleasant. They found skid marks on the road.'

'Skid marks? But you were stationary.'

'Where you grabbed the handbrake.'

'Oh crap.' More guilt. 'What did they say?'

'That they could tell there'd been a skid earlier up the road, as if we'd jackknifed across the road – and what was that all about?'

'Oh.' Some of their questions suddenly made sense. 'That was why they kept going on about whether you'd been driving erratically, and had there been any skids prior to the "incident". What did you say? Did you tell them it was me?'

'No! Of course not. I said that the brakes had suddenly come on all by themselves. I thought that'd add to the story of the brakes being dodgy. And I said that was why we'd decided to stop the truck, because I was worried about the brakes.'

'Ooh, clever! I wish we'd thought of that for our parents.'

'I was worried though, saying it, in case it contradicted what you told them. Does it?'

I tried to think back.

'N-no . . . I don't think so. I just said that you stopped the truck, and they asked me why, so I said I couldn't remember. I thought that a bit of confusion might be understandable, considering what happened after.'

'Thank goodness, well done.' He squeezed my hand. 'Well it looks like we're in the clear . . .'

'Ugh, I'm so sorry, Seth. I never thought they'd blame you.'

He shrugged and kissed the back of my hand, on the mark where my veins were still bruised from the IV.

'Well, you can't blame them. It wouldn't be the first time some teenager with a big car got carried away. And my history doesn't help. I think they were pretty pissed off they didn't manage to convict me over the fight, so this probably seemed like a second chance to lock up a menace to society.'

I shuddered.

'I would never, never let that happen.'

'I can take care of myself,' he said softly. But I knew that wasn't true.

'Only Mr Brereton now,' I said, half under my breath.

'What?' Seth looked amused. 'Are you worrying about our History project?'

If only.

'Look, there's something you need to know about Mr Brereton . . .' I began.

'Oh. My. God.' The girl came up to us as we were walking to History. 'I heard the news. That is just *so* amazing. Like something off *Casualty*. Did you see a tunnel and a white light and all that? Everyone thinks you two are *so* cool, it's unreal.'

I was thoroughly fed up of gawping students who wanted to congratulate Seth and me on our near-death experience and tell us how amaaaaazing we were. This one I didn't even know.

'You ought to get some kind of medal or something,' she continued. 'It's just, like, so cool!'

Seth's temper snapped.

'Yes, really bloody cool. Anna almost died in my truck. We were hospitalized. So please, just shut the hell up and leave us alone.'

'Sorry, sorry!' The girl backed off, her eyes wide, and I heard her start telling her friends about how the whole business seemed to have pushed Seth Waters, like, off the *edge* or something.

'I can't bear this.' Seth slumped at his desk, his head in his hands. I knew he didn't only mean the girl. It was the whole thing. The suspense. The goldfish bowl feeling. The wait.

I was a wreck myself. As Mr Brereton entered and began the lesson, Seth noticed my hand trembling and took it gently in his. It was only his calm grip that stopped me from turning tail and running.

'I can't do this, Seth,' I said, under my breath. 'I don't think I can stand it.'

'You can do it.' He squeezed my hand under the desk. I looked up at the clock.

Only another half hour. Quarter of an hour. Ten minutes. Five . . . and then the bell was ringing with a cacophony that set my pent-up nerves jangling.

'Thank you everyone,' Mr Brereton called, over the scraping of chairs and general chatter. 'Until Monday then. Don't forget the homework.'

Then, as if as an afterthought: 'Ah, Anna. Yes, we had something to discuss, didn't we? You may go, Seth.'

'I'll wait outside.'

'Please don't,' Mr Brereton said dismissively. 'Anna may be some time and I'd hate to make you late for your next class.'

'I'll wait.' Seth's tone was implacable. Mr Brereton

wavered for a moment, and then shrugged as if to say: *What does it matter anyway?* He waited until Seth had left and then turned to me.

'So, Anna, my dear, none the worse for your accident?'

Suddenly I hated him. I hated his bullshit chit-chat, his false concern for me, his horrible tweedy jacket and everything else about him. I felt burning anger at the Ealdwitan – not just for what they were doing to me, but for their callousness towards Dad, towards Seth – using the people I loved as human pawns in their pathetic little game.

'Let's cut to the point.'

He blinked, as if taken aback, and said mildly, 'If you wish. What point would you like to make, my dear?'

'What's going to happen?'

He sighed. 'Well, I won't pretend that my friends weren't surprised and disappointed at finding that you broke your word so quickly.'

'Surprised!' I spat. '*Surprised?* You know very well they *made* me break my word.'

'I have not the least idea what you're talking about.'

'Oh please! My dad has a near fatal choking accident and then barely an hour later, Seth's truck plunges off a cliff? You're telling me that was coincidence?'

'I'm telling you nothing, my dear. But I am morally

certain my friends had nothing to do with these distressing incidents. Perhaps there are others who wish to cause you harm?'

'Rubbish! Who?'

'Well, you have,' he coughed, 'contacts, shall we say, who are less than desirable. Friends who have their own reasons for disliking my colleagues, and who may have their own reasons for turning you against us.'

It was so staggeringly audacious I nearly gasped out loud. Was he really pretending that the Pellers were behind all this?

I struggled to regain control of my temper, then said coldly, 'I won't dignify that suggestion with a reply. All I want to know is, what do the Ealdwitan propose to do now?'

'*Do?* Well, the fact that it took less than twenty-four hours to break your word has certainly strengthened them in their opinion that you need a guiding hand.'

'You know very well, I had no choice,' I said bitterly. 'If it were up to me I'd never practise magic again.'

'We always have a choice,' he said coldly, and there was something reptilian in his hooded eyes. 'No single life is more important than the safety of our entire community. Your actions jeopardized that safety, Miss Winterson. Your little trick with the car was seen, by a walker. It was *extremely* fortunate he happened to be one of our community. You may not be so lucky next time. And then there may be blood shed.'

'Whose blood?' I gasped.

He shrugged.

'It is sometimes necessary, in order to maintain our safety. Members of the outwith are sometimes unfortunate collateral damage, if there is no other way. But,' he leaned forward and spoke emphatically, 'but we never spill a drop of blood – our own or that of others – willingly or without reason. And that is why it is so very, very important that you are not permitted to continue to put lives at risk.'

'I put lives at risk? *I* put lives at risk?' I was so angry now that I could barely speak. I felt the power and rage rise inside me, threatening to spill out, annihilate this dry little man with his cold, reptilian eyes and soft voice. I forced it down and spoke quietly. 'I'm sorry, Mr Brereton. I will do my utmost to never endanger another person – outwith or witch,' he flinched at the word, but I carried on, 'but I don't intend to be blackmailed.'

'Blackmail!' He gave a gentle little laugh. 'That's a very strong word. Anna, my dear, there is no suggestion of blackmail. But you are young – gifted. Please, won't you join us? You could be great, Anna, with our help. We would show you wonders, reveal undreamed of secrets, give you powers beyond imagination. We only want to help, to guide, to lift the burden of your magic from your shoulders and turn it into the greatest gift you have ever had . . . Anna, please, won't you let us help you? Won't you join us? You would find yourself among friends.'

His voice was honeyed, persuasive, and for a moment I felt myself waver. Would it be so bad? Was it *really* worth endangering Seth and Dad's lives, when all the Ealdwitan seemed to want to do was help me?

Then I realized there was magic in his tones, some kind of subtle music running beneath the words designed to bind me and shape me to his will. I shuddered and struggled under the haze and said, thickly, 'N-never . . .'

Then my powers flexed and I thrust off the stupor, and said more strongly, 'Never! I don't know what you or your "friends" want with me, but they chose the wrong way to persuade me. I might have considered it until you started picking on innocent people – but having seen how you treated my dad and Seth, I'd rather – I'd rather *die* than join you.'

He looked at me for a long moment as if considering, then sighed.

'Is this the answer you wish me to convey to my friends?'

'Yes.'

'For all our sakes, Anna, I beg you to reconsider.'

'That is my answer.'

'Then I am sorry for you, my dear.' He stood, his small hooded eyes unreadable, ancient and dark. 'And your friends.'

CHAPTER FIFTEEN

At the sight of Seth and me, Maya turned the shop sign to 'closed' without a word. Then she ushered us upstairs and turned on the kettle.

'You must be Seth.' Even in the midst of all this she managed a smile. 'I'm very pleased to meet you at last.' Then she turned to me. 'Bad news, Anna?'

'Very bad.' I gulped. 'I think this is probably war. And they know about my friendship with you and Emmaline.'

She paled, but only said, 'I see. Why don't you tell me what happened.'

I related the conversation and she grew whiter still, but stayed composed. At last, when I'd finished, she folded her hands and said, 'Well, it doesn't sound good, I admit, but I think there's little we can do but wait for them to make the first move.'

With that, there was a sudden banging at the door

below. I jumped convulsively but Maya shook her head reassuringly. There was a yell from below.

'Ma, Ma, it's us.' Sienna and Simon came running up the stairs. 'What happened?'

'Sienna saw something,' Simon said, breathlessly, as they came up to the landing. Then he saw Seth and did a double-take. 'Who's this?'

'Anna's Seth,' Maya said, wearily. 'Don't worry. He knows most of what there is to know.'

'Is that wise?'

'It's fine,' Seth said, with slight acidity. 'I'm not about to go to the Witchfinder General, if that's what you're worried about.'

'Stop bickering, you two,' Maya said. 'What did you see, Sienna?'

'Trouble,' Sienna said soberly, but before she had time to say more there was another slam from below and I heard Emmaline's voice calling up.

'Is Anna here?' She burst into the flat. 'Thank goodness. You weren't in English and I thought . . . Was it bad?'

I nodded and gave all of them the gist of the conversation.

'I'm so sorry,' I finished. 'I never meant to drag you all into this. I never thought . . .'

Maya patted my hand. Her fierce expression sat oddly

272

on her kind, maternal face. 'Don't worry, Anna. We set our course with the Ealdwitan long ago, I think. It was bound to come to grief sooner or later.'

Just then, Emmaline's face changed as if she'd received an electric shock. Her eyes went blank, focussing on something I could not see. Then, just as suddenly, she was back.

'Someone's coming. One of them.'

The pounding on the stairs made us all jump. Sienna moaned, grabbing for Simon's hand.

'Is it one of them? Can anyone see?' Simon asked frantically, but before anyone had time to respond the door slammed open again and Abe stumbled in, gasping for breath as if he'd been running.

'What's happened?' he said hoarsely. 'What's going on?' And then, 'What the hell's *he* doing here?' He pointed at Seth.

'Abe, I don't think Seth's the problem,' Emmaline said.

'What do you mean? The way I see it, he's the root of the whole bloody thing. Whatever's happened, I'm not discussing this in front of an outsider.'

'He knows what's going on.'

'I don't care if he knows my mother's maiden name and pin number. You,' he pointed at Seth, 'out.'

Seth picked up his bag and shot me a questioning

273

look, but I shook my head vehemently.

'No! Seth's staying, this concerns him as much as you, Abe.'

'It doesn't concern him in the least. He's not one of us. He's an outsider and he can't be trusted.'

'I'm an outsider too,' I said hotly. 'Do you trust me?'

Abe laughed bitterly. 'You're one of us, Anna, as well you know. Or is that a fib for the benefit of your boyfriend here?'

'Seth knows what I am.' I was shaking with anger. 'If he goes, I go.'

'Then go,' Abe snarled.

'Stop it, both of you!' Maya broke in. 'This is pointless and it's not getting us anywhere. Abe, this is *my* house, and as far as I'm concerned, Seth can stay. He's in as much danger as any of us, if not more. The question is, what's going to happen? Can anyone tell who's coming and when?'

There was a sudden silence – all eyes turned to Emmaline and Sienna. Emmaline shook her head.

'I don't know. I just got a glimpse, a dark car with blacked-out windows. I don't know where it was.'

Sienna's eyes glazed and I knew she was searching, frantically looking for answers. Simon held her hand as if willing her on, but when at last she trembled and turned her gaze back to the room she shook her head.

'Nothing. Whatever Emmaline saw, I can't get a fix on it.'

'Try the bones,' Simon suggested, and Sienna nodded. She took a small bag out of her pocket and shook some small objects, like dull irregular white pebbles, into her hand, chafing them with her palms. Then she whispered something to her closed hands and flung them on to the table. Everyone craned to look – but her face crumpled in fear.

'They're only showing darkness and water. They're telling us to be afraid. Oh God, what shall we do?'

'I'm so sorry,' I whispered. 'What can I do? Should I go? I could leave – go somewhere else . . . Maybe I should just give in to them. Give them what they want.' I put my head in my hands.

'No!' Emmaline yelped. She banged the table, making the bones jump and skitter. 'You most certainly can't give in, Anna! Where's your spine?'

'Do you *want* to join them?' Seth asked.

'I don't know.' I stared into his wide grey eyes, calm in spite of this madness. 'I don't *know* any more. How can I tell what I should do? I could never live with myself if they hurt you . . . Dad . . . any of you.' I looked round the room at the faces of all my friends, the faces of all the people in danger because of *me*. Seth took my hands, enclosing them gently in his larger ones, and I realized my fingers were shaking.

'Look, ignore the threats,' he said quietly. 'If it were just you – just you here now – what would you do? Would you join them?'

'No.' Suddenly I knew that for sure. 'No. Never. But I can't ask everyone else to bear this for me – this is my problem. I'll – I'll go away.'

'No,' Maya's voice was firm. 'We will fight this out beside you, Anna. This *isn't* just your problem. If we let them get away with this, who knows what'll be next? Whatever their motives, the Ealdwitan have gone too far this time; we must stand up to them. Everyone,' she turned to the others, 'I suggest you contact whoever can be trusted and give them the facts. There must be people out there unwilling to let the Ealdwitan ride roughshod this way.'

'I know at least a dozen people who would be quite glad to see the Ealdwitan get their comeuppance,' Abe said, and there was a cruel smile on his mouth that I didn't quite like.

'I can think of a few people,' Sienna put in, 'and there are others, who might come just to see fair play.'

'I'll contact the Dean at my university,' Simon

276

said. 'He's no friend to the Ealdwitan and he'll know of others. I just wish . . . I just wish we knew what their intentions were and when they'll make contact.'

Some two hours later we found out. There was a quiet knock at the street door and we all looked up; Seth and I from cooking supper, which had been delegated to us as the most useless members of the party, and the rest from their various methods of contacting their friends, colleagues and contacts.

'Who's that?' Emmaline said sharply. 'Is anyone expecting visitors?'

All heads shook, and Maya straightened from the map she had been poring over and stood, stiffly.

'Everyone, keep calm and stay here. I'll go and see.'

She left, and Emmaline stood up and went to the window to look out. Her face, when she turned back to the room, was frightened.

'It's the car. The one I saw, with blacked-out windows. It's in the street outside.'

Just then we heard footsteps on the stairs and Maya's voice saying, 'This way, please.' The door opened, and in came a small, balding man in his fifties, wearing a grey suit and holding a briefcase. He looked like nothing so much as a solicitor, or a middle-ranking civil servant.

Behind him was a woman, slightly younger but similarly dressed, and behind her a very tall man wearing black jeans, a pullover and impenetrable dark glasses. They made an incongruous trio.

'Please sit.' Maya gestured to a group of chairs. The two civil servants sat, though the tall man remained standing behind them. His manner, I realized suddenly, was that of a bodyguard.

'Let me introduce myself,' the little man said, in a dry nasal voice. 'Mr Peterson, and Ms Revere.' He held out a small, very stiff card. It bore the name Peterson. But it was not the name that made my heart jump. It was embossed with the silhouette of a black crow.

'From which organization?' Emmaline asked, pointedly, tapping the card. The man shot her a weary glance.

'Please, Miss Peller. Let's not play games. We are fully aware that you were expecting contact. Ms Revere and myself have come to set out our employers' position. The girl—'

'Her name is Anna,' Maya interrupted acerbically,

'Quite so. The girl has been given ample opportunities to join the organization freely and of her own will. Unfortunately she has chosen not to take advantage of these offers, so my employers must now press the point. Should she refuse again, they will be compelled to avail themselves of her powers by, ahem,' he coughed and continued, almost under his breath, 'by force.'

I gasped, and the sound was echoed around the table by the others. I saw Seth's fists clench and – was it my imagination? – a tiny satirical smile break out on the woman's face at the sight of his anger.

Mr Peterson did not smile, he looked pained.

'It is of course a highly undesirable situation – very painful, I do appreciate. But there are larger issues at stake, matters which I am not permitted to reveal.'

'Issues? What issues!' Emmaline scoffed. The little man spread his hands with what looked like real regret.

'Unfortunately I cannot disclose more. Suffice to say that my employers would like your co-operation, Miss Winterson. I have been tasked with securing that co-operation.'

'And if I refuse?' I whispered. He spread his hands again, and his face was more regretful than ever.

'Then they will be compelled to take action. Against you, and against any members of our community who collude in your refusal. Unfortunately the collateral damage to the outwith bystanders is also likely to be considerable and unavoidable.'

'By collateral damage, I take it you mean deaths?' Abe said brutally. Mr Peterson said nothing, but he inclined his head in acquiescence.

'No!' I could not suppress the sobbing, outraged gasp that escaped my lips.

'I very much wish it were otherwise. But may I emphasise that my employers are as eager as you to avoid this – they would be happy to accept a change of decision at any point.'

'So what you're saying . . .' I said slowly, 'is that unless I come over to your side you'll harm my friends and family?'

'Certainly not!' The little man looked almost comically shocked. He adjusted his tie fussily. 'Any collateral damage would be deplorable and entirely accidental. But my employers might be compelled to remove certain . . . privileges that this community has enjoyed. Certain . . . protections. And it would be dishonest of me to deny that there may be . . .' He coughed again. 'How shall I put it? *Unfortunate* consequences as a result.'

He turned to Maya and her family.

'My employers would like me to make clear that they have no quarrel with you, Ms Peller. If you care for this girl then may I suggest that you do your best to persuade her into a more sensible course of action. Or of course,' he shrugged, 'you may simply wish to relocate for the near future.'

'How dare you,' Maya crackled, visibly, with fury. There was a hum in the air like the sound of angry bees. 'We stand with Anna, in spite of all your threats.'

He shrugged again.

'Very laudable, I'm sure.' His voice did not give any impression that he thought it laudable in the least; it was dry and had an unpleasant note of bored sarcasm. 'I would caution you, however, not to make the mistake of relying on her protection. Her power is admittedly impressive for one so young but it's certainly not extraordinary in any way.' He nodded at Emmaline. 'Your own daughter could probably do as much, given time.'

'Really?' Abe said sarcastically. 'Then why are you so anxious to recruit Anna and not the rest of us?'

'Oh,' he waved a dismissive hand, 'our interest is purely . . . technical. An operational specific, nothing more.'

'Care to elaborate?' Abe smiled.

The little man made a small, apologetic moue. 'Would that I could, but service protocol, you know . . .'

'And what about *him*?' Abe nodded at Seth. 'Haven't you got anything to say about his role?'

I hissed through my teeth at Abe, too furious to speak.

281

But the little man only shrugged.

'He's of no importance. Loose ends will be tidied up after the main business is concluded.'

He looked at his female colleague and they exchanged a glance.

Both stood up.

'Well, I can see that this discussion has covered all that may profitably be said for the moment. My employers would like to give you until midnight tonight, Miss Winterson, to consider your position. After that point they will regretfully have to take enforcement action. Ms Peller, I suggest that you and your family would be safer elsewhere, but no doubt you will take your own views upon that point. Well, if there are no further questions?'

He looked at his watch like someone concluding a board meeting.

'Get out!' Maya said, with magnificent anger.

'Certainly.' The little man extended his hand and then, with a small, secretive smile, dropped it. 'Well, perhaps it was not to be expected. Good day.'

And they left, shadowed by the man in black.

As soon as he was gone, Maya burst into tears, and Emmaline and Sienna crowded round to try to comfort her. I felt a fierce stab of jealousy of their cosy family unit and that mother-daughter relationship that I'd never know. I heard Maya saying, 'Oh darlings, darlings, it'll be OK, it'll be OK, I promise,' and I longed for even that false reassurance, for someone to love me so much they'd lie in the face of all the evidence, just to try to protect me.

I could remember the last time I'd whinged about not having a mother; it had been school sports day, when I was ten, and I had no one to run with me in the mother-and-daughter three-legged race. The sight of Dad's face as I moaned had shut me up; I had one amazing parent. That was a lot luckier than some of my friends, and I'd vowed never to make Dad suffer over what I'd never missed, never to harp on pointless might-have-beens.

But I'd never felt my loss so strongly before today. If only, if *only* my mother were here. This whole mess might never . . .

But there was no point in wishing, or in blaming my own mistakes on someone long-gone. Instead, I put my head in my hands and shut my eyes against the horror of what I'd caused.

All this – all this I'd brought on the people I loved, just by being here. And I could do nothing but wait as the clock ticked towards midnight, while that horrible phrase, 'collateral damage' echoed and scrabbled inside my head.

Poor Dad – happily oblivious to all this and pottering

at home, all unconscious of the sword over his head. I thought of him, sitting with his feet on the Aga, chewing his thumbnail and reading the paper, waiting for the axe to fall. I thought of Elaine, and June, Prue and Liz, of Caroline, Madeleine, all the kids and teachers at school, the fishermen at the harbour, everyone in Winter, all of them equally blameless, all of them innocently awaiting the carnage, all on my account.

Maybe I should just give in. It seemed as if giving myself to the Ealdwitan was the only way of averting disaster – and really, was it such a high price to pay? Not when weighed against the safety of everyone I loved.

Except, what did they want from me? Why were they so very desperate? I was scared to find out. I knew they'd want more from me than I was prepared to give. Not least, I was pretty certain that if I joined the Ealdwitan, I'd never see Seth again. Their contempt for the outwith was too strong, and he knew too much.

I raised my head from my arms and looked at Seth. He was sitting quite still, an expression of black rage on his face. There was no despair at all, he just looked furious. Somehow his anger pulled me back from my bleak acceptance of defeat. Seth didn't look like someone facing destruction, he looked like someone preparing to fight.

Very well then. I would fight beside him.

CHAPTER SIXTEEN

To my surprise, the others felt the same way as Seth. There was no question of accepting defeat, or of persuading me to give myself up – they were ready, even eager, to fight. The only discussion was how and when.

'You'd better stay here,' Maya told me. 'Call your dad and tell him some story to explain it.'

'But I can't abandon Dad,' I said, thinking of him all alone and defenceless at home. 'Who'll protect him? I should be there in case something happens.'

'At this stage I think your presence is only going to endanger him,' Maya pointed out reasonably. 'It's you they're after. They may even overlook your dad if you aren't there.'

'But then I'll only be endangering all of you!' I said despairingly.

'We, at least, have ways of defending ourselves.' Maya

looked grim. 'As for Seth, I think his safety is probably compromised whether he stays or goes, given what he knows, so it's up to him.'

'I'll stay,' Seth said flatly.

'Do you need to call your mum?' Maya asked.

'I'll tell her I'm staying with a friend. She won't ask questions.'

Dad on the other hand did ask questions – a great many – but I told him that Emmaline had broken up with her boyfriend and was inconsolable, and had asked me to stay the night to have a shoulder to cry on. I made a mental note to tell Emmaline the story in case Dad ever mentioned it. Assuming, of course, we were all here in the morning to tell the tale.

And then, it was just a question of passing the interminable hours until midnight. The others spent the time in various ways – contacting friends and colleagues, cooking, drinking. Sienna was desperately scanning the future for some inkling of how the Ealdwitan were going to proceed. But she moved from runes, to tarot, to scrying water, and her expression grew more and more defeated.

'Nothing,' she said at last. 'Nothing at all. It's just darkness – chaos and darkness.'

'Well that's just super,' Abe retorted. 'Thanks for the morale booster.'

Out of everybody, Seth was the most cheerful, bossing me around the kitchen and knocking out a very creditable pasta sauce. The food was hard to force down at first, but while we ate the others started turning up, and whether it was the food or the company or both, the mood seemed suddenly to turn.

First came a crowd of Abe's friends: half a dozen bikers who arrived, crashed into the flat reeking of smoke and petrol, then almost immediately left for the pub. Maya's friends were more diverse; they ranged from a comfortable middle-aged couple who looked as if they might run a country tea-shop, to an extremely elderly man who walked with a stick and had the air of a retired librarian. Sienna's friends were all young and very beautiful; and Simon introduced only two contacts, a professor and a research fellow, both from his university, and promptly went into a corner with them to conduct a deep academic discussion.

And all the while the clock ticked on. At eleven-thirty Abe's crowd came back from the pub and the flat was suddenly filled with a crush of bodies, a haze of cigarette smoke, and a hum of talk and laughter. It felt like a grim New Year's Eve party; all of us sitting round, watching the minute hand inch towards vertical and our remaining time tick away.

287

At last there was only five minutes to go, then one minute. The couples drew together unconsciously, and I found Seth's hand in the crush and held it tight. He squeezed back, and I realized there was something I needed to tell him. Something I needed him to know before the end, if that's what tonight was.

'Seth, listen,' I began. He turned to me, his beautiful face warm in the candlelight, his grey eyes golden with reflected flames, 'Seth.' I drew a breath, my heart suddenly loud in my ears, 'Seth, I—'

But suddenly my voice was drowned out by a cheer as the clock-hand entered the last five seconds.

'Five!' shouted someone satirically. 'Four!'

Others joined in.

'Three! Two! One . . .'

'Seth,' I said urgently, 'I lo—' But Seth kissed me. The sounds of the room grew faint and far off, and all I heard was his breath and mine, ragged with adrenaline, the insistent beat of our hearts thudding together with the same reckless anticipation.

'Midnight!'

There was a burst of nervous laughter and a cork popped. One of Simon's friends said fiercely, 'For heavens' sakes! Will someone tell these young idiots it's not a bloody party. We need our wits about us!'

At that the noise died away, and there was silence, apart from the sound of wind at the window, and rain lashing against the pane.

Nothing.

I could hear my heart beating in my ears so loudly I wondered if everyone else could hear it too. The seconds ticked past, and there were murmurs from the crowd, and a couple of suppressed giggles.

Still nothing.

'Bring it on!' shouted one of the bikers. There was more laughter – guffaws this time.

Then, 'They're here,' Emmaline whispered. 'They're at the castle.'

'What's happening?'

'What can you see?'

'What are they doing?'

Emmaline shook her head frantically, trying to get a clearer picture I supposed, then said, 'Damn, it's gone.'

'I can tell you what they're doing.' Maya looked up from her palm. There was a bee there, sitting quietly, its wings glinting in the lamplight. 'They've smashed the harbour protections. The waters are rising.'

There was a hasty discussion over whether to go or stay put, with fierce argument from each camp, but eventually most of the group surged out on to the street and began to walk down through the town. Seth and I followed, still holding hands, shielding our eyes from the driving wind and rain. When we reached the foot of the high street we could see the sea was already over the harbour wall and lapping at the foundation stones of the fishermen's cottages along the quay.

A group of men coming out of one of the harbour pubs did an astonished double-take and almost tripped into the rising waters.

'It's flooding!' one of them yelled over his shoulder, back into the bar. 'The harbour's flooded!'

At that, more drinkers came out, and soon the quay was full of people splashing through the water to secure their boats, or hurrying home to dig out long-disused sandbags. Someone in one of the harbour cottages tuned a radio to the forecast and we all craned to listen.

'Reports are coming in of a freak storm in the Channel, with gales expected in the shipping areas of Sole, Lundy, Plymouth, Portland, Wight and Dover. The Met Office has issued a severe weather warning. On-shore winds combined with rain and high tides may cause localized flooding in coastal areas. Residents are advised to—'

A church bell began to toll in a mournful distress signal, followed by another, and then another, until the town was filled with a discordant clangour that mingled with the wail of the wind to form an eerie lament.

Doors were opening all up and down the row, and I saw a face appear at the window of the furthest cottage. It was a girl – she looked familiar. I squinted through the darkness trying to make out her features. It was with a shock that I recognized her: Caroline. I knew that she'd seen me too, for her face hardened, but she opened the window and leaned out.

'Seth,' she cried above the noise of the bells. 'Seth, what's happening?'

I squeezed Seth's hand, pointing with my free one. He looked up and his expression changed.

'Take your mum to your gran's, Caroline. You can't stay here, the waters are rising.'

'What are you doing out?' she called back. 'Didn't you hear the forecast?'

But Seth only shook his head. 'Go to your gran's,' he repeated.

'Seth, please,' Caroline said. 'I – I'm scared, Seth. Come with me.'

I let go of his hand.

'Seth!' Caroline's voice was low, pleading, but it reached us, even over the sound of the bells. 'Seth, I still – please . . .'

Seth turned his back and stared out to sea. Caroline stayed, leaning out over the dark waters, but then her eyes met mine and her expression changed.

'I hope you drown,' she spat. The glass in the window rattled as she slammed it shut.

'Seth,' I said. He turned, but whatever he might have said was interrupted by an almighty splash as one of the drinkers fell over a submerged mooring ring, cannoning into Seth.

'Sorry, mate. Christ, it effing stinks,' the man grumbled.

It was true. The water smelled. Not the fresh, clean smell of the sea, but a foetid stench of rotting fish. It was was dark with weed and silt, and there were creatures in it, deep-sea creatures: white, sightless fish, coiling eels and sucking, tentacled things that I couldn't name. And it was rising all the time. The benches, which had been dry when we first came down to the quay, were half submerged.

I looked round for Maya – and realized with a shock that she was no longer behind me, that there was nothing there but a dark expanse of choppy water. Seth, Emmaline, Abe and Sienna were all with me, so were Abe's biker friends Bill and Carl. But Simon and Maya were on the other side of the quay with the rest of the group. We'd been edging away from each other, forced apart by the rising water – and now we were cut off by the swirling black mass that was now the quay. We were trapped, and the only way out led up to the castle, to the Ealdwitan.

'Ma!' Sienna yelled.

'Don't worry,' Maya yelled back, 'we'll find a way round. Just – just stay out of the water . . . Oh God!' She recoiled sharply as a thrashing thing darted out of the dark waters. It snapped at her hand, then fell back with a splash. 'Stay away from the water, do you hear me?' She was backing away from the rising tide, up the high street. 'We'll get the others from the flat and come to find you.' Her voice was now almost too faint to hear above the rising wind and the tolling bells. 'We'll find you!'

And then they were gone, forced round the corner and out of sight by the rising sea.

'Well,' Abe said, flatly. He looked at Bill and Carl, and then shrugged.

'What do we do now?' Sienna asked.

'Move up the hill, I suggest,' Emmaline said distastefully, watching the murky ooze rise closer.

We all jumped as there was an enormous crash and the small hut where the fishermen sold whelks off the harbour arm swept suddenly into the sea. We watched as the sea battered it into shreds of broken planks – then it disappeared beneath the waves. Emmaline looked shaken.

'Thank goodness we live up the hill, is all I can say.'

'Grandad,' Seth muttered.

'Sorry, what did you say?' Sienna asked, cupping her ear against the wind.

'My grandad. He lives on the Spit.' He pointed out to sea. Abe, Sienna and Emmaline all looked at each other, and then Sienna turned back to Seth.

'I'm very sorry.'

Just then Emmaline gave a gasp and staggered, putting a hand to a gash on her cheek.

'You're bleeding!' Abe shouted, over the roar of the wind.

'I was hit,' Emmaline said in wonderment, 'by something hard.'

She looked down at her feet. There was a huge green barnacled crab scuttling away.

'Time to go, I think.' Abe jerked his head towards the road. We nodded and began to climb.

It was the route I walked home from school, but the familiar path looked very different in the moonlight, slashed with fallen branches and driftwood. As we walked, straining into the wind, Seth's eyes kept drifting out to sea, and I knew he was thinking of his grandfather, trapped out there with the rising waters. My heart tore for him – and suddenly my mind was made up.

'We have to do something,' I said. 'We can't let them destroy Winter like this. The town's cut off – we're the only people who can reach the castle now. It's up to us.'

'We have to wait for Ma,' Sienna said. I shook my head, 'There's no time. It'll take them hours to get round the headland to find us. The whole village could be under by that time.'

'But there's only six of us,' Abe said. 'Seven, if you count the useless one.' He jerked his thumb at Seth. 'Emmaline, how many did you see up at the castle?'

'I only caught a glimpse,' she said, 'but at least twenty – more perhaps. I don't know.'

'Considerably more,' said a dry voice and, turning, we saw Mr Brereton in our path. His hair was plastered to his forehead and his glasses were misted with salt, but he was standing upright, in spite of the tearing gale.

'Mr Brereton!' I cried, stupidly.

'I take it, my dear, that you haven't come to tell us of your change of heart?' he asked. I shook my head vehemently. 'Then I'm sorry, my dear, you leave me with no choice.'

Somehow, although his voice was as calm and quiet as

ever, he had no trouble in making himself heard above the storm.

'I command you to stop.' He held out his hand and suddenly my feet were rooted to the ground. 'All of you, stop.'

I couldn't move. I literally couldn't lift a foot. It was the strangest feeling. I tried pulling cautiously, then harder, and finally I wrenched with all my strength, but it was like my shoes had been glued to the tarmac. My skin might have been part of the road, for all the good straining did. Turning, I could see by the expressions of the others that they'd suffered the same.

'Mr Brereton,' screamed Emmaline, 'let go *now!*'

She flung out an arm, palm outstretched towards him. Mr Brereton staggered; for a moment my feet grew lighter and I almost stumbled forwards – but then he seemed to recover.

'Ah, Emmaline Peller, if I'm not mistaken,' he said smoothly. 'You always were a most unpleasant child. Little girls should be seen and not heard.'

He pointed towards her and she opened her mouth to retort – or tried to. As I watched, her eyes bulged and her face contorted in distress, but she seemed completely unable to open her mouth. Only muted sounds of horror came from her sealed lips as she tore at her face with her hands.

'You bastard!' Abe bellowed. He raised his hand and a bolt of lightning struck Mr Brereton squarely on the forehead. He was flung into the air, back towards the edge of the cliff, and before he could rise Abe hit him again with another crack of lightning.

Just as he was about to try a third, Mr Brereton scrambled to his knees and howled, 'Terrethum!' Abe tumbled, like a felled tree, and lay on the ground as if stunned.

'Kveykva!' Bill drew back his hand and flung a ball of white light. Mr Brereton cowered to the ground, but it passed overhead harmlessly. Then, stumbling to his feet yet again, Mr Brereton drew himself up to his full height and drew a circle in the air. A rope seemed to shimmer there, and he caught both ends in his fist, drawing them tighter, and tighter.

A band of steel closed around my chest. My lungs were being crushed, and I looked around me in panic, but had no breath to call for help, and no one to help me anyway. Beside me Seth was doubled in agony, tiny shallow breaths hissing between his teeth. Emmaline had her arms wrapped around herself and a look of mute terror in her eyes. It was like being held in a vice; with every breath I exhaled the band drew tighter around my ribs until there was no air left at all. Finally I could only heave uselessly, my ribs straining with the effort, but totally unable to get any oxygen to my lungs. There were stars in front of my eyes, and a dull hissing in my ears. My vision grew black, began to fracture. Through the black mist I saw Seth fall to the ground beside me.

As my head spun, I tried to recall the surge of power I'd had before, the surge of rage and love which had let me dive to Seth's rescue without needing oxygen, without needing anything except magic. I'd done it then, I could do it now.

I summoned all my powers – and took a breath.

It was like silver light gushing through my lungs – a breath so wonderful, so glorious, I felt I'd never take life or lungs for granted ever again.

'Get off them!' I screamed at Mr Brereton. He looked round at me, startled. It was almost as if he'd forgotten I was there. Suddenly I could move my feet and beside me Seth, Emmaline and the others were moving too, stumbling forward with choking gasps, inhaling air as if it was the first breath they had ever taken.

'Get away!' I thrust my hands out and Mr Brereton staggered back, towards the cliff. 'You hateful, hateful man!' He stumbled from my searing rage, shielding his eyes, doubled up against the fury of my attack. 'Leave them *alone!*'

One last time he quailed, and one last time he stepped back – into nothing. We heard a scream, and a hideous, dull cracking: the sound of a body ricocheting off rocks. And then nothing.

'Are you OK?' Emmaline was sobbing. 'Oh Anna! Are you OK?' She flung her arms around me, her face wet with tears and sea spray.

'I'm fine,' I was shaking. 'But – but – Mr Brereton!'

'Gone,' Abe said succinctly. 'And good riddance. C'mon. Let's get up to the castle and get stuck into the rest of them.'

'Oh God.' The horror of it suddenly struck me and I sank to my knees. 'I've killed him; I've killed a man.'

'A man!' Bill spat on the ground disgustedly. 'He's not what I call a man – barely human. I'd sooner spare a rat's life. He would have killed us, Anna. All seven of us. It was one life or seven.'

I knew he was right, but it didn't stop me turning with a backward glance to look at that spot on the cliff edge where I'd seen him last, as we started our walk up the road, towards the castle.

I'd taken only a few steps though, when I realized Seth wasn't beside me. I looked back and he was standing, staring out to sea, still where Mr Brereton had rooted him. I ran back and plucked at his arm.

'Are you OK?'

'No,' he shouted back above the gale. 'I can't come, Anna.'

'Your feet!' I turned to call to the others, to tell them to stop, to come back, help me release Seth. 'Don't worry, Seth, I'll get the others. We'll get you free.'

'It's not that.' He put a hand on my arm to stop me. 'I have to go back; I have to get Grandad.' He nodded towards the Spit, almost invisible behind the lashing rain and enormous waves.

'What!' I was horrified. 'Seth, you're mad. Look out there . . .' I swept a hand towards the churning black sea, filled with who-knew-what kinds of nameless, snapping creatures. 'Look at the sea – you'll never survive!'

He shook his head.

'Grandad needs me – he's an old man, Anna. I can't just abandon him.'

'Seth, please, please no. If there was any chance, I'd tell you to go, but there's no way any boat could survive out there, let alone land on the Spit. You'll die. You know it.'

He nodded, but his face was set and I could see my words had had no effect on his resolve.

'There's a chance of that, I admit.'

'A chance!' I felt a sob rise in my throat, 'A chance? A certainty you mean.'

'No, it's not a certainty; boats have weathered as bad, or worse. I wouldn't go if I thought it was suicide.'

'Seth,' I said desperately, 'please don't go. Please, please, I'm begging you. It would break my heart to lose you. I love you – I always have loved you. I should have told you that long ago.'

Seth only stood very quietly in the pouring rain, water streaming over his skull and down the bridge of his nose. Then he smiled so that my heart lifted and twisted and ached all at once.

'I know,' he said very softly, so quietly I had to strain to read his lips. His words should have sounded arrogant, but they didn't, and his face was full of a fierce sadness and joy. 'I know you do. But Anna, you know there's a chance that you won't come back from the castle. Would you turn back from there, if I asked you?'

'Yes!' I sobbed, knowing I was lying but not caring.

'OK then.' He put his arms around me, and they were warm, strong and infinitely comforting. I put my head on his shoulder and it felt like coming home. He held me close, so that I could hear his voice, softly, through his chest, in spite of the waves and the wind. 'Come back with me. Inland. I won't go to the Spit if you turn back from the castle. We'll run, away from all this.'

I pulled away. I buried my face in my hands, unable to answer.

'Well?' Seth said, his voice almost lost under the shrieking wind, 'Will you do it? Will you turn back?'

Wretchedly, I shook my head. Not even for Seth could I abandon Winter to its fate. If there was even a small chance that I could help save the town I had to lend my strength to the fight. And of course Seth had known that all along. He smiled and stroked a lock of wind-whipped hair behind my ear.

'Come on, Anna, we both know there's no chance of you running now. I know what you have to do, and I'm not going to try to persuade you out of it. Let me go.'

I could not find words, so I only hugged him, winding my arms so tight around his neck that he almost choked. Then he laughed, an incongruously joyous sound in the bitter, shrieking storm, and wrapped his arms around me, lifting my feet off the ground.

'Come back safe,' I choked in his ear.

'I'll try. I love you, Anna.'

'I love you too.' I buried my face in his shoulder. His skin smelled of salt and sweat and soap. 'I love you, Seth. If you die,' my heart clenched cold with the effort of even uttering the words, 'if you die I'll – I'll – I'll never forgive you. Do you hear me? Come back, come back safe, do you promise?'

'I promise,' he said, and there was something in his voice that made my tears spring afresh. Then from up the hill I heard a bellow.

'Anna, Seth, what's going on? Are we going or not?'

'I'm not,' Seth shouted back, his words ripped and twisted by the winds. 'I've got something else to do.'

He kissed me again, quick and fierce, then he was gone, running down the slope towards the harbour, into the dark.

I turned back to the others, wiping the tears from my face with my sleeve.

'OK, let's go.'

As we climbed, shapes began to resolve themselves out of the murk. First was the dark hump of the castle headland, then the gap-toothed, tumbledown towers of the castle itself.

'My God,' Abe muttered under his breath, 'they've made it into a bloody fortress.'

And then I realized what they had done, and why the Ealdwitan had chosen this place for their stand. Not only was the castle the highest point in Winter, protecting them from the rising waters, but it was still, in spite of its age, an impressive fortification. The Ealdwitan had gathered on one of the farther battlements, where they could see both the sea and the town of Winter.

It was the perfect place to co-ordinate their attack. They were shielded from outwith eyes, invisible behind the castle walls as they lashed the town with wind and waves. But just as importantly, they were shielded from attack; shielded by the castle's imposing moats, battlements and towers, and by its ancient magic. They'd twined their spells about the castle walls like a fantastic mesh of magical barbed wire and before we could even touch them, we'd have to penetrate a dark web of spell and counter-spell.

A wave of despair washed over me. We might as well turn back. We might as well give up. We were all doomed.

Beside me I could see from their devastated faces that Emmaline, Abe and Bill were having the same thoughts.

'We're lambs to the slaughter,' Emmaline said bleakly. 'Is it even worth trying?'

'Of course it's worth trying!' Sienna snapped. 'What's wrong with you all? Have we come this far to give up now?'

'It's a spell, you fools.' Carl grabbed Emmaline's shoulder and turned her to look at him. 'Emmaline!' He shook her. 'Emmaline, Anna, resist it, do you hear me? This feeling – it's just a spell, they're messing with your minds.'

I shook my thick head and felt the despair lift a little, then settle again.

'Come on,' Sienna urged. She shook Bill's shoulder. 'Bill, listen to Carl, he's right. This is *not* hopeless, do you hear me? Abe, Anna, snap out of it – you're falling into their trap.'

The effort of resistance was like wading through treacle. Every cell of my mind wanted to give in to the black washing despair and just lie down and weep, but Sienna and Carl's nagging voices kept telling me to keep pushing, keep resisting, keep the black tide back. And gradually it began to ebb . . . I saw Emmaline surface with a gasp, shaking her head like someone with water in their ears. Then I pushed out of the thick goo of the spell, breathing hard, as if I'd been swimming against the tide.

'For goodness' sake,' Sienna said, and her voice was grim, 'that was just the first line of defence. You'll have to be a bit tougher than that if we're going to get anywhere.'

'It was so real,' Emmaline said, still slightly dazed.

'Anna's got an excuse, she's never encountered this kind of thing, but you,' she stabbed a finger at Emmaline, 'and above all *you*, Abe, should be ashamed of yourselves. Now pull yourselves together.'

'What a kids' trick to fall for,' Abe said disgustedly, as we began to walk. 'I deserve everything I get after that.'

'Look.' Sienna put a hand on his shoulder. 'It was the right spell at the right time. Which, as the saying goes, is half the work done.'

'What do you mean?' I said, confused. 'What saying?'

'One of ours, not one you'd know. "The right time and tide does half the work, the wrong makes half again". What it means is that magic works best when it works *with* the tide, not against it. We were already despondent and depressed – coming on top of that, the spell worked far better than it should have done.'

We trudged on up the hill, the castle glowering over our heads, and when we reached the top I looked back. The sight that lay below was both beautiful and terrifying. Where the small harbour had been, cosily surrounded by cottages and dotted with small boats, there was now a great spreading mass of black water which had overflowed the harbour confines, flooding the quay and the gardens of all the cottages round about. Thread-like tentacles of sea were spreading across the rest of the village, penetrating the streets of Winter with probing oily fingers, until the whole town was enmeshed in a dark, glittering web of water, spreading and growing with every passing minute. Soon only the roofs of the harbour cottages would be visible. Then, not even the roofs. The river would break its banks and rise through Wicker Wood to taint our house with all its muck and murk. Its waters would merge with the sea and together climb the high street, flowing into every living room, gushing under the doors, overflowing windows – welling unstoppably out of the plugholes and toilets as even the sewers became overwhelmed.

I thought of Dad, asleep in his bed and unconscious of the dark waters creeping towards him through the night. And of Seth, somewhere out there, fighting the waves.

'Anna.' Emmaline pulled softly at my sleeve. 'Anna, come on. We need to keep going.'

I nodded and together we crested the hill, to stand in the shadow of the castle.

CHAPTER SEVENTEEN

Whether they were really oblivious to us, I don't know. But as we stood, staring up at the castle's sheer granite walls, I felt like we were less than ants to them, ants in the path of their destructive flood, about to be swept away by the waters.

'What now?' I asked in despair.

'I don't know,' Emmaline said. 'Sienna, any ideas?' Sienna shook her head. 'Carl? Bill?'

'I have an idea,' Abe said. We all turned. 'It's like Sienna said, right time, right tide. We have to use the weapons they've supplied, weapons we can turn against them.'

'Which are?' Sienna asked.

'The weather. They've whipped up this storm to suit their own ends. But I think we can control it – turn it back against them. They're in a really exposed position up here, very vulnerable. I think we could make them very uncomfortable.'

'It might work,' Sienna said, with a kind of dawning hope in her voice.

'We all know what you can do with the weather,' said Carl, 'and Bill's not so bad with electricity either. We could do some pretty effective stuff with lightning I reckon.'

'No!' I said instinctively. They all turned to me, surprised.

'But, Anna,' Emmaline said, 'it's a good plan. Plays on our strengths and their positional weakness. What's the problem?'

'Seth!' I said desperately. 'He's out there, on the sea, he's gone to fetch his grandfather. If we whip the storm up now . . .'

They all looked at each other, uncomfortable. I could tell they were weighing the life of one outwith against the safety of the entire community of Winter – and finding the balance unequal.

Sienna cleared her throat, and I couldn't bear to hear what she was going to say.

'I know, I know!' I cried. 'All those people, all those innocent people, but Sienna, it's *Seth*. Emmaline – can't you understand?'

'I understand, Anna. But it's not just Seth we have to consider,' Emmaline said softly. 'It's your dad . . . Seth's mum . . . my mum . . . all our families. You know that.'

Of course I knew that. And I knew she was right, which made it all the more bitter. But agony welled up inside me and I snapped, 'If he was a witch you wouldn't be so bloody cavalier about risking his life.'

I regretted the words as soon as I said them – the more so because I didn't really believe them. Emmaline flinched.

'Is that what you really think?'

'No,' I said wretchedly, 'no, I'm sorry, I'm sorry. But Emmaline, you don't feel about Seth the way I do . . .'

'No, I don't.' She looked at me steadfastly, her brows furrowed with compassion. 'But I understand how *you* feel.'

But I wasn't sure if she did. I wasn't sure if she knew what she was asking of me. I knew she was right, but my heart felt like it was tearing in two, ripped between love and duty.

Abe took my hand.

'*I* understand, Anna,' he said, very quietly, and something about the way he said it made me believe that he did understand, perhaps had stood in my shoes once upon a time. 'It's a terrible choice; one I wouldn't wish on my worst enemy. But you need to ask yourself, what would Seth tell you to choose?'

I snatched my hand away, turning my face to

the storm. Because I knew, of course I knew, what Seth would say.

'And Anna,' Sienna put in, 'even if we held back, it might not save Seth. Look at it.' She waved a hand at the sea, and she was right. It was impossible to imagine any craft surviving out there. Perhaps he was already gone and I'd be sacrificing Winter for a dead man.

I nodded brokenly.

'Are you sure?' Abe put in gently. 'We can do this without you, if you prefer.'

'No.' Suddenly my voice was strong. I couldn't take the coward's way out. 'No, you're right. I'll help. But please, *please* spare the Spit as much as you can.' I directed my plea to Abe, knowing that if anyone had the power to shape this storm, it was him.

He nodded. 'You have my word.' He looked around at the others, 'Ready?'

They nodded.

'Then follow my lead.'

He shut his eyes, bowed his head, and his shadow seemed suddenly to grow about two feet, lengthening across the grass. The clouds boiled and coalesced overhead and thunder rolled. Then the storm erupted.

The first thing to change was the wind. It veered round to our backs and began to pick up pace. I would have thought it impossible for it to blow with any more violence, but it did. The pitch increased to a scream, small trees bending, ripping in the force of the gale. Stones and branches flew ahead of its path and I saw that it was turning, shaping, massing upon a vortex directly above the castle. True to his word, Abe was concentrating all his energies on that one single spot, forcing the storm's devastation down on the Ealdwitan.

'Bill,' he snarled under his breath. Bill raised his hands and brought them down as if cracking an invisible whip. Lightning struck at the towers and stones rained down. There were shouts and cries from the castle, and great balls of St Elmo's fire raced up and down the battlements.

Sienna and Carl each put a hand on Abe's shoulder blade. They had their eyes closed too, and I sensed the flow of their strength running invisibly into Abe's arteries, feeding his power as he in turn fed and shaped the storm. Emmaline's eyes were wide and both her hands stretched out towards the castle's defences, ripping and tearing the distant threads of power. But as fast as she stretched and strained at the web, it meshed and grew. The witches inside were repairing and strengthening their defences, far faster than Emmaline could penetrate them.

'Anna.' Sienna spoke with her eyes still closed. 'Anna, you're not helping . . .'

I was not. In fact, I suddenly realized that a part of me was even hindering, damping down Abe's storm in spite of my intentions. I was fighting the winds that ripped across the bay, smashing the small boats out there to matchwood. Oh, Seth . . .

With a great effort I tore my mind back from Seth and Bran and threw my power into the fray. Once I did, it was both terrifying and exhilarating. I was swept into the torrent of Abe's violence, all my rage caught up and whipped into the swirling storm, with one target – the Ealdwitan. I threw everything I had at the castle, and the huge structure groaned.

For an incredulous, joyous moment I thought we had them – their spells flickered and frayed, and a cry of shock and fury went up from their ranks. And Abe had the storm right within his grasp – every twig, every hailstone, every drop of rain had become a weapon to smite the Ealdwitan as hard as we could.

But, after the first shock, they began fighting back. The wind veered round and we, too, were buffeted and shaken. Bill's lightning, instead of striking with precision, fractured into a dozen forks, smiting trees, rocks, all over the countryside. The rain howled in our faces instead of at our backs. And all the time they huddled behind their fortress of protection and we had nothing, nothing but the shirts on our backs.

'Give her to us,' a voice came from the castle, howling above the storm. 'Give up the girl, surrender, and the rest of you will go free.'

'Never!' screamed back Emmaline into the teeth of the gale.

And then came a crack of lightning so close and so devastating that we all fell back, shielding our eyes, feeling our bones rattle with the living shock of it. A smell of scorched earth and burned hair, and a bright blindness that burned and bore into my skull long after the crack had sounded.

We were all stunned, I think. Then as we came to ourselves, peering through the blinding darkness, a fear fell upon us. One by one we scrambled to our feet – all except Bill.

He lay against the scorched earth, his face pale and untouched, but the zips and buckles of his biker's jacket were melted and twisted beyond recognition. Sobbing, Sienna knelt beside him. She touched his face, then snatched her hand back as if scorched. Emmaline made to follow but Sienna cried, 'Don't touch him, he's burning.'

The rain that fell on his body hissed and turned to steam as we watched, the grass curling and wilting beneath.

'Is he . . . ?' Emmaline asked.

Abe nodded. Carl gave a great sobbing cry and put his head in his hands. Then suddenly Abe ducked and flung his arm out defensively, and barely a moment later the lightning stabbed again. It hit Abe's shielding arm, shattering into a thousand flaming fragments, and Abe staggered backwards as if he'd taken a great blow to the heart.

'Abe! Are you OK?' Emmaline ran to him and flung her arms around him, supporting his weight so that he tottered but didn't fall. He nodded, dazed, and when he spoke his voice was cracked and hoarse.

'This can't go on. They're so much stronger than us. I can't shield and fight at the same time.'

'Fight,' came a cry from the woods behind us, and we all turned. Maya was forging up the hill against the tearing winds, her hair streaming out like a Medusa's in the gale, her linen dress soaked dark with rain. Behind her came the others. 'Fight, we'll shield you.'

'Ma!' screamed Emmaline, and she and Sienna ran to embrace her. Maya hugged them fiercely for a moment, then suddenly broke away and shouted, 'Everyone, shield!'

She flung out a hand and a huge rock, tossed by the winds, smashed harmlessly into shards above our heads.

'That was a bit too close,' she yelled. 'Come on now, everyone, let's get on with this and give them space to work.'

At Maya's signal her party spread around in a circle and suddenly it was as if a cool breeze had wafted over us. The fury of the winds ebbed, the rain no longer lashed in our faces, and when the lightning cracked again it broke harmlessly above our heads.

Abe gave an enormous grin and I saw him gather the threads of the storm together. Then he flung them at the castle and the granite stones groaned.

For what felt like hours the storm raged to and fro, buffeting the castle with all its might, and then turning, twisting back, shaped by the magic on either side according to the cunning and strength of each. But we were tiring. More and more of Maya's half of the party stepped forward to help Abe's attack. Now expressions were grim and the rain was lashing us again, while the castle stood, impenetrable as ever, and there was a note like mocking laughter in the wind that blew in our faces.

I was standing at Abe's shoulder, adding my strength to the attack, when I heard a voice in my head. 'Anna, Anna,' I turned. It was Maya. Her eyes were shut and her lips weren't moving. She looked totally concentrated on the task of shielding her family, but inside my head I heard again, '*Anna, stop a moment, pull back.*'

I stopped.

'*It's never going to work this way.*' Her voice inside my head was short, breathless, like someone trying to speak while holding up a great weight, but it was calm and gentle as ever. '*Their protective charms are too strong. They've used the old magic on the castle – ancient charms – to their advantage. We need to break it; break their protection. I know you can do it.*'

'Maya, help me,' I begged. 'Show me how. Like you did before – you lead and I'll put all my power behind you, but I can't do it alone, I don't know how.'

She shook her head, an almost imperceptible movement, but I caught it.

'*Too much. Have to shield.*' Her voice was staccato now, as if the effort of holding the shield was almost too much. '*You can do it. You. Alone. You* must *do it.*'

I looked down at Winter, drowning by slow degrees. I looked out at the blackness of the sea where somewhere Seth was fighting his own battle against the storm. And I looked at my friends, ranged around me with expressions of desperate concentration – at Emmaline, her face twisted with effort; at Abe, crouched against the force of the storm; and at Bill's body, lying where he had

317

fallen. Everyone I loved would perish, just as Bill had done, unless I could find a way of shattering the protections that the Ealdwitan had hijacked for their own.

I shut my eyes and looked inside, into the inner well where I imagined my magic bubbling up, longing to break free. I tried to think about everything Maya had shown me, everything I'd seen and learned in these few short weeks. It seemed pitifully little. I was scared. I was scared of myself. But what else could we do? If I couldn't do this . . .

I stopped. I *had* to do it. There was no other option.

I opened up and let the magic out. Then I flung it at the castle with all my strength.

A cry went up from the battlements. I opened my eyes to see the torn threads of charms hanging loose and limp where I'd seared them – but it wasn't enough. It wasn't nearly enough. The mesh was too strong, too old, too cunning for one person to break.

'Maya, I'm sorry,' I started, and she turned to look at me. As she did, a huge ball of magic came hurtling across the sky from the castle, and crashed into her shield. Maya gave a gasping cry and fell to the ground.

'Ma!' Sienna screamed, and all around us now hail and rain and lightning bolts were falling, our shields in disarray, our defences completely abandoned.

'Are you OK?' Emmaline ran to crouch beside Maya, but Maya was beating her off, pushing her away.

'Leave me, you fools. Don't stop shielding!' She heaved herself up on one arm, blood pouring down her face, and then scrambled to her feet. 'Sienna, get that shield back right *now*. Emmaline, give me your scarf; I can't see for blood.'

She grabbed the scarf from Emmaline's neck and swiped frantically at her eyes, until the worst of the gore was clear, then stumbled back into position, her shielding arm at the ready as if nothing had happened. 'Get on with it, Anna,' she cried, and then ducked as a huge rock sailed inches above our heads.

I had to end this. I had to end it *now*, or we were all going to die, witches and outwith alike. I took a deep breath, drawing into myself all the power and rage and love that I possessed. I forced it down into the dark well at the centre of my heart. Down, down, I pushed it all, concentrating every feeling, every emotion I had ever had, into a single thought.

And then I let rip.

A blinding light seared across the sky. It was a blast like an atomic bomb, rippling out from the centre, devastating the magic that lay in its path, tearing through the charms of centuries, ripping through the Ealdwitan's protective forces, slashing, cutting, rending everything in its path. The earth shook and groaned as if torn by an earthquake, and the group around me fell to their knees, stunned for a moment by the force of the explosion.

Then Abe howled, 'Their defences are down! *Now!*' And he flung the wind and rain back to the castle with a terrifying violence.

Rocks were crashing into the sea – and more than rocks. Large parts of the headland began to crumble away, taking bushes and trees down too. As we watched, one of the castle towers groaned and tottered, and then the granite blocks, which had stood for more than a thousand years against the sea-wind and rain, fell with a thunderous roar into the crashing waves beneath, taking the castle's seaward battlements with it.

With their protections shorn we could see the Ealdwitan now, what was left of them. They were scrambling back from the precipice, those still able to run dragging the hurt and maimed with them; and from the weeping and screaming that reached us on the wind I guessed that more had gone to their deaths in the sea. The thought should have made me sick with horror – but it didn't. I only felt a fierce delight in my own power of destruction.

The Ealdwitan were running now; we could see figures

disappearing over the headland, some running, some hobbling, some loping like wolves, others swooping through the air over our heads. Their silhouettes were like huge black crows against the pearly sky.

'That's right – run, you damn cowards!' yelled Abe, fierce with exultation.

He turned to me and crushed me in a grip of iron, his hug so fierce I could hardly breathe.

'Anna, you genius!' He gripped my face between his hands. 'God, with a woman like you beside me I could—' he stopped and laughed exultantly, and then out of nowhere he kissed me with a hunger and fury that took my breath away. For a moment I was too stunned to do anything. Then I struggled out of his grasp, but before I could demand what the hell he thought he was doing, Emmaline was on me, leaping and yelling and kissing me.

'We've done it!' she shrieked. '*You* did it, Anna!'

The air was full of the exultant shouts of the others, dazed and dazzled with our success. All around people were slapping backs, crushing each other in rib-cracking hugs, laughing and shouting with the joy of being alive.

'I'm proud of you, Anna.'

I turned. Maya stood quietly behind me with a smile of utmost weariness and pleasure. 'I am so proud.'

I smiled back, my heart almost too full to speak. I was

searching for the words to try to express the gratitude I felt, for protecting me, helping me, believing in me – when the harsh scream of a crow cut through the air, impossibly loud, and we all turned to look.

Dawn was rising, a sliver of red over the water, and the sea was strewn with storm-ripped debris and pale creatures of the deep flung up by the tempest's violence. At the foot of the cliffs lay the smashed corpses of the Ealdwitan, their blood seeping into the dawn-red water.

Above towered the black mass of the castle ruins. They were empty now, but for a great black crow, wheeling and crying above the scattered stones and shattered bodies.

It seemed to be half mad with fury and loss, diving to the waves and then back up to the ruined towers, and screaming its agony and loss to the heavens in a voice that echoed across the bay.

At last it flapped its inky wings and then swung round towards us, skimming low over the turf. Closer and closer it came, and I wanted to duck, but pride held me steady. It was only a bird.

Pride was a mistake. The cruel grey claws extended like talons and it dived, dropping like a hawk, right above my head. Scaly claws tangled in my hair, the curved black beak gouged and pecked at my face, stabbing for my eyes. I screamed, battering the bird with my hands and feeling

322

the blood come as its beak sliced into my flesh.

'Get off her!' Emmaline yelled, and she flung a ball of fire at the creature, but I ducked, instinctively, and it missed us both. The creature turned its malevolent black head towards her, opened its beak, and screamed. A pulse of power ripped through the air and Emmaline flew back, her body smashing into a tree trunk. For a moment she hung, held there by the rough bark. Then she slipped to the ground, her head lolling, terrifyingly limp.

The bird struck again, its reeking breath hot in my face. I remembered my power, but I was tired, too tired – it felt like there was nothing left. It was all I could do to shield myself from its spells, let alone drive it off.

Through a dim whirl of claws and feathers I saw Abe flinging hopeless spells, Sienna with her arms outstretched – but the creature clung closer, gripping my hair and scalp with vicious strength. The stench of its breath was foul in my face – it smelled of carrion, of death, and I heard its harsh, gasping croak against my cheek.

Your mother died a traitor and a fool – and so will you.

Shock pulsed through me, breaking my concentration, breaking my shield, and suddenly my body ripped with pain as the creature's spell engulfed me. The crow's claws sank deep into the flesh of my shoulder and I felt my feet lift from the ground.

At that moment the air was blasted with a searing red light. Something red hot, burning with a fierce red flame, shot past me, just inches from my ear. It hit the crow square in the breast and the creature gave a scream of pain, a sound more human than corvid. I dropped from its claws and it flung itself into the air with desperate strength. A burning red-white light blazed in the centre of its chest.

It flapped its huge wings, wrenching itself skyward, and within moments there was nothing left but the smell of burning feathers.

I turned, to see Seth and Bran standing on the track that led up from the beach. Bran was leaning heavily on his crutch and Seth was holding something in his hand. It was a flare gun, the kind that fired a distress flare for ships in trouble. As I watched, his hand shook, the gun fell to the floor, and he ran across the short turf, into my arms.

'Anna.' His words were sobbing gasps, hot against my forehead. 'Anna, oh Anna!'

'You saved me!' was all I could think to say. 'Seth, you saved me.'

Words welled up inside me – words of love and thanks and unquenchable joy that he was here, back, in my arms. But before I could say any of them, we heard a dreadful cry from behind us. We all turned, to see Maya, crouched on the grass beside Emmaline's body.

'She's not breathing! Oh God! Someone please – please . . .'

Sienna crouched beside her, feeling for Emmaline's pulse. Her face when she looked up was grey with horror.

'Oh Ma, oh Simon – what can we do? What can we do?'

I remembered Abe's words – they seemed like a hundred years ago: *If there's one thing witchcraft can't do, it's make you immortal. Or raise the dead. So it's all pretty bloody useless at the end of the day.*

So many of us, so many witches, so much power – and all so useless.

'Get away.' Bran spoke roughly. He hobbled across the turf, his crutch under his arm, and shoved Sienna out of the way. His knees creaked as he knelt in front of Emmaline, and he put his hand under her nose, then listened to her heart. Then, pulling open her shirt, he put both hands on her chest and began CPR.

For what felt like hours, Bran thumped Emmaline's heart, then pinched her nose, breathing into her mouth. Nothing . . . nothing . . . I began to feel desperate.

Above the roar of the surf I could hear Bran monotonously counting to thirty under his breath, then breathing into Emmaline's mouth. Every few cycles he stopped and felt for a pulse. And nothing. Still nothing.

Stop it! I wanted to shout. *It's not working!* But I didn't. I just stood, with the tears running down my face, while Bran pumped Emmaline's heart and counted to thirty. *Please live*, I told her in my head, willing her, urging her heart to start again. *Please, please live.*

Again Bran stopped and put his fingers to Em's neck. But this time, for the first time, he paused. His fingers rested there and his lips moved almost . . . almost as if . . . A thread-like moan floated on the still air.

'Emmaline!' Maya sobbed.

Emmaline gave a kind of retching, coughing choke.

'Oh, Em!' Sienna fell to her knees and grabbed Emmaline's hand, pressing it to her mouth. 'Em, darling Em.'

'Get off my sodding arm, Sienna . . .' Emmaline moaned weakly. 'I think it's broken. Ahh! Oh Ma . . . make it stop hurting . . .'

'Oh darling . . . shh . . .' Maya stroked her forehead and her hands glowed with a white light. 'Sleep, sweetie . . .' Emmaline's muscles slowly went slack and her sobbing breaths became even and deep. The whole company of witches exhaled a tremulous sigh of relief.

'Thank you.' Maya stretched out her free hand towards

Bran. 'Bran Fisher, thank you, I—'

I don't know what more she would have said, for he cut her off with a hawk of spit at her feet.

'Fagh, witch. Don't give me your thanks. I want nothing from you. You and your kind have done enough harm tonight. Get away, get back to your holes to lick your wounds.'

'Bran Fisher, please.' She spoke softly, still holding out her hand in supplication. 'You've saved my daughter's life. Won't you let me repay that debt?'

But Bran said nothing. He turned and hitched his crutch under his arm, preparing to begin the walk back to Winter.

'Please,' Maya said. 'We have no quarrel with you. Is there nothing we can do to win your trust, show our thanks? Your leg . . .' She indicated his stick and his limp.

'Bring the dead men of Winter back to life,' he said bitterly. Maya shook her head. I could see there were tears in her eyes.

'You know that is the one thing beyond all our power. If I could . . .' She stopped, brokenly, and gestured towards Bill.

'Get away,' Bran repeated disgustedly. 'I want nothing from you.'

He turned his back on her and hobbled painfully down

the path towards Winter. Seth looked from his grandfather to me, then back again, and I saw the anguish in his eyes.

'Seth,' the old man called, without looking over his shoulder, and then louder, 'Seth!'

'Grandad,' his voice was pleading, 'please, don't make me choose . . .'

Bran turned at that, his face full of contempt.

'Stay then, stay with your witch. But she'll never be yours. Our kinds are oil and water.'

'Don't be like this,' Seth cried.

But Bran only turned and limped away.

CHAPTER EIGHTEEN

We made our slow and painful way back to town, the bikers carrying Bill's body on a piece of driftwood and the unconscious Emmaline slung across Abe's back, her poor arm supported by Maya's scarf.

The sight that met our eyes was devastation beyond anything I had expected. The water was receding, but in its wake was a trail of filth and destruction. Sand, silt and seaweed covered everything – roads, trees, flowerbeds, cars. Even the children's playground down by the library was ruined. The sandpit had been transformed into a miniature lagoon, full of crabs, eels and hag-fish marooned by the ebbing waters, all thrashing about in their death agony. Seaweed hung festooned from the swings like Spanish moss.

We stumbled through the streets, our feet slipping in the muddy filth. As we passed the fishermen's cottages I shut my eyes, feeling sick at the sight of their smashed windows and pulverised doors. There was no sign of inhabitants. I could only hope that Caroline had taken Seth's advice and got to safety. Then we turned into the high street and I saw Prue, hopelessly sweeping drifts of soaked books and cushions out of her front door. Her chubby face was white and streaked with black mud.

Maya's shop was knee-deep in mud, a tidemark around the counter and cupboards, the floorboards dark with damp and filth. But the flat had been spared. We staggered wearily up the flights of stairs and through the door, then crashed on to any soft surface, desperate for rest, any kind of rest.

I was too tired and stupefied to find myself a bed. I staggered to a quiet corner in Maya's study where I sat, then slumped to the floor, resting my head on the bare boards. My last memory was of Seth gently tucking a pillow under my cheek and curling beside me, his coat over us both.

I was woken from a deep, deep sleep by a shrill buzzing close beside my hip. I swatted at it and it stopped, only to begin again. Unwillingly I raised my head, trying to focus sleep-dulled eyes. Of course, it was my phone. I squinted at the screen. *Dad mobile*. Oh crap.

I picked up the call.

'Hi, Dad . . .' My voice was slurred with sleep, but I had barely time to draw breath before Dad interrupted, his words tumbling over themselves.

'Anna! Oh thank heavens – I've been through hell. Are you OK?'

'I'm fine. Is the house OK?'

'I knew Maya would take care of you but your phonelines were all down and I kept thinking, what if the shop flooded or you got anxious and tried to get home and got caught somewhere in town . . . ?' He slowed and gave a laugh. 'Oh dear, it's a miracle I escaped a heart attack. Sorry my dear, it's parental anxiety I'm afraid. You'll understand if you ever have kids. So you really are OK?'

'I'm fine,' I repeated dully. 'Sorry you were worried, Dad. How're you? How's the house?'

'Oh fine, it was a pretty near thing – the river burst its banks, but the water stopped just before it reached us. The beech blew over though, I'm afraid.'

'The beach?' I echoed.

'The beech. You know, the tree where the rookery was. The birds have just disappeared – I've no idea where they all went. It's rather quiet without their incessant cawing, actually. But that was the only real

331

casualty here. How's Maya's?'

'Wet . . . a bit. Only the shop. I'm glad you're safe . . .'
I wanted to be more effusive, but my brain simply couldn't
process the words. 'I don't know what time I can get
back . . . There's lots of clearing up . . .'

'Of course, of course. No hurry. I expect they could
use a hand, and now I know you're safe I won't worry. Do
you need a lift?'

'M-maybe later . . .' I was so tired I could barely speak.
'Goodnight, Dad – I mean, goodbye.'

'Are you OK, sweetie?'

'Fine, just late night . . .'

'Oh, OK. Well I'll let you get back to sleep. See
you later . . .'

'Bye, Dad. Love you.'

'Love you too, sweetie.'

I hung up and slept again.

When I woke again it was late and I could tell by the
soreness in my bones that I'd slept for a long time, perhaps
hours. I was stiff and my mouth was dry, but there was a
delicious smell coming from somewhere. I opened my
eyes. Seth was crouching beside me with a plate of pasta
and pesto, peering into my face.

'Oh! You're awake anyway.' He smiled, that wide,

enchanting smile that always tugged at my heart. 'I was just wondering whether to wake you.'

'Hello.' I smiled back, then struggled upright and looked at the plate. 'What's this?'

'Breakfast. Lunch. Whatever you want to call it. It's three p.m. so afternoon tea might be nearest the mark.'

'Three!' I was shocked. I pushed back the hair from my face and tried to get my senses back together. 'How long do you think we slept?'

'I've been up for a couple of hours. You slept from six a.m. until now.'

Then memory came back, and with it a dull feeling of dread.

'Where's Emmaline? Is she OK?'

'She's all right. Maya and Simon took her off to A&E. She was swearing like a trooper when they put her in the car, so I think she'll live. They seemed to think her arm was broken, but that she'd be OK.'

'Thank God.' I felt weak with relief, and suddenly starving. 'What's that? I could eat a horse.'

'Well, I can only offer penne.' He gave me the plate and a spoon, then sat back, watching with a smile as I shovelled the hot pasta into my mouth. It burned my tongue but I barely noticed, I was so hungry. At last I sat back with a contented sigh and Seth laughed.

'You looked like you needed that.'

'I did. Thank you.'

'You're welcome.' He sat beside me on our makeshift bed and ran his hand tenderly through my tangled, sticky hair. 'Anyway, it's me that should be thanking you.'

'What? Why?'

'I spoke to Abe. It sounds like you saved us all, Wonder Woman.'

'Please don't joke about it,' I said uncomfortably. I suddenly felt wretched, fraudulent. 'Anyway I didn't. If anything it was all my fault. The Ealdwitan were after me, don't forget.'

'You're not responsible for what those – those people . . . did, Anna.'

'But that horrible crow!' I cried, shuddering again at the memory of it. 'You saved my life with that flare gun. And Emmaline – Bran was amazing. If anyone saved our skins it was you and Bran.'

'Let's just say, we saved each other. Thank God it's over, and we're both safe.' His arm tightened around me.

Was it over? I wished I could be so sure. But Seth was probably right; the Ealdwitan had staked everything on this throw of the dice – exposure, defeat, destruction. Well, we hadn't destroyed them. But we'd shown them that the Winter witches were a force to be reckoned with

– and I didn't think they'd be returning for a long time, perhaps never. So why did I feel so sad?

Perhaps because although last night had been terrifying, it had also been wonderful. With death looming over us, I'd been freed from the responsibility of tomorrow, free to love Seth. And now . . .

I sat, watching him, as he looked out of the window. Maya's study faced down the hill, towards the harbour, and Winter was spread out beneath us, the houses tumbling to the sea, and the sea stretching out to meet the horizon, both so perfectly blue that you could hardly tell where water ended and air began. It was completely tranquil; I found it almost impossible to connect it with the strength and fury of last night.

I could have sat all day, watching Seth's face, as he in turn gazed at the shifting loveliness of the waves. But perhaps I moved, for he turned and his eyes met mine, and his face was full of a naked, fearless love that almost broke my heart.

I *knew* he loved me. I knew it, with every bone in my body, every nerve, every cell. I just didn't know why. And no matter what I did, no matter how many charms and countercharms and enchantments and remedies I tried, I'd probably never know why, not for sure. I'd never know whether he'd have found me in the first place without that ill-fated spell, or if we might have walked on separate paths for the rest of our lives. I remembered his voice, sobbing, urgent: *You can't change someone's soul with a spell, Anna – you can't make them* love, *not real love, not like this.*

'Seth,' I said hesitantly, and I drew a breath.

There was a sudden knock at the door and I jumped, biting my tongue painfully.

'What? Who is it?' I snapped.

Sienna's head came round the door, her expression apologetic.

'I'm sorry it's just – they're taking Bill. And I thought . . .'

'Of course.' We both stood up. I straightened my clothes, and we followed Sienna out into the hall where two ambulance officials stood, their heads formally bowed over Bill's covered body on the stretcher. As they lifted him I felt the tears well up unstoppably. It could have been me or Seth on that stretcher. We had started this – *I* had started it with that stupid, stupid spell. And yes, I'd finished it too. But Bill had paid the price, while I was safe.

Bill had given me that. He'd given me my life and Seth's. Now it was up to me what I did with them.

Abe, Carl and Sienna followed the crew down the stairs to the ambulance. As the door closed behind them the noise of their feet on the stairs faded, until it was so hushed I could hear my heart beating.

I turned and found Seth looking at me, his grey eyes wide, full of quiet waiting. And suddenly I knew what to do. I owed it to Bill not to waste a second longer.

Two weeks later and the sombre memorials had been held for the lost townsfolk, Bill and Mr Brereton numbered among them. It broke my heart to hear the short reference to Bill, 'A stranger among us for only one night, an innocent bystander like so many others, caught up in the violence of the storm,' compared to the long, sickly eulogy to Mr Brereton: 'A remarkable man, a steadfast friend, a devoted teacher who guided so many of the townsfolk, old and young through their education, growth and development . . .' intoned the officiant. I had to clench my hands to stop myself from standing up and shrieking out the dreadful accusations that would put the record straight, expose Bill's true heroism, giving his life for a town full of strangers, and Mr Brereton's dreadful betrayal. Beside me I could see Emmaline was having the same dark thoughts. Her eyes were closed, the hand not in plaster was clenched until the knuckles were white, and she was muttering something under her breath.

It seemed cruel in the face of Bill's death, but of course

life went on. Dehumidifiers hummed in the harbour cottages, soaked belongings were stacked up outside houses for removal, loss adjusters patrolled the town, and delivery lorries arrived daily with new sofas, carpets and appliances. Some families – Caroline's and Prue's among them – had moved out to relatives, but further up the hill others were back in their homes already. The shops had signs in the window saying: *Damp, But Still Trading!*

As the elderly fisherman down by the quay pointed out to all passers-by, it was not the first time Winter had been flooded, no, not by a long chalk.

'We've scrubbed these here cottages down before, and we'll scrub 'em again,' he said sagely. 'Aye, we'll scrub 'em again. T'would take more than a pint o' seawater to drown Winter.'

It was Emmaline who indignantly asked how much scrubbing *he* was doing.

'My daughter'll see to it,' he said imperturbably.

Impossible though it seemed, things were starting to get back to normal.

One thing was decidedly *not* normal though. It was Friday night and I was going out on a date.

The whole thing was just excruciating, and to make matters worse Seth had been so mysterious that I had no idea where we were going or what was going on. I'd

338

asked him what to wear and he'd said vaguely, 'Oh, something nice.'

I'd spent the day sorting through filthy, sodden books in the school library and, despite showering, I still felt grubby as I riffled through my wardrobe, resolving, not for the first time, that I really had to get back up to London soon, if only to get something new to wear. I'd grown to love Winter in many ways, but I doubted I'd ever be resigned to shopping at Winter-Wear – Ladies' and Gents' Outfitters of Quality.

At last I found something I was reasonably happy with and dragged a comb through my unruly hair. Then I glanced at the clock and realized I'd better get going, Seth would be here any minute.

Dad gave a little clap as I walked downstairs. 'You look *extremely* nice, my dear. I haven't seen you look so dressed up in a long time. Where did you say you were going?'

'Out,' I muttered, rebelliously.

'With?' Dad prodded. I sighed. I wanted to roll my eyes and tell him to get lost, but I realized it wasn't totally unreasonable to want to know where your only daughter was off to at nine p.m. on a Friday night.

'Seth.'

A slow smile spread across Dad's face. I wanted to kick him. 'Really?' he drawled.

'Yes.'

'Well I never. So would this be what they called in my young day *a date*, then, my dear?'

'Mmph,' I muttered.

'Sorry?'

'Yes! Yes it's a damn date. We're going out. Happy?'

'Yes.' Dad's broad beam said it all. Something in his proud grin made me smile, sheepishly.

'So, do I look all right?' I asked. He put a hand out and touched my hair.

'You look *more* than all right, my dear. In fact you look like your . . .' He stopped, and although he was still smiling, I saw there were tears in his eyes. My heart began to thud.

'Who, Dad? Who do I look like?'

His lips pursed, though whether in an effort to speak, or to keep silent, I didn't know. He only shook his head. I took his hand pleadingly.

'Dad, please. Please tell me. I look like Mum, don't I?'

He shut his eyes and a tear traced his cheek.

'Dad? Why don't you ever talk about her?'

'I'm sorry,' he whispered at last. 'I'm sorry, Anna. I want to tell you. I *will* tell you. One day. Just . . . I *can't*. Give me a bit more time. Please?'

The door knocker rang out suddenly in the quiet house

and we both jumped. Dad wiped his eyes and coughed, and I went to answer it.

'Hi.' Seth stood on the doorstep. I groaned.

'Seth – how could you?'

'What?'

'You're wearing a *suit*! Why didn't you tell me?'

He looked, quite honestly, breathtaking. The suit was completely plain, black with a stark white shirt, but it made Seth look anything but. The snowy-white shirt made his tan look all the deeper, and the severe, beautifully cut lines of the jacket somehow only served to emphasize the lean strength of the muscles underneath. It could have made him look like a fisherman dressed up as a stockbroker. Instead it made him look like a panther in evening dress.

He shrugged. 'Sorry, I didn't think of it.'

'Do I have time to go and change?'

'Why? You look amazing. Anyway, the answer's no, you don't.'

Despairingly I looked down at the little dress I had on, which had seemed perfectly adequate up until Seth's arrival, and then I realized that nothing in my wardrobe was going to match up to Seth's severe perfection, so this would probably do as well as anything else.

'OK, whatever. Bye, Dad.'

Dad came into the hallway, his smile back in place. Seth's appearance always seemed to put him into a sickeningly good mood.

'Hello, Seth. Good to see you.'

'Hi, Tom.' Seth grinned back. The fact that they were already on first-name terms still hadn't stopped annoying me. 'See you later.'

'Drop in any time, Seth. We're always pleased to see you around.'

Grrr. Yes, he was pleased I was going out with Seth. I got it. Now could he please stop acting like my personal matchmaker? Surely dads were supposed to hate their daughter's boyfriends?

'Where are we going?' I asked as we climbed into the replacement for Seth's truck, a much quieter but equally battered Mini.

'Wait and see,' was all he said. We drove down the cliff road, past the shattered remains of the castle and I averted my eyes – I still hadn't got used to the sight of the devastation yet, perhaps I never would. Then down the hill towards the harbour. Waiting at the quay was Seth's little boat – or was it his after all?

I looked uncertainly as Seth stopped the car. It looked like Seth's boat – but it was hung all around with lights, tiny twinkling fairy lights that glittered and sparkled in the calm reflection of the waters. Where normally there was a rough plank for a seat, now there lay a snowy cloth. And in the footwell was a basket.

'What's going on?'

'Picnic,' Seth said. He turned off the engine and we got out. 'Better leave your shoes,' he added, smiling at my heels. I kicked them into the back of the car and he leaped lightly into the boat and then held up his arms for me. I hesitated.

'What is it?' Seth asked.

'It's just . . .' I knew I was being irrational but I couldn't help it. 'Seth, the last time I was in a boat with you, I ran up such a storm we nearly died.' That was true but, too, I was thinking about the Ealdwitan's flood – those strange, deep-sea creatures that lurked in the deep ocean, about my terrifying dive through the fathoms to release Seth from a watery grave in his truck, about Seth fighting for his life on his desperate race to the Spit.

Seth gazed up at me steadily. He looked as if he knew what I was thinking, and after all, he'd come even closer to death than I had, but his face was quite calm, no trace of fear at all.

'I understand. If you don't want to, we'll do something else, it doesn't matter. But it's a completely calm night – we won't even be able to sail. I'll have to row us, it's so calm. I've triple-checked the forecast. But most of all, I know the sea. I've been in it, on it, around it every day of my life since I was a tiny kid. I love the sea, and I know you've seen its terrifying side, but I want to show you how lovely it can be.'

I hesitated a moment more, then jumped – and the movement sent a thousand glittering sparkles across the bay as Seth caught me surely and set me on the stern.

'Shouldn't I wear a life jacket?' I asked as Seth picked up the oars. Seth smiled.

'Well, if you like. But I've seen you dive to fifty feet without oxygen. So if you don't want to, I *think* you'll be OK. Plus, I'm here to pull you out.'

We sat in silence while Seth rowed us slowly out of the harbour and on to the night sea. It was nearly the longest day and, although the sun had set some time ago, the sky was still infused with a wash of lemon towards the west. Above the horizon the shades deepened, through aquamarine, turquoise, azure, to a glorious midnight blue. Stars began pricking out as Seth rowed.

At last, far out across the bay, he stopped and set the oars to drip. We drifted with the current, watching the lights of Winter, very small across the bay, and the lighthouse making its lazy searchlight-sweep every few minutes. Everything, every glittering light, every cottage and house, even the moon, was reflected in the clear waters of the bay, and the waves rocked us gently with an almost imperceptible swell.

'It's so beautiful,' I whispered.

'I know.' Seth smiled. He opened the basket and the sight and smell made my mouth water: dressed crab, crayfish, crusty rolls, strawberries and cream. I could have eaten the whole lot that minute. But it was for something else that Seth was searching. He dug in the basket and came up with a bottle of wine and two glasses. Then he laughed. 'Damn, I thought I'd packed so carefully! I've forgotten the corkscrew.' He examined the bottle for a moment and then shrugged, 'Oh well, I'll have to cork it.' He pulled off the foil and pressed. There was a short, silent struggle, then wine spurted up his sleeve. He licked it off and then poured two glasses, the cork bobbing in the bottle.

'Well, Anna.' He held one out to me. 'Here's to us. And love.'

'To us,' I echoed, and we touched glasses.

To *us*, I thought. It had a nice sound. No, better, it had a wonderful sound. A magical sound. I set my glass carefully on the plank and leaned across towards Seth. Then I kissed him.

I didn't think about the Ealdwitan, or Bran, or my

mother, or any of the troubles that might lie ahead. I just kissed him, letting my fingers wander through his hair, under his shirt, up his forearms, so that he shivered and tightened his grip. I kissed him the way I'd been wanting to, ever since we'd met; until my blood seemed to turn to molten gold and the whole world shifted and rocked and rearranged.

'Whoa! Steady, steady.' Seth pulled back, laughing, and set his hand to the tiller to right the rocking boat. I laughed too, looking at the waves that had suddenly sprung up around us, stirred up by the force of my desire. As my heart calmed, so did the waves, and the little boat slowly steadied.

Seth let go of the tiller, put his arm around me and we lay back against the stern, side by side in the deepening night. I rested my cheek on his shoulder, and a happiness so deep it was almost terrifying began to unfurl inside me, as the moon set and the stars came out over the sea.

Behind us, as the boat drifted, the starlight shimmered off a beautiful iridescent trail. A trace of petrol from the boat's motor floated on the sea, making broken rainbows of our lazy wake. It was a thing of beauty, a little piece of magic out of nowhere. From just oil and water.

346

A WITCH in WINTER

Did you love
A Witch in Winter?
Then we'd love to hear from you!

Text 'WITCH'
followed by your review
in less than 20 words and first name to
60777

We'll also let you know when there's more exciting
news about the next book from Ruth Warburton –
A Witch in Love – coming July 2012!

Hodder
Children's
Books

AN INTERVIEW WITH RUTH WARBURTON

How did you come to write *A Witch in Winter*?

I've always written stories; the first one I can remember writing was when I was about seven and it was about . . . witches! Surprise, surprise. I can't recall the title but I do remember it was about a factory caretaker called Cardy. He's sweeping up the factory one night after dark when he's surprised by a mother and daughter appearing on one of the walkways high above the factory floor. Strange things start to happen and he realises that it's Hallowe'en . . . It was all told from the point of view of the sixty-year-old Cardy, which in retrospect was a bit of a strange choice for a seven-year-old, but I remember my teacher liked it.

I wrote lots more stories after that, and they got longer and longer, but it took me a long time to come back to witches as a subject. One day I was listening to a programme on the radio about romance in literature, and one of the interviewees said that the challenge is finding original reasons to keep the hero and heroine apart – because there's no story if they just fall into each other's arms and live happily ever after on the first page. I listened to it, thinking that for me, the most compelling reason not to fall into someone's arms is because you don't know if they really like you or not. And suddenly the idea for *A Witch in Winter* came into my head – a girl who enchants the boy of her dreams to fall for her, but then has to live with the fact that she'll never know for sure whether he truly loves her.

Can you tell us a bit more about the spells in the book – how did you research them?

A lot of them are based on real beliefs, for example the idea of putting a broom across the door to stop an evil-doer from entering is found in lots of cultures. And the piece that Liz reads aloud about a wife putting blood in her husband's wine is actually an old voodoo spell (although in voodoo tradition you add the blood to his coffee).

The reducing spell is based on an old Hebrew spell for banishing spirits and demons. You take the demon's name and reduce it, letter by letter, until the demon is vanquished.

So there are a lot of seeds from folk traditions and different witch-craft practices, but I adapted them to suit my purposes, and nnone of the spells that Anna performs are real.

The incantations look like they're written in a foreign language – are they?

Sort of, yes. They're mostly written in Anglo-Saxon (also known as Old English – the English of *Beowulf*, the *Dream of the Rood* and the *Anglo-Saxon Chronicles*). This is the language that was spoken in England before about 1000 AD. Later it mingled with Norse, French and other languages to become first Middle English (the English of Chaucer and Malory) and finally Modern English (which is Shakespeare's English, and also our own).

I studied Anglo-Saxon as part of my English degree and found it really hard! It's basically a completely foreign language and almost impossible to read without a dictionary and a grammar guide, although some of the words sound like their modern equivalents when you read them aloud. For example 'sc' is usually pronounced 'sh' so the Old English word 'Sceadu' is pronounced quite similarly to what it means in Modern English; 'shadow'.

Lots of the words in the spells are borrowed from Anglo-Saxon poetry, particularly *Beowulf* which is beautiful and full of evocative words and phrases: the sea is a 'hronráde' which means 'whale-road' for example. Several of the phrases used to describe and summon the storm demon are taken from *Beowulf*, including the word 'Hwat!' which introduces the spell. This is a word used in Anglo-Saxon poetry to begin a poem, and means something like 'hey!' or 'listen!'. Seamus Heaney gives it as 'So' in his trandition of *Beowulf*. It's completely inauthentic to use it for a spell, but I loved the idea of a poet casting a spell upon his listeners, summoning them to be entranced, like Anna summons the demon.

Is Winter a real town?

No, but it was inspired by several real places. The seaside setting comes from holidays in Cornwall, Devon and Brittany, but the town of Winter itself was influenced by Lewes, where I grew up. Lewes isn't exactly like Winter – it's bigger for one thing, and it's about five or six miles inland – but it does have a lot of similarities. It has a very long history, including an Iron-Age fort on Mount Caburn above the town, and a spooky ruined castle almost a thousand years old, which partly inspired Winter Castle (although Lewes Castle is in the middle of the town, not overlooking the sea). Lewes was also heavily flooded in the year 2000 while I was still living at home. My dad's house, which overlooks the river, was flooded almost a metre deep and some of those experiences found their way into *A Witch in Winter*.

Who is your favourite character?
Oh this is really hard! I'm not sure I can pick one – I do have a really soft spot for Emmaline. Partly because she has the same faults as me – I can be equally sarcastic and impatient – and partly because she's all about the sisterhood. I love an unapologetically strong woman who stands up for her friends.

But I also love Anna – she tries so hard to do the right thing, even when it's painful. And she's courageous, even when she's full of self-doubt, which is the highest form of courage really.

And of course I heart Seth – for loving Anna in the truest way – not wanting to change or limit her, or make her less than she can be, and for not being fazed by the prospect of a girlfriend who could kick his ass several times over, if she wanted to. I could never write a book where only the guys get to have cool powers and do fun things, and the girls just sit around and get saved – in *A Witch in Winter* Anna is the one with the cool powers, and she and Seth both save each other in different ways.

Actually I really like all the girls in the book – even Caroline, who gets a pretty raw deal in my opinion.

Is there going to be a sequel?
Yes – A Witch in Love. Stay tuned . . .

Can readers contact yoo with their own questions?
Yes! Absolutely, I love to hear from readers. You can find me online at www.ruthwarburton.com, or if you prefer pen and paper, you can write to me c/o Hodder Publishers, Hodder Children's Publicity Dept (their address is at the front of the book). Please come and say hi!

A WITCH in WINTER

Did you love
A Witch in Winter?
Then we'd love to hear from you!

Text 'WITCH'
followed by your review
in less than 20 words and first name to

60002

We'll also let you know when there's more exciting
news about the next book from Ruth Warburton –
A Witch in Love – coming July 2012!

*Hodder
Children's
Books*

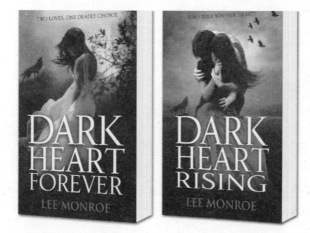